Wildflowers and Wide Receivers

Tampa Tarpons Football Team

Kathryn Andrews

Wild Flowers and Wide Receivers

A Tampa Tarpons novel

Copyright © 2024 by Kathryn Andrews

Published by Kathryn Andrews, LLC

www.kandrewsauthor.com

Ebook - ISBN: 979-8-9889147–7-8

Paperback - ISBN: 979-8-9889147-8-5

Hardback - ISN: 979-8-9918379-1-0

Cover Design by Heart to Cover, LLC

Editing by Editing4Indies

Proofreading by Judy's Proofreading

For Karla -
Thank you for inspiring, supporting, and pushing me
everyday. Love you...

Bryan Brennen – Quarterback
Camden Drake – Running Back
Chase Sullivan – Defensive Back
Darius Jenkins – Offensive Tackle
Dylan Henderson – Safety
Jack Willett – Former Wide Receiver
Jonah Dallmann – Wide Receiver
Miles Mitchell – Linebacker
Reid Jackson – Wide Receiver
Rico Williams – Cornerback
Ryder Monroe – Linebacker
Titan O'Neil – Tight End
Tyler Quinn – Tight End

Prologue
Jonah

New Year's Day

I'd just had the best night of my life.

The clean vanilla scent of her hair, the softness of her skin, and the taste of champagne on her lips . . . it was the kind of night that songs are written about and poems are penned; one that had the ability to change the trajectory of life. I'd felt free and exhilarated, and grounded and home at the same time. I was certain I'd found that feeling we all long for and hope to find, the one that usually comes when you're not looking for it and least expect it, and it whispers, "Soulmate."

Only, as fast as a mirror shattering and the vibrating of my cell phone, that feeling disappeared with the first rays of sunlight, and my best night was replaced with my worst morning.

In fact, worst isn't even a strong enough word to

encompass the overwhelming emotions I felt. What anyone would feel.

Life is funny like that. Well, I shouldn't say funny because there's nothing funny about the many voicemails I discovered on my cell phone first thing this morning—the endless slew of text messages from people wondering where I was or what I now have to do today.

I thought I'd be reliving the buzz from the night before, getting a strong workout in, cleaning up my condo a little bit, then finding myself back at the home of the most incredible girl. They say magical and fabulous things can happen on New Year's Eve, and they weren't wrong. Only that magic instantly evaporated, as did the vision of me with the gorgeous, funny blond girl I had just met the moment I picked up my tux jacket from her couch and walked out her front door. As it turns out, horrible and unthinkable things can also happen too.

My first call had been to my offensive coordinator, Marcus. He immediately answered and said, "This had better be damn good, Dallmann."

In return, I barely choked out the words, "I need you."

Outside of him, I wasn't sure who to call, but of all the people in my life, I knew he would be the right choice. And he was. While I headed home to shower and change, he got on the phone with our travel department, and they worked their magic.

Keeping my head propped against the plane window and my eyes closed, I can still see her large, beautiful smile with bright pink lips, but as the miles grow farther between us, even that becomes blurry. Then again, maybe the blurriness is from the tears.

Tears.

Tears that started hours ago and just won't stop. Endless and leaking from my broken heart to my eyes and then dripping down my face. Do I care that I've been photographed repeatedly in this emotional state? Yes, but what can I do? When you live in the public eye, there's no way to hide from it, no matter how desperately it's sometimes needed. And of course someone is always waiting for a moment just like this.

A moment that should be respected and allowed to remain private. Instead, I'm certain it's already splashed across the internet and sports social media sites, with the world wondering, "What's happening to Jonah Dallmann?"

"Please bring all seats and tray tables to their upright position. Our crew will be coming down the aisle one last time before we land," says a voice over the speakers. I thought this would be the longest flight of my life, the three hours from Tampa to Boston, but as we're about to land, I realize it isn't long enough.

I'm just not ready for any of this to be my reality.

As the plane pulls into the gate, I lower my hat even farther on my head and pull the hood of my sweatshirt over it. Standing, I retrieve my bag from the first-class overhead compartment and feel the stares on my back. If they follow football, my face might be recognizable to some, but my size has always intrigued people. I'm not a small man. I'm six foot three, weigh two hundred and forty-five pounds, and my wingspan is eighty-one inches, almost seven feet. People stare because they know I'm an athlete, and more often than not, people love to ask me for who. They get excited about the prospect of meeting a professional athlete, and I usually go along with it. After all, I've worked hard to be where I am, but today is not the day. Today, I wish I could just blend in.

Stepping out of the airport to meet the car service, I'm met with frigid, damp air. In my rush to book the flight, pack a bag, and leave, I'd somehow overlooked that January in the Northeast is miserable and forgot to grab a coat.

Of course.

Immediately, I think I can borrow one from my brother. He's not quite as big as I am, but he's still large enough that I can manage for a short time with his, but then I remember why I'm here, and my heart seizes so bad it feels as if my chest is caving in on itself.

Twenty-five minutes later, we pull up to his house, and I find my uncle standing on the front porch smoking a cigarette. I thought he'd given them up, but then again, given the situation, who can blame him?

After climbing out of the car, I glance up at the sky's darkness. It's overcast and thick with winter clouds. Its somberness is fitting. It's a random thing to notice, but the gloominess matches the moment, and as irrational as it is, I'm grateful that the day isn't sunny and bright. Something about that would feel wrong.

Ice crunches under my boots as I make my way up the

short sidewalk to the house. It's a standard South Boston row house: upright, crammed between the neighbors, tiny front porch with a metal railing, and faded green siding. Christmas lights remain hung around the inside of the window, and a small lopsided snowman sits on the front lawn, or should I say snowwoman since it's decorated with a pink hat and scarf, and has long eyelashes. The aching is so painful as it constricts and squeezes that I feel like I can't breathe.

After I signed with my first NFL football team, I tried to buy a new house for my brother, John, but he and his wife, Ashley, loved this one, so I just paid it off. They'd already lived here for a few years and made it their home. I wanted to do something nice for him. After all, he's always been there for me as my biggest fan and staunchest supporter. Being drafted after all those years and all the hours of practices and games wasn't just my dream coming true; it was his too.

John was with me at the draft. Carolina selected me in the second round. When they handed me the team hat to put on my head, I asked for two so he could also have one. That hat and a photo of us at the event in Dallas still sit on his mantel today.

Trudging up the steps, I stop in front of my uncle, but no words are said. His eyes are red-rimmed, the deep grooves of his wrinkles are more pronounced, and he looks as if he's aged ten years. My heart doubles down on the pain. He embraces me, and we take a moment to cry with each other at the grief that's filled every space inside us.

Death.

Unexpected tragic death.

Death of the one person who means the most to me in life.

Stomping my boots to free them from any leftover snow or ice, I walk into the house, and the smell of pine greets me from the leftover Christmas tree still sitting in the corner of the room. Its lights are on. My guess is that they were never turned off last night.

When I look around, nothing appears out of place. Their home looks like it does any other day, and just like it did a week ago when I was here for Christmas. The dining room table is decorated with winter colors. Boots are lined up next to the front door with coats hanging on the coatrack, and the crackling fireplace makes it all warm and cozy.

And that's when I spot her next to the fire.

Time stops, and the air rushes from my lungs as the world around me goes silent.

There, wrapped in a fuzzy pink blanket, being rocked by someone I don't know, is Vivi. Even though it's early afternoon, she's still wearing pink unicorn pajamas, and she's clinging to a stuffed dolphin she got from the aquarium when my brother and sister-in-law came to Tampa to watch me play a few months ago. Her white-blond hair is sticking out everywhere, and at this moment, my bright, full-of-energy, little light of my life looks dull.

"Uncle Jonah," she says when she sees me standing in

the doorway. Her eyes are so large and watery, and her voice is so sweet and so small and so broken.

"Wildflower." My voice cracks on the syllables, just like my heart.

Cutting the distance between her and me, I scoop her little body up into my arms. She wraps around me like a koala bear and cries.

I cry with her, breathing in her sweet scent of lavender from her kiddie shampoo.

She's so small and soft. She's so sweet and perfect.

How do I make this better?

How do I ease her pain?

I can't because there's only one thing she wants. The one thing I can't give her. And her next six words slice me to the core, causing permanent damage.

"I want my mom and dad."

Chapter 1
Jonah
2 Years Later

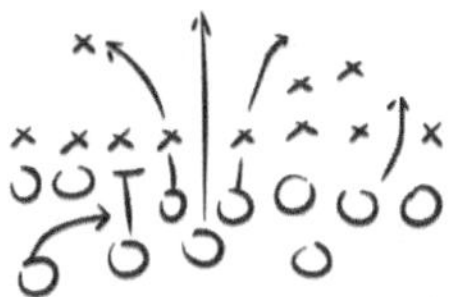

Sweat rolls down my back as I stand under the free-frame squat rack and begin my third set. It's March, we're in the offseason, and I've stuck to my plan of hitting the gym and training hard. I'll be starting my fifth season in the league and, including the trade, soon to be fourth with the Tampa Tarpons. Do I do a lot of squats? Yes. Any athlete will tell you that the movement of the squat strengthens the tendons, muscles, and ligaments in the legs. This one exercise lowers the chance of injuring the knee or ankle, both of which I can't afford to have happen, and as a wide receiver, my position leaves me highly susceptible to both.

Tyler stands next to me. He's equally as sweaty as I am, and his near-black hair is plastered to his face. He's there for a spot if I need it, but I don't, and neither does he. He's a tight end for the Tarpons and, ultimately, my person. Since day one on the team, we've practiced, worked out, studied film, and roomed together when the team won't allow us singles. We also spend a lot of time with one another outside the organization. He's my best friend, and I wouldn't have it any other way—even if he is a big clown, always forgets something, and eats way too much of my food.

I rip the set off, one through twelve, and the bar clunks loudly as I drop it back onto the rack and breathe in the scent of rubber and metal. At least it seems loud since the gym is fairly empty. Most of the team likes to come in earlier in the day, but with Vivi's busy school and dance schedule, the calm around lunchtime works best for me.

"How's my girl doing today?" Tyler asks as I move out from under the rack. He wipes a towel over his face, then grabs a standard-issue green-and-orange Gatorade bottle and squirts water into his mouth.

"You know you ask me this every day, and the answer is always the same." I chuckle, eyeing him as I grab my towel and run it over my shoulders and head. The bar was heavy today, and the burn in my shoulders lingers just like the burn in my legs. "Plus, you just saw her last night."

"Yeah, I know, but something exciting will happen one day, and you'll want to tell me when I ask." He grins.

"Well, today is not that day." I pick up an identical bottle to his and take a long pull of water.

A little over two years ago, my brother and his wife tragically and unexpectedly died, leaving me their five-year-old daughter, Vivianne, or Vivi as everyone calls her. Everyone except for me. To me, she's Wildflower.

It was New Year's Eve, and their car was struck by a drunk driver while driving home from a late dinner. We were told that they died instantly, but on more nights than I care to say, I've lain in bed and wondered if that was true. Because what if it wasn't? What if they lay there, one not moving but the other still watching? Was there panic? Was there pain? And would that pain be the physical kind or the emotional kind, knowing what is happening and what they were leaving behind?

I know I shouldn't have these thoughts. They aren't healthy or relevant anymore. It's not like I can change the outcome, but I do. I can't help it. I tell myself that everyone has these thoughts about their loved ones who've died this way, and somehow that makes it okay. At least for me, but then I worry about Vivi having these thoughts, too. The only comfort I have is knowing that she didn't see any pictures of the wreckage, and she was too young to ask anyone to describe the details of the accident.

"You never know. There's still plenty of time left," Tyler says, breaking me from my thoughts. "So what's for dinner?"

I almost laugh.

At twenty-four, I became a full-time parent. As Vivi's godfather and with the legal wishes in my brother's will, it wasn't contested by anyone on our side of the family, which is just my uncle or his sisters-in-law, who weren't that involved with them anyway. Not that I ever would have said no; Vivi was the light to my brother's life, and in front of God at St. Timothy's Cathedral and all their friends, I vowed to be there for her for every moment needed, so that's what I'm doing. Especially since he can't be now.

"I'm making a chicken noodle soup in the slow cooker. Lots of vegetables and a salad. Maybe some peanut butter bread or cheese toast for her, too."

"Sounds delicious." He grins. "I'll be there at six." He whips me once with his towel and walks off toward the locker room.

I follow, shaking my head.

"When are you going to start contributing to the food bill?" I call after him. It's become a running joke that I repeatedly ask him. He eats with us at least five nights a week before heading out to wherever or with whoever.

"I'm not." He laughs as he strips off his shirt.

"Bro, I've seen you eat. You should definitely be contributing," Sully chimes in. He's just come from the cold tub, so his skin is red, and my junk shrivels at the thought of having to sit in it.

Sully is a defensive captain. He's our lead defensive tackle and shares that spot with Miles, our middle line-backer. Sully is quite possibly the nicest guy I know, and instead of just sticking to his side of the team, he goes out of his way to be friends with us all.

"Sully, you're one to talk. We've all seen what you put down at that Brazilian steak house you took us to earlier in the season," Tyler fires back. Sometimes I feel bad for the steak house. Considering it's unlimited food, it's become our go-to spot, and we can put down some food. But word has gotten out that we can be seen there, so I'd like to think we've increased business for them, too, as fans always show up just hoping for a sighting or an interaction.

"I'm not arguing that. Linemen eat differently," he says, dropping his towel and his wet shorts to put on dry clothes. "I'm just saying, buy your own food for a change or contribute. Jonah is taking care of our girl, and you're freeloading." He winks at me.

As much as he's a nice guy, he's also an instigator.

Tyler scoffs. "It's not freeloading if he invites me over."

Sully looks at me. "Did you invite him over?"

"Nope," I answer, stripping out of my wet clothes and wrapping a towel around me.

Tyler's jaw drops as he looks at me. "Bro, why are you doing me dirty like this?"

I chuckle. He's so easy to rile up.

"Just saying." I shrug. "Maybe one night I'd like to come home to a home-cooked meal, too."

Tyler studies me for a moment and then looks back at Sully, who's stepping into a pair of joggers. "Fine. Point made. Once a week, I'll bring dinner to your house for the three of us."

"Now we're talking," Sully says, grinning.

"I said the three of us. You're not invited," Tyler tells him while scowling, and Sully laughs. It's one of those laughs when you can't help but smile and want to laugh too.

"We'll see," he taunts, wiggling his brows.

After Vivi came to live with me and the prepared meals from my teammates' spouses stopped arriving, I had to learn how to cook. Like really cook. Sure, I knew how to use a blender and a grill, smoothies and chicken all day long, but to no one's surprise, that is not the diet of a five-year-old girl. I'd also convinced myself that if I was giving her good, solid, healthy meals, her emotional recovery would waver toward the better side. But so far, her shine is still the same—as dull as the day we finally said goodbye to Boston.

It took three weeks to have the funeral, pack up their belongings, and sell the house. Three weeks to make it seem as if my brother, the best person I'd ever known, never existed, and three weeks for Vivi's personality to close in on itself. Where she was always a curious, bubbly, and happy child, she's now composed, quiet, and in many ways emotionless. Even after all of the therapy, which is still ongoing, and fun activities, I keep waiting for her to snap out of it or finally have that emotional break, but so far, she hasn't.

"I'm thinking of taking the boat out this weekend. You and Vivi wanna go?" Tyler asks as he grabs his bag from his locker and pulls on a clean shirt. Instead of showering, I know he's going to head home to drop off his car and then go for a run down Bayshore Boulevard. I swear he loves fresh air and the water more than anyone I've ever met, and it's the perfect time of the year in Tampa for that.

"No big plans?" I tease.

His dark brown eyes connect with mine, and he gives

me this look that says I'm crazy. I can't help but crack up while moving my bag to the chair in front of my locker.

Tyler doesn't do serious, and he'll tell anyone who'll listen that spending excessive time with someone gives false hope. Hope he wants no part of. He loved a girl all through college, but that didn't work out. Now he's so casual there's almost no point to his social life, and as for me, I don't have one at all. Not that I need one. Right now, I'm where I'm supposed to be.

"The only plans I want are sweeping my little sweetheart away on the boat to go see if we can find some dolphins."

I smile at him. "I'm sure she'll love it. Count us in."

Vivi might be mine, but Tyler has made himself a steady constant in her life too, and I will forever be grateful to him for that.

"Perfect." He slings his bag across his chest and heads for the door. "See you for dinner," he calls out over his shoulder while tossing up the "peace out" sign as he walks out.

"You tell me when he's bringing dinner, and I'm definitely coming over," Sully says, smiling conspiratorially.

I laugh. "I will."

After taking a quick shower, I've just returned to my locker when I feel the haptic vibration of my watch on my wrist. Looking down, I see that the school is calling. Uneasiness instantly sweeps through me, and my stomach drops out because why would they be calling? It's stupid that unexpected phone calls give me a flash of anxiety, but after John, I can't help the momentary irrational panic that ensues. Trying not to let myself get too worked up, I dig my phone out of my bag and take the call.

"This is Jonah." I hate my shaky voice.

"Mr. Dallmann, this is Ms. Rice from Vivi's school." I start pacing on the pewter carpet in front of the cherry-wood team lockers.

"Yes, how can I help you?" I ask. I can't see Vivi being bad or getting into trouble; she's nearly perfect. So maybe she got sick?

"Well, it seems Vivi had an accident today . . ."

Accident.

The word rings through my ears, and I stop hearing anything else she's saying. Accident, that's what they told me about John. They said there had been an accident.

"What?" I pause, feeling fear's fingers wrap around me and start to squeeze.

"It's nothing serious, but we will need you to come pick her up. She hurt her ankle, and it's quite swollen."

I let the words register and sink in.

Her ankle.

If emotions were tangible, mine would be like a balloon that grew larger with every passing second on this call. Only it pops just like that, and relief rushes over me like a cool breeze.

Will it always be this way?

Will I always have this type of reaction?

"How?" I ask, tossing my water bottle into my bag and zipping it up.

"I believe she tripped on the stairs and stumbled."

Stumbled? She's so graceful and coordinated, this surprises me.

"Is she okay?" I think about her being in pain and crying, and it makes me want to damn near burst out of my skin.

"Yes, she's fine. Just upset about how this will keep her from going to dance tonight."

I almost laugh. Almost. Of course that's what she's worried about.

"Alright. Thanks for calling. I'm on my way."

With my bag in tow, instead of heading for my SUV, I detour to the offices of our sports medicine staff. One of the athletic trainers will know what to do.

Pushing through the double doors, I find Ryan sitting at his desk in the back of the room. He's been a trainer with the team for at least five years, so he should know a lot of different people in town.

"Hey, Jonah. You okay?" he asks, scanning me to see if he can spot an obvious injury.

"Yeah, I'm fine. But I just got a call from Vivi's school. I guess she's hurt her ankle. What should I do?"

"Did they say how bad?" He frowns as he leans back in his chair and tilts his head.

"No, just that I should come pick her up. Where should we go?" I mean, it's a legitimate question. Should I take her to the emergency room, an urgent care, call her pediatrician, or a specialist? I have no idea.

"I've always heard great things about TBPO, Tampa

Bay Pediatric Orthopedics. I know a lot of the high school athletic trainers refer their kids there. There's a female doctor there, Dr. Black. She's young and new, but Vivi would probably like her best. Just call and see if you can get her in this afternoon."

"Perfect. Thank you," I tell him, taking a step backward toward the door.

"No problem," he says, calmly smiling. "Let me know what she says, and if you need to bring her in, I'm here too."

"I appreciate it," I say to him as I turn and start jogging toward the parking lot.

Turns out, I'll have something to tell Tyler about after all.

Chapter 2
Sophie

Coming out of my office, I look down at the iPad and see I'm finally on my last patient for the day, one that's been recently added. It's been a long day, but that's to be expected. Youth sports in Florida ebb and flow, and currently, we are on the upswing of ebb as high school lacrosse, track and field, softball, and baseball seasons are all underway. But I don't mind. I love my job, and I love my patients even more.

It's been almost a year since I finished my pediatric orthopedic fellowship, and I am thankful that I get to work in this practice every day. While my dream has always been to get back home where I'm from, not many physicians end up staying and working in the town where they finished their training. Do I see myself here long term? No, but there are no openings up north at the moment, so I'm learning what I can, seeing patients, and biding my time.

I'm from Minnesota. In fact, my dad still lives there,

but fortunately for me, I love Tampa, too. I loved it from the moment I stepped into this growing, kind of quaint, beautiful city. From the weather, the beaches, the history, the food, to the professional sports teams, I really can't think of a better place to be until something opens up and I can move. So when I heard TBPO was expanding and had an opening, I jumped at the opportunity. Fortunately for me, one of the attendings I trained under is also one of the founding physicians of this practice, and we get along swimmingly. He was delighted when I asked about the position, and it just kind of became mine. I'm now one of seven, along with five physician assistants, and we have two locations. Occasionally, I have to fill in at our St. Petersburg office, but I mainly work here in our Tampa office.

"Hey, Sophie. Hold up a minute." I turn to find Dr. Blair, or Isaac as I call him, walking my way. He's smiling, which makes me smile too.

Isaac, one of the seven in this practice, and I have been casually dating over the past couple of months. In general, I have a very strict "don't mix business with pleasure" policy, but when he asked me out, I didn't want to say no. He's a few years older than I am, but there's something so boyishly handsome about him that I just want to hug him every time I see him.

"Hi," I say as he comes to stand next to me. I grin at his tie. He's notorious for wearing funny kid-friendly ties, and this one has Goofy all over it.

"Hey," he says, smiling back at me. "How's your day

been? I've been so busy, I haven't had two seconds to check in on you."

He does this. At least once a day, he always comes and asks how my day is. It's sweet.

"My day is great. I'm about to see my last patient, finish up some notes, and then head out."

"Pilates tonight, right?" he asks as he runs one hand through his hair, and it fluffs up before settling down.

I smile because of course he remembers. Every Thursday, I meet my friend Camille for Pilates. Her schedule is just as crazy as mine. She owns her own business called Vintage Soul, where she refurbishes old furniture to make them shabby, modern, or whatever the client wants. Her wait list is a mile long, but she's so good at what she does. How could it not be?

"Yep. My bag is packed and in my car."

His smile grows. "Well, I won't keep you. Just wanted to say hi and I hope you have a good night."

"Thank you, and you too," I tell him as he runs a hand over my shoulder, affectionately squeezes my arm, and walks in the other direction. It occurs to me that I didn't ask him about his night. I feel a little guilty over this, but we'll catch up tomorrow.

"Hi, Dr. Black." I turn to see Polly, a recent patient of mine, leaving the physical therapy room.

"Polly!" I give her and the therapist both a wave. "How's it going?" I ask as Polly walks over, wraps her arm around my waist, and hugs me. Polly tore her rotator cuff at the beginning of the winter season while playing volley-ball, and she should almost be done with recovery.

"Very well," the therapist says. "I'm predicting a lot of serving and spiking will be happening real soon."

"I'm happy to hear that," I tell her, my smile widening even more.

These kids and their resilience—it's just another layer to why I love my job. Adults tend to make recovery a dramatic experience. Kids, though, are back at it in no time. It's inspiring.

As they walk past me to the waiting room to meet her mom, I look around the office. It's your standard doctor's office with two hallways full of patient rooms and another hidden hallway with physician offices. We have imaging in the middle that connects both patient hallways and a large nurses' station. Our floor is large gray-and-white checkered tiles, our walls are a pale gray, and they are covered with pictures of sea life. It's always decorated or themed if there is a holiday, and today, pastel Easter eggs hang from the ceiling and all around the office. It's almost Easter, and whereas in the past I've gone home to spend it with my dad, I'm staying here this year. Isaac sort of hinted the other day that we should make plans for this weekend, so maybe we'll spend it together.

Turning down the hall toward the patient rooms, I look back at the iPad and spot the last name of the patient, Dall-mann. I pause as my excitement for the weekend dissi-pates, and an unwanted feeling of rejection sweeps over me. I know it's irrational to feel this way after all this time, but does one ever really get over being stood up? Especially after having already spent the night with that person and thinking it was amazing.

I know one-night stands happen all the time, and I did set myself up for one, but I didn't see myself becoming one after the night we had. It was New Year's Eve into the following morning, and we had made plans for later that day. He was going to come back over, and I went out of my way to prepare food for him, clean my townhouse, wash and dry my hair so it looked casual yet pretty, and spent the day giddy with excitement that I was going to see him, but then I didn't. He did not show, did not call, and it burned badly. I put myself out there, exposed a few vulnerable sides, and then was left with that icky feeling of not being good enough for someone. It's a terrible feeling and pretty much sums up most of my dating life: nonexistent and ghosted.

Well, until Isaac. But then again, when I say casual, except for him kissing me good night each time we go out, I would say we are so casual that it's almost not even dating. I don't know. I'm just going with the flow and not over-thinking it. Time will tell.

Shoving those memories to the side, I walk into the room, wondering if this person might be a relative of Jonah's. I spot the little girl sitting on the examination table and smile at her. Her back is straight, and her arms are crossed over her chest. She has dried tear tracks down her face, and she's frowning. She's wearing a blue-and-white private school uniform and has on a navy satin headband, pulling her hair off her face.

"Hi, Vivi," I say softly, hoping to defuse some of her tension.

"Sophie?" I hear whispered from the parent chairs. It's a voice I would recognize almost anywhere and still hear in my dreams at night. It's like I conjured him with my thoughts in the hallway, and my back goes ramrod straight.

Turning slowly because he's sitting, I come face-to-face with tanned skin, a jaw that should be used in men's razor commercials, and large, surprised hazel eyes. The same eyes from that night, which were a mixture of kind and heated. So heated, I can still feel the track of how they raked over me once my clothes fell to the floor.

My stomach tightens.

Suddenly, this ten-by-ten room is shrinking, and I wish for nothing more than to be able to slink out of it. That feeling of not being enough for this guy burns through me. I can feel my cheeks and ears turning pink, and then I get angry with myself. This is stupid. My reaction to him is stupid. He's just a guy. A guy who chose not to include me in his life, and that's on him, not me.

He's also the same guy who gave me one of the best nights of my life. The night was filled with dancing, laughter, and intimacy that still leaves me blushing to this day when I think about it.

It's then that I notice he looks good. Like really good.

He's wearing a black baseball hat pulled down over his forehead, a white T-shirt with the Tarpons logo on it, black athletic shorts showing off his muscular legs, and a nice pair of running shoes. These past two years have been kind to him, and suddenly, self-consciousness slips under my white coat, and I wish I could pull it tighter around me. It's not that I think I look bad. In fact, I think I'm in the best shape I've ever been in, but like Maya Angelou said, "People will forget what you said, people will forget what you did, but people will never forget how you made them feel."

He made me feel lied to and inconsequential. If he didn't want to see me again, he just could have said so. Instead, he gave me false hope with zero regard for how his standing me up would ultimately make me feel.

"You're a doctor?" he says, more like a statement and less like a question. There's confusion on his face as two distinct lines form between his eyes.

"Yes. Surgeon, actually," I tell him with an unwavering voice.

Pride defuses through me at him finally knowing this. The night we met, there wasn't a lot of getting-to-know-you happening. I don't know why I didn't mention that I was a doctor. I just didn't. But I worked so hard to get to this point, and while I do think I'm an all-around catch, it feels great to let him know that he missed out on someone amazing, driven, incredibly smart, and successful.

Silence engulfs us as his confusion slowly slips to

something that looks like a mixture of esteem and regret. My mind must be playing tricks on me because, deep down, I know that's not true. Not at all. While he might be impressed with my professional accolades, this man has no regrets, or he would have found a way to reach me a long time ago.

"You know her?" the little girl asks.

Her voice breaks our staring contest. I'd forgotten she was even in the room, and I can feel the heat under my skin climbing up my neck and into my face.

I turn to look at her, and an unfamiliar pang jolts me.

One that feels a lot like jealousy, longing, and unrequited heartache.

She looks just like him.

Well, not just like him. But her hair color, eye color, and a few of her features are identical, and I have to work hard to hide my shock.

He has a daughter. A seven-year-old daughter, according to the chart.

And suddenly, it's really easy to answer her question.

"No. We do not know each other. We only met once at a friend's house several years ago."

In my peripheral vision, I see his shoulders slump just a little. I mean, what did he expect my answer to be? We were together for less than twelve hours in total, and most of that time, we weren't speaking.

Clearing my throat, I look back at the iPad and see they're here for her ankle.

"So, Vivi, my name is Dr. Black, but you can call me

Sophie, too. How about you tell me what happened today." I pat the back of the exam table to get her to scoot all the way back so both feet are out in front of her.

Jonah stands to move next to her, and I swear the room shrinks even more. Why is he so tall and so wide? His broad shoulders and chest, combined with his long arms, means he's bigger than the examining table, again sucking up more space in the room. Space I desperately wish I could sneak out of.

Is it hot in here?

"I don't know. I was walking down the stairs, and then I fell. My ankle twisted, and I kind of landed on it."

"Do you lose your balance frequently?" I probe her swollen ankle a little to see how she reacts. A few winces here and there from tenderness, which is better than her crying out, but with the location and the purple bruising, this tells me all I need to know.

"No," she replies.

"What kind of shoes were you wearing?"

"White tennis shoes. Those." She points at the pair on the floor.

Moving to the small desk next to the sink, I lean against the edge to put as much distance from Jonah and me as possible. Glancing down at the chart details, I look at her extracurricular activities. "It says here that you're a dancer."

"I am." She sits a little taller and tilts her head, almost in defiance.

Interesting. Most little girls by this age tend to be in

dance because their parents tell them they should be. It's routine more than a passion, but I see that's not the case here.

"Did you perhaps roll your ankle or injure a leg muscle this week that might have contributed to falling?"

"No," she says, her back now arching in defeat.

Jonah's head is yo-yoing back and forth between the two of us. His blond hair curls out from under the edge of the hat. I hate that I notice that detail.

"Okay. So just a freak random trip, then?" I ask her.

She nods her head. "Yes."

"Hmm." Sitting at the desk, I pull up her X-ray films, which she had taken before I came in, and review the radiologist's notes even though I already know what they are going to say. There's a monitor for the patients to see the images, but I don't take the time to explain anything. Instead, this gives me a minute to breathe and collect myself even though I know both of them are staring at the back of me.

Taking a deep breath, I move back to the examination table. The poor little girl is so tense, I think about how to best explain what is going on in words she'll understand. I glance at Jonah, who's intently watching me, and look away as quickly as possible. Butterflies awaken inside me and stretch their wings.

I hate that I react this way to him.

"Currently, which I think you're probably hoping for, your ankle presents as a sprain. But do you see the swelling here?" I point toward the bottom of her leg. "This bone is the fibula or the calf bone, and right here, where the tenderness and the bruising is, is a growth plate. Often, fractures of the growth plate don't show up on an X-ray, but given the location, the bruise coming in, and the symptoms, it's safe to assume there is a fracture, so we'll treat it as such. We can do advanced imaging if you'd like, but the course of treatment and therapy will be the same."

"And what is that?" Vivi asks; her hands are clenched tight into fists by her side.

"I'm thinking you look pretty responsible and can be trusted to use a walking boot instead of being placed in a cast."

"But I don't want to wear that!" She turns to Jonah, panicked.

He steps closer to her, which means closer to me. Internally, I'm reeling. Then he places a hand on her good leg, and flashbacks of those hands on me flip through my mind: on my lower back when we danced, on my stomach as he slid it across my bare skin, and how he gently wrapped them around my head as he brought his mouth to mine.

Another blush burns through my cheeks, and I blink to clear the images and bring myself back into this room.

"Vivi," I call to get her attention. She looks at me, and big tears are floating in her eyes. "If we don't treat it and it gets worse, there could be long-term damage, such as growth arrest, where the bone stops growing."

"What does that mean?" she asks.

"What do you think it means?" In school, we are taught that with adults, it's easiest if you just state the obvious, but with kids, the outcome is easier to absorb if they tell you what is happening. It makes them feel more in control of the situation and the diagnosis easier to swallow.

"One leg would be longer than the other?"

"It's possible." I nod.

She frowns and looks down at her legs. Jonah and I both watch as she wiggles her hips, stretching her legs as far as they will go, and she points her toes on her uninjured leg.

"Do either of you have any questions?" I ask.

Jonah shakes his head, but Vivi asks, "How long will I have to wear it?"

"Six weeks," I tell her, and those large tears start to drop.

Jonah, sensing her distress, moves closer to her, wraps her in his arms, and she turns to bury her face in his chest. I hate it when they cry, and this little girl is breaking my heart. At this moment, any looks he might have been giving me stop. He is fully committed to consoling the broken child in his arms.

"Well, someone will be right in to get her fitted. If you think of any questions, if her ankle gets worse, or if you need anything, please don't hesitate to call the office. Otherwise, I'll see you in six weeks."

I put on my best fake smile as I look at them both. Vivi doesn't acknowledge me, and Jonah's eyes catch mine and hold. His gaze is intimate, as if he is concerned for Vivi, and gratitude pours out of them. My stomach dips. It might have been over two years since I've seen him in person, but I remember his eyes as well as his hands and how they feel when trained on me. They are hypnotizing and lethal, which I cannot be a victim to once again. And it's with that thought that my fight or flight kicks in, and flight is telling me to get out of the room as fast as possible.

Chapter 3
Team Chat

Sully: Anyone else notice there's a strange odor coming from Darius's locker?

Darius: Bro, what are you going on about now

Sully: Your shit stinks

Darius: No, it doesn't. And why are you lingering near my locker in the first place?

Dylan: You know he does this. He gets bored and starts sniffing around, literally, making sure we're up to code

Sully: It's like you left something in there from the postseason, and it's died

Ryder: Code for what?

Dylan: Rookie, did you not read your welcome packet?

Ryder: Are those crickets chirping?

Sully: Ryder, I gave it to you when I gave you the tour

Ryder: You mean there are things in there you didn't go over?

Titan: 😆

Sully: Bro. You have to read the code of conduct for the locker room.

Titan: Just give him a candy bar, and he'll quiet down

Sully: 👍

Darius: Stay away from my locker

Sully: But what is that smell?

Darius: Could be my lucky potato

Sully: WTF is a lucky potato

Darius: My son gave it to me. He drew a face on it and gave it a red cape. Said it would bring me luck.

Titan: 😂

Sully: All capes belong to Camden

Camden: Why are you dragging me into this

Sully: Your locker is near his. How do you not smell it?

Camden: Oh, I smelled it. It's just none of my business

Darius: I bet it rotted

Sully: 🧹 Clean that shit out.

Darius: Fine. No need to get your panties in a wad

Sully: Code.

Sully: Make that code black after my favorite color of panties

Chapter 4
Jonah

I can't stop thinking about her.

Surprised doesn't even begin to cover how I felt seeing her walk into the room yesterday. I had no idea she was a doctor. We didn't share those details during our night together. All I knew was that she was wicked smart, funny, confident, and the most beautiful woman I had ever seen. Throw in her career and her bedside manner with Vivi, and now she's out of this world. The fact that she works with children amplifies my regret over how things ended. I can't help but wonder if things would have been different had I sucked up my pride and grieving heart, gotten her number, and made that call I owed her. Could she have made a difference or an impact on the progression of Vivi's emotional state? On mine?

Of course I've thought about her over the past couple of years. I did a lot in the beginning, but like all things, it became less and less over time.

I had thought about reaching out to her before the funeral. I was aching for her to be there with me, this person I barely knew, but as much as I wanted to, I couldn't bring myself to actually do it. It didn't seem fair to drag her into this horrible, tragic event. I didn't have her number, but it would have been easy enough to get it from Reid and Camille. We barely knew each other, and it wouldn't have been right or fair to throw her into the mix of all that I had to do with the funeral, house, and Vivi. To her or to us. No one should start a relationship like this. Then again, I assumed she had wanted to when maybe she didn't.

Once we were settled back in Tampa, I again thought about reaching out to her, but I just couldn't. I knew if I explained what had happened, she would understand, but so much time had already passed, and I felt like I missed my window and that ship had sailed. Also, I may be Vivi's uncle, but for all intents and purposes, I became a single dad. I couldn't love her any more than if she were my own. In fact, from the moment John told me they were pregnant, a spark for her permanently branded itself to my very being.

"You should get her a dog," Reid says out of nowhere as we watch Vivi sit in the hot tub of his pool with their dog, Izzy. She may be limping around and moping because of the boot, but allowing her to be in the warm water and jet bubbles makes her happy. So does their dog, which is how we ended up here on a Friday night.

"Because I have so much time for a dog," I say bluntly.

Crossing my legs on the black-and-white-striped lounge chair, I look out past Vivi, over the dock to the houses on the other side of the water. Taking a long pull of the beer I'm holding, I don't tell him I haven't thought about it because I have. It's been over two years, and Vivi's still closed off. Things don't excite her anymore, at least not like they used to. Yes, she loves ballet to the point of it being an obsession, and she loves going out on the boat with Tyler to hunt for dolphins, but there's really nothing else.

Well, ballet, dolphins, and Izzy.

"Ehh, you can make it work," he says. "Plus, she's old enough and responsible enough to help out."

The outside lights flip on. Camille must have turned them. The sun has dropped low enough on the horizon that it falls behind the houses across the water, and we can no longer see it. Being lovely like she is, when we showed up at their door after school, she must have seen something on my face because all she did was smile big as she opened the door wide, cooked dinner for the four of us, and left Reid and me alone out here to chat. I know Reid's right about the dog, but that word responsible gets me. I feel like I've had an overload of responsibility, and the dust is just now settling.

"Maybe." I really should just pull the trigger and do it. All kids need a pet, and I'm allergic to cats, so those are out.

"How did her spring party at school go today?" He's asking because Vivi and Camille spent several hours cutting out paper flowers for each classmate last weekend. They had to write something nice about each kid on them. In the class, they glued them on large sheets of construction paper so each of the sixteen kids could have a bouquet.

"Good. I was surprised they let us come in for it. Usually parents aren't allowed. Each kid read a poem they wrote, we played a few games, they gave their parent a present—a sunflower seed that had sprouted in a painted flowerpot—and we ate a snack. One little girl named Heather talked to Vivi a lot."

"Oh yeah?" he asks, turning to look at me surprised and delighted.

Outside of Tyler, we are closest to Reid and Camille, Bryan and Lexi, and Camden. Reid is also a wide receiver, Bryan is our quarterback, and Camden is a running back. As we are all on the offensive side of the team, we spend a lot of time together. When Vivi came into our lives, even though I had only been with the Tarpons for a few months, we found ourselves wrapped in their love, along with a few others from the team, and in our own unique way, we became a family. A family I will forever be grateful for.

"Yeah, I asked her about it later, and she just said they were friends. I asked if she wanted to invite her over, and all she said was maybe, but I'll take it. Maybe is definitely better than no." I take another pull of the beer and finish it off.

Other than the guys on my team and a few of the wives, Vivi hasn't made any friends—not at school and not in her dance class. I saw the team psychologist about this around a year ago, and he said it was normal and fine. She was likely having a hard time emotionally connecting due to a fear of loss, but he assured me she would come around. People all handle grief differently, especially children. This really didn't make me feel any better, but I needed another opinion besides the one from Vivi's therapist. I'm just waiting for the day her joy returns. He warned me that it might not, that she experienced trauma at a young age, and she may have changed, but I would recognize when some of the heaviness she carries wore off.

"Absolutely," he agrees. "I wonder if this girl is in her dance class, too?"

"I'm not sure, but now that you mention it, I'll have to ask her. How's Camille feeling?" I ask him just as Vivi laughs. Izzy has licked her in the face. Her laughter makes my heart sing. It's so beautiful and so rare these days. I feel like I cling to these moments, hoping the next one will come sooner than the last.

Lifting my phone, I take a picture of her with Izzy standing over her.

"Good. It's been crazy watching the way her body has changed and also the way she eats. She's always been a good eater, but man, this whole eating for two has taken her to the next level. I swear she eats more food than I do, but the doctor says that's normal." He chuckles as he picks up his phone and fires off a text, which I'm sure is to her. He's constantly checking in with her.

I've also recently seen Camille eat, and I'm pretty sure she eats more than I do.

"Speaking of doctors, you both know the one we saw yesterday." I eye him like he should already know where I'm going with this conversation, and nerves fire under my skin. I wasn't sure if I was going to mention that we saw Sophie, but I can't hold it in.

"Oh, yeah. Who?" he asks. His phone vibrates, and he glances at it before flipping it back over and placing it on his leg.

"Dr. Sophie Black," I state. Just saying her name out loud has my stomach tightening.

A grin splits his face. "I didn't even think to ask who you saw. Camille loves Sophie. She comes over occasionally, but mostly, they go out at night after Pilates." His grin turns mischievous, and he raises an eyebrow. "Didn't you hook up with her a couple of years ago?"

"Yep," I say, looking down at my bottle. I really do hate how things ended.

I also hate the word "hookup." It makes it feel like it was cheap, quick, and easy, but that night, I had more of a life-alerting epiphany. Life-altering in that she would be in it indefinitely if I'd had my way.

But fate had a different plan.

"What happened there?" he asks, watching me for a reaction while taking a sip of his beer.

"Nothing." I shrug one shoulder. "That following morning, I found out about John."

Saying his name makes my stomach tighten again, but for a different reason.

He remains silent. Nothing more needs to be said.

I met Sophie at a New Year's Eve party that Reid and Camille had thrown. I didn't want to be there. I was bitter after being traded from Carolina a few months prior, I'd been working my ass off to prove myself so it wouldn't happen again, and I was tired. I'd only gone to that party to show solidarity with my teammates and had zero plans to meet someone, but the second my eyes landed on her, no one else there mattered. She wore this little gold-and-silver dress, high heels that made her legs look long and toned, and bright pink lips. Her lips and smile were like kryptonite to me, breaking down every wall I had around me. I had to meet her. I had to know if she could be mine.

And she was . . . until she wasn't.

"Well, what did you think? I'm pretty sure she's just biding her time and not dating anyone seriously."

Dating anyone seriously. That means she's dating someone casually, and I find that thought makes me regretful. But what could I do, or what could I change? Vivi needed me, Vivi still needs me, and she's my number one priority.

"Does it matter?" I say, defeated, running my hand through my hair.

"Of course it does. Your life may have changed, but you still have a life," he says.

"I don't know. I'm not sure that I'm ready for any more change."

But would it change, or would it just get better? And what I'm most unsure of is how Vivi would react. Not that

I think she would respond badly, but is she ready for change? Can she handle a new person in our life?

"I think you're wrong. I think now is the perfect time," he states, letting his comment linger between us in the cool air.

What I don't tell him is that after we got home last night, I impulsively ordered thank-you flowers and had them delivered to her office. I didn't hear from her today, not that I expected to, but secretly, I had hoped I would.

"What makes you say that?" I ask, curious to hear what he thinks.

"What makes you say it's not?"

Lifting my bottle, I take another sip as I think about this. The obvious excuses trickle through my mind, but even I recognize them as excuses.

Then I think about Sophie. This new Sophie. Same blond hair, same bright blue eyes, wearing green scrubs and a white coat. She may have been at work, but she was even more beautiful than I remembered.

Can I do this?

Can I ask for more?

That's assuming she'd want this too, which, after how I left things, I'm not so certain that she would.

Chapter 5
Sophie

I'm not sure what to think of the dark pink roses sitting on my kitchen table.

When they arrived at work two days ago and my medical assistant brought them into my office, I was pleasantly surprised. Although Isaac and I have been seeing each other, I didn't think we were at the place in our relationship where he would be sending me large romantic bouquets.

And then I opened the card.

Thank you for being so good with Vivi. It was great to see you. Jonah

Jonah.

What in the world is he doing sending me flowers, and dark pink ones at that?

Of course I immediately had to look up the meaning, and dark pink stands for appreciation, gratitude, and a great way to say thank you, but these don't feel like a thank-you; they feel like more.

Of course Isaac saw them sitting on my desk and gave me a brief "what the hell" look before dropping it. He didn't say anything because they really aren't any of his business, but I can understand his confusion. He asked me to dinner—just like he had every week since we started seeing each other, albeit he was hesitant with the glaring siren of scented roses situated between us—and I instantly said yes.

Yes.

I had been so excited about Isaac asking me out again this week after our date last week, but as soon as he walked out of my office, I realized my heart didn't leap for joy like I thought it would.

It took eight minutes of being in Jonah's presence for him to derail my life.

Rubbing my forehead, I shake my head, wondering what is wrong with me, and then reach for my glass of wine on the counter where I poured it. Isaac will be here soon to pick me up, and I need to shake out of this weird place I'm in.

Jonah was just being nice, nothing more.

I look at the roses again and try to remember the last time someone bought me flowers, and I can't remember. They really are beautiful. I'm not sure where he got them, but they look expensive, and despite who they're from, I really like them.

Feeling drawn to them, I move to the table, bend over, and smell them. So floral and so pretty.

I again shake my head.

I hate that I'm confused by them.

After all, they were just thank-you flowers.

Needing to talk to someone, I pick up my phone and call Camille. She answers right away, and instead of saying hello, I blurt out, "So I saw Jonah Dallmann the other day," and then squeeze my eyes shut. Yes, I saw him before we had our Pilates class, but then, I didn't really have anything to say. People run into past hookups all the time and don't make a big deal of it, but then he went and sent me flowers.

"Oh really? That's great! Was Vivi with him?" she asks.

At that, I open my eyes and picture the blond little girl with big hazel eyes.

"She was. I saw them in the office." I take another gulp of the wine.

"Oh, she was your patient. He didn't mention it to me, and I should have thought to ask. Isn't she just the cutest thing ever? Jonah brought her over yesterday after school. My heart hurts for her to be in that boot. She's pretty serious about ballet and cried over not being able to do all of the things in her class. I guess they've started rehearsing for the spring recital, and she was worried about not being able to perform in it. How long do you think she'll be in it?"

"Vivi," I mumble, seeing her sitting on the examination table, straight posture and unflappable scowl, and then I think about them at Reid and Camille's house. Suddenly, Camille feels like a traitor to me, and she wouldn't even know why. I understand that Reid works with Jonah, but she's my friend. "You know I can't talk about patients with you, but if I was not her doctor, I'd tell you most breaks heal around six weeks." This time, I find more self-control and take a sip of the wine.

"Oh, that's good. Poor Jonah, too. If it had been any more serious, I think the poor guy would just lose it," she sighs into the phone.

"That seems a little dramatic," I tell her, moving to the couch where I've tossed my shoes and purse for dinner and set my wineglass on the coffee table. Isaac said he made reservations for us at a trendy yet fancy place, so I'm wearing a dark-green dress that hits at the knees and high-heeled black ankle boots.

"Probably, and I should give him more credit. He's been amazing with her and definitely handled this situation better than I would have. So tragic what happened to her parents. I still think about it every time I see her, and it's been over two years."

Her parents.

What?

I freeze as I'm bent over to zip up one of the boots.

Her last name was Dallmann too, so that makes her his niece.

This word drops through my head like an atomic

bomb. The high, whistling pitch slides through the octaves of a musical scale until it deepens and then hits the ground. The ground beneath me that seems to shift. Not his daughter. I never even considered this, and then her word tragic registers.

"What happened to her parents?" I finish zipping the boot, slip on the other, and then turn to stare at the flowers as if they have all the answers.

"How do you not know this? We had to have talked about it at some point. It was a huge deal for a while, and the entire Tarpons organization rallied around him."

"I don't know, and no, we've never talked about him. Not once. And you know I'm not on social media."

Well, at least I'm not anymore. After waiting for him for an entire day and feeling like the stupidest person in the world because I believed our night together meant more, I stopped looking at anything to do with sports, especially Tarpons football and deleted any app that might show him. Surprisingly, I didn't miss them and never redownloaded them.

"Are you sure we've never talked about this?" she asks skeptically.

"We haven't."

"Oh my God, Sophie. You remember our silver-and-gold New Year's Eve party, right?"

How could I forget? Visions of him laughing in a tux and then naked, sweaty, and above me flash through my mind.

"Of course." I have to clear my throat.

"It was that night. His brother and sister-in-law were killed in a car accident. He got the news when he woke up on New Year's Day and had to fly out to go to his niece."

New Year's Day.

I gasp.

Dread and guilt fall heavy into my stomach, and I sink back into the couch. The same couch we made out on, which feels like ages ago and yesterday at the same time.

I had no idea, but thinking back, he turned his phone on right before he left, and it lit up and chimed with messages. And through the window, I watched him sit in his car with his phone to his ear. Nothing seemed out of the ordinary, but then again, I didn't stand there long enough to get caught staring at him. I had no idea he was getting devastating life-altering news.

Camille ignores my silence and continues. Internally, I'm freaking out.

"He's her next of kin. It was awful. A lot of us flew to Boston for their funeral. I've always thought a grown man crying is sexy, but watching him, his uncle, and Vivi lose themselves while trying to hold it together at the same time was one of the saddest things I've ever seen."

Tears fill my eyes, and I close them, feeling this foreign pain for him and most definitely for that little girl I just met.

"Why didn't you tell me?" I ask.

"I don't know. I just assumed you knew like everyone else. But call me curious. Why would I?" she asks.

Right, because she doesn't really know about us. No one does. At least I didn't think so. I was so hurt and embarrassed after he stood me up that I didn't tell anyone. Yeah, I'm sure a lot of people saw us, but no one did afterward. Just me and my foolish heart.

"Because I know you saw us together the night before at your party. It just seems like something we would have talked about." I look around my townhouse and remember Jonah being here. After I received my offer to stay on with TBPO, I thought about buying my first home, but then changed my mind, as I have no intention of staying here.

"I guess it just didn't occur to me. That time was crazy. It was all over social media and news outlets for weeks. He was photographed at the airport on New Year's Day. Even though he dressed in disguise, he was spotted. Dark circles under his eyes, tears on his cheeks, and grief so strong you could feel it from just looking at the image. ESPN followed the story through the funeral, and players from all across the league sent flowers and donations to a college fund for Vivi. Reid, Bryan, and Tyler found him a house in our neighborhood on the island, and while he closed down his brother's home in Boston, Lexi, Missy, myself, and team members moved him out of his condo and got the house ready to go. We decorated a room for Vivi. We all wanted her to have a safe place when she got here. She still isn't doing too well, and it's been over two years. Then again, can you blame her? How sad."

They moved him into a house.

They decorated her room.

I could have helped.

"I didn't know," I say, just more than a whisper.

Then again, I guess he didn't want me to since he didn't bother calling. Well, that's not fair for me to say. Clearly, I'm finding out that there were a lot more important things on his mind at that moment, as they should have been.

"Yeah, but they're hanging in there. One day at a time. I'm really proud of him. At twenty-four, he stepped up in a way not many others could."

Twenty-four . . . that makes him twenty-six or maybe twenty-seven now. He's six or seven years younger than me. I had no idea there was such an age gap.

Thinking of the two of them, I remember the way he wrapped his arms around her and she cried into him. The love between them was evident. Maybe that's another reason I just assumed she was his daughter.

"She's lucky to have him," I say, meaning it but also because I feel like I have to say something.

"She is. So are you going to see him again?"

I jerk at her question and start shaking my head even though she can't see me.

"I don't think so. Oh wait, I will when they come back in for the six-week follow-up."

Six weeks.

I'll see him again.

"That's good. He really is such a great guy."

I don't say anything because I wouldn't know. I just let out a hum, and she continues.

"Speaking of follow-up, Reid and I had an appointment with the OB this morning, and she says the baby is the size of a large banana or a cantaloupe. Isn't that exciting? I found a comparison picture on the internet and sent it to Reid. He was not as impressed as I was."

I laugh. Leave it to Camille to change the mood of the room. It's the Southern in her, and I love her for it.

"I think that's exciting."

"Exactly. Listen, I have to run. Reid cooked dinner." I can hear his deep voice in the background, but not his words. I smile at the thought of him laboring over a meal for her. It's cute.

"Yum. Tell him hi for me."

"Will do."

With that, she's gone.

Moving through my house, I head to my office to find my laptop. Just thinking about them, I'm reminded of something I've never done before. I'm kind of ashamed of it, but at the same time, not really. From Vivi's chart, I wrote down Jonah's address. I don't know why it feels like an invasion of their privacy, but I was thinking about dropping by and bringing them something at the time.

That is until I got the flowers.

Until I felt weird.

Opening the laptop, I google Jonah Dallmann and flip to the images page. Sure enough, there to be preserved forever are pictures of him from that morning after at the airport, the funeral, and others.

All this time, I thought I had been stood up.

All this time, I had filed away the memory as just an incredible one-night stand.

All this time, I tried not to resent him for leaving me waiting even though I have.

I know he didn't have my number. It's not like he could have called to let me know he wasn't coming, but I always knew he could have gotten it if he really wanted it.

Now I feel selfish.

Now I feel like a shrew.

Did it cross my mind that something had happened to him? Yes. But instead of reaching out, I tucked my tail, licked my wounds, and assumed the worst. Meanwhile, he'd been dealing with the most horrific thing.

Flipping through the pictures, I see a lot of him playing football, but others are interspersed. From my cold black desk chair, I get a montage of the biggest loss of his life.

The photo that breaks me the most is one of them at the gravesite, and he's holding Vivi, who's younger and openly crying. Camille meant it when she said that a lot of the team flew to Boston for the funeral, as they were all standing in the background. And they were getting ready to start the playoffs and knee-deep in practices and meetings that year.

To think, all this happened just days after we were together, and I could have been there for him too. If only I'd set my stubbornness aside, called Camille, and asked for his number. She would have told me everything. I know she would have. Instead, all this happened, and I knew nothing.

The doorbell rings, startling me, and I slam the lid shut, feeling somehow caught.

Standing, I smooth down the skirt of my dress, take several deep breaths to clear my head, and move through the house to open the door. There on my doorstep in a dark gray suit with no tie is a smiling Isaac.

"Wow, you look beautiful," he says, his eyes wandering over me from head to toe.

"You look pretty handsome yourself." I smile back at him. And he does.

Leaning forward, he gives me a kiss on the cheek, then holds out a box of chocolate.

"I figured since you already got flowers, chocolate was the next best thing," he says sheepishly. I hate that he's been thinking about these flowers and what they might mean. I should tell him that they were a thank-you from a parent of a patient, because they were, but somehow that doesn't feel right, so I choose not to say anything at all.

"Thank you. You know how much I love sweets." And he does. Sales reps are constantly coming into our office and bringing goodies. More times than I care to count, he's found me stuffing my face with cookies or donuts in the office break room.

"I do." He smiles at me again.

"Let me grab my purse, and we'll be on our way," I tell him.

Leaving him at the door, I head to the kitchen and place the chocolates on the table next to the flowers. Glancing at them one last time, I let out a sigh. Even though I learned a whole lot about Jonah tonight, it doesn't change the past or how things went down. I tell myself that everything happens for a reason and decide to forget about Jonah Dallmann.

Chapter 6
Jonah

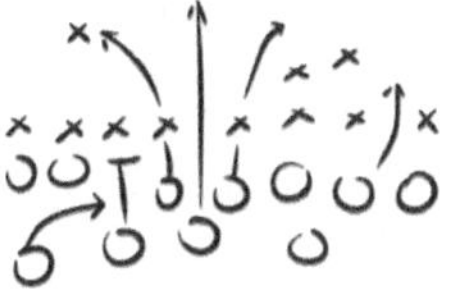

I would be lying if I said I wasn't nervous about walking into Sophie's office today.

I've spent so much time thinking about her over the past couple of years, and now that she's here and about to be in front of me, I'm not sure what to do or say.

Well, that's not true. I know I need to start with an apology.

For six weeks, I've been scripting conversations in my head. They've covered a full spectrum from completely avoiding what happened two years ago and hoping the chemistry we shared is enough to move us forward to some semblance of something to full-on begging for forgiveness.

After our night together, she went out on a limb the following morning and invited me back over later that day for dinner. We planned to watch the college bowl games and eat black-eyed peas and collard greens for good luck and prosperity. I was so excited too. Just the thought of her cleaning up her place, making food, and then having me stand her up still makes me want to wither inside myself.

Then again, I just don't know. There's also the real possibility that she really didn't care all that much that I missed our date. I may have been way more into her than she was me. But regardless, I still think some things need to be said.

Except . . . when she walks into our room, I can't find the words.

I heard her come down the hall before I even saw her. The click of her heels got louder the closer she came to the door, and with her stride, my heart pounded in my chest. When she opened the door, walked into the room, and her eyes found mine, I felt my heart fall to my feet.

Damn, she is so beautiful.

For ten solid minutes, she talked to Vivi, examining her ankle, reviewing the new films the radiologist person took before she came to see us, and watching her walk on it. With my short answers and grunting in agreement as she spoke, one would think that I was illiterate, but I just couldn't get my tongue to work with my brain.

Six weeks.

I've been counting down to this day again for six weeks, and as the seconds tick by, I know I'm about to lose the opportunity, but I can't stop staring at her.

Her hair is longer than when we met two years ago. That night it was shoulder length and now it's a little past her shoulders. It's still the same gorgeous blond color, and her eyes are just as blue as I remember them. She's wearing a dark purple dress under her white coat and nude-colored heels. Her hands, which have been all over Vivi's ankle, are not adorned with jewelry, but her nails are painted a light pink, and my mind drifts back to what those fingers felt like buried in my hair as she kissed me.

I haven't been with anyone since her.

It's not like I haven't had opportunities. Quite a few of the women at Vivi's school have made it known there are options, but that's just not my thing. Plus, I haven't really had time. My life revolves around Vivi and football. I'm not complaining, it is what it is.

"Okay! I think you're good to go. It may be a little stiff for the first couple of days, but I'm confident with some stretching and the routine exercising I know ballet is known for, you'll be as good as new in no time." She smiles at Vivi, and Vivi smiles back.

It's so rare to see her smile that I instantly whip my phone out.

"We need a celebratory photo. Vivi, hold up the boot, and you two smile," I say to them, sounding like a lunatic.

Sophie looks at me strangely, but she steps next to Vivi, and they both smile as I take the photo.

"All right, then," Sophie says, as she glances at Vivi and then turns to me. "Like I mentioned before, if anything changes or if she feels any discomfort past what you think is normal, just give the office a call."

"Will do," I say, standing. This move makes me much taller than her, and she has to look up. "Ryan from the team said he would help her, too."

She gives me another small smile. "It wouldn't hurt, and I firmly believe in never turning down free healthcare, therapy included."

I smile back at her, and the heaviness of this goodbye moment weighs me down.

"Well, it was nice to see you both. Take care of yourself, Vivi," she says, looking at her and gathering her iPad. "No more falling," she teases as she reaches for the door and opens it.

My heart rate picks up to a gallop.

Our time is over.

"No more falling," Vivi repeats, pushing the boot aside and putting on her regular shoes.

This is it.

Sophie's eyes flick to mine and hold for a long second just before she walks out the door.

"Actually, Sophie"—I clear my throat and move to the doorway—"do you mind speaking with me for a moment?"

She stops in the hallway and pauses before she turns to look back at me. Her eyes flick down to Vivi before rising back to mine.

"Sure. Vivi, why don't you head up to the checkout counter? I know there is some candy, and then you can wait for your uncle in the lobby."

Uncle.

So she knows.

Of course she does. She probably did last time, too. Everyone knows about John's death and Vivi coming to live with me.

"Okay. But just this once. Dancers don't eat candy," Vivi says as she turns to go to the lobby.

Sophie chuckles. "Got your hands full there, I see," she tosses over her shoulder as she looks at me and proceeds down the hall.

"You have no idea," I mumble behind her as I follow.

"How did she really do in the boot?" she asks as we enter an office. Her office.

"Well, it didn't deter her." A small smile escapes me. "She still went to her dance classes. Turns out there's a lot she could still do, so she was happy."

"Wow. Most kids rejoice when they get to take time off from their sports. Good for her for sticking with it."

"She is committed, that's for sure," I say proudly.

Laying the iPad down on her desk, she turns to face me. "I was really sorry to hear about the loss of your brother," she says as she leans against it, and I briefly take in her space. Her glass-topped desk has a computer, a coffee cup, and a few other things placed on it. She has two windows with standard business blinds, a bookshelf covered with books and items, a section of her wall dedicated to mail and art children have made for her, and her degrees. She completed her undergraduate degree at the University of Minnesota Twin Cities, her medical degree from the University of Florida, and completion certificates for orthopedic surgery residency and her pediatric fellowship from the University of South Florida. There are other certificates showing her accolades and whatnots, and I find I'm just so proud that I could burst.

Proud for a woman I don't really know, but proud all the same.

I'd like to think that I'm a good judge of character, and while I knew she was sweet and funny the night we met, knowing now that she's gentle and kind as a caregiver to children makes my esteem for her grow even more.

I press my lips together and tell her, "Thanks."

"I found out way after the fact, and I'm sorry that I wasn't able to be there for you," she says, crossing her arms over her chest. It's defensive. She's closing herself off.

I hear her words, and they sound sincere, but her body language lets me know how she feels about what happened and that I never reached out.

Guilt swamps me. She didn't know. She thought I stood her up because I wasn't interested.

I take in her beautiful face. There's tension around her mouth and eyes, and I know I did the right thing by asking for a few minutes. "No. I'm the one who's sorry. I should have reached out to you or at least had Missy or Camille let you know what was going on. I hate that I stood you up," I say, frowning.

She unfolds her arms and moves behind her desk to sit down. "I didn't understand at the time, but I do now, and, Jonah, you have nothing to be sorry about." She looks up at me.

Shaking my head, I push my hands into my pockets and tell her, "That's not true."

I want to tell her that I'm sorry for so much more than just not showing up. I'm sorry for making her feel like what happened between us wasn't important. I'm sorry for hurting her feelings, when next to Vivi, she is the last person I wanted to hurt. And I'm most sorry that I've let all this time pass, time that might have created an us.

"I understand," she says.

My eyes rise to find hers, and I tell her a truth. A truth she deserves to hear. "I was really looking forward to spending that day with you. For what it's worth, I want you to know that I was coming back. I remember thinking that wild horses couldn't keep me away, but it turns out that wild cars can." My heart constricts.

Silence surrounds us as we both stare at each other.

"Well, for what it's worth, I was looking forward to seeing you, too." Now she just looks sad.

And I hate it.

Next to her, the iPad dings. She looks down and then back at me. "I have to go. My next patient is ready."

I nod and take a step back, which puts me in her doorway, and my heart starts banging in my chest.

"Can I see you again?" I ask, fear almost preventing me from asking, but I have to know. No more regrets.

She hesitates and then quietly says, "I'm dating someone."

Right.

The pressure around my heart releases and deflates. The nerves I'd felt this whole time dissipate as I realize I've lost my chance. I knew this outcome was a possibility. I'd just hoped for the alternative. I mean, who wouldn't want to be with her? She's funny, smart, and beautiful. The complete package. I look at the ground as I try to keep myself and my composure together, and then back to her.

"I'm happy for you," I tell her. And I am. I only want the best for her.

"Thank you," she says quietly, tucking a piece of hair behind her ear.

"So maybe I'll see you around?" I give her a smile, trying to lighten the mood, and she smiles back.

"I hope so."

And that's my cue to leave.

"Hey, Jonah?" she calls out, and I turn back. "Thank you for the roses."

I give her a closed-mouth smile and soak in the details of her one more time.

A coach once said, "Regret is the pain of knowing we could have done better." That's always stuck with me, and at this moment, he's right. I have a lot of regret over how things turned out between us, but I don't have any regrets for asking today. I put myself out there, and I'm glad I did.

Coming out of Sophie's office, I pass another doctor in the hallway. I give him a nod, and his eyes flare just a bit with recognition before he nods in return. After he passes, I glance back to see him walk into Sophie's office, and quietly, I hear him ask, "You do know who that was, right?"

Chapter 7
Sophie

I t's been four days since I've seen him.

Four days for him to completely upend my life.

After he left my office, Isaac popped in, and he was so excited to have passed Jonah Dallmann in the hall, wide receiver for the Tarpons, that I didn't really have time to process my and Jonah's conversation or how he made me feel before I saw my next patient.

But the minute I got home and every one since then, that's all I've done. I've replayed in my mind every move, every face expression, and every word.

"Can I see you again?"

What does he want to see me for? He's had over two years to find me and see me, and now by some random chance, he runs into me again and thinks now is the time? I know this isn't fair, but it's how I feel.

Actually, I feel like a rutabaga.

I know that's a terrible comparison, but everyone has

that one crazy relative who makes a rutabaga casserole as a holiday dish for the family get-together. We always eat it, and every time I think to myself, this vegetable doesn't taste too bad, but then I forget about it once the dinner is over until the next holiday when I'm like, "Oh yeah. I forgot I like rutabagas."

Out of sight, out of mind.

But even though I liked the casserole, it wasn't memorable enough for me to seek out rutabagas in the store to make them for myself. So aside from being confused as to why he would ask to see me again, I'm also irritated. Because, rutabaga. No one likes being a rutabaga.

"You're quiet tonight," Isaac says, pulling me from my thoughts. He's looking at me, but the second my eyes catch his, he looks down at his plate.

Inwardly, I flinch. He's right. I'm here on a date with him, but I'm not here at the same time, and now, I feel bad.

"Am I? I'm sorry. I just have a lot on my mind." I try to blow it off and ease his thoughts.

Earlier today, Isaac asked me if I wanted to grab dinner after work, and of course I said yes. I told myself I had no reason not to want to grab dinner, that I should want to. After all, we are dating. So here we are, even though I'm still out of sorts and kind of wishing I was just at home in my pajamas.

"Anything you want to talk about with me?" There are wrinkles between his smoky-gray eyes as concern moves over his expression.

I swear, this man is too good to be true. He picked a

tapas place, which is perfect in that it's noisy and not super romantic. The ambience is upscale, and all of the food has a Spanish name, like pollo al chilindron and arroz caldoso. They have the best sangria, which he said he knew I loved.

"No," I tell him, and disappointment slips over his features.

"I see," he says, leaning back, taking his sangria with him to pull a long swallow of it.

The problem is, there is nothing to talk about. At least nothing that he needs to be made aware of, and certainly nothing he can help me with. No guy wants to hear about another guy.

And I don't get it. I really don't.

Jonah and I are not a thing. We never were. Our time together wasn't even twelve hours. I met him sometime around ten at night, and he was gone before nine in the morning. Now, years later, after two barely ten-minute conversations and a bouquet, I'm so out of sorts I don't even know where to begin.

Actually, I do.

Nowhere. There is no place to begin.

"You know . . ." He sets his glass down, readjusts the napkin sitting in his lap, and then looks at me, like really looks at me. "All these months, I've been waiting for you."

My breath catches, and deep down in my gut, I know he's about to steer this conversation to a place I don't think I'm ready to go. I don't like confrontation or uncomfortable situations, and by this one statement, he's surprised me and made me wary. "What do you mean?"

I watch as he pulls at the collar of his pale-blue dress shirt as if it is trying to strangle him. He wore the same shirt to work today, but it was buttoned up and paired with a tie covered in bears. "I don't know. I've always felt like you needed time. Time for what, I'm not sure. I just never got the feeling that you were as into me as I was into you."

I think about what he's saying, and he sits back and sighs deeply as he sees the confusion on my face. I'm into him. I have been since the first time he asked me out almost six months ago. I always say yes, and we do everything he suggests. I can't think of one time I've told him no. I want to make him happy, so I always go with the flow.

"I've been trying to give you space to get used to the idea of us, of me." He runs his hand over his head. It disrupts his perfectly styled hair, and suddenly, I feel worse than I did before. I'm messing him up when normally he's so put together, and I didn't even know I was doing this. "I don't know, Sophie. In the beginning, you came off almost like a skittish cat. You took the job with us, still wired from coming out of the fellowship, and I waited as I watched the contentment slowly settle. I get it. We've all been there. I didn't want to push you too hard or too fast, but then I was afraid I might miss my shot." He lets out another deep breath. "I feel like I'm always walking on eggshells around you. I hate it, but it's been months, and I feel like we're stagnant. Are we?"

"I didn't think so, at least I didn't until just now," I say, frowning, balling up the fabric napkin lying on my lap.

The very first time he asked me out was to our office

Christmas party. Dr. Stone, who was my attending and who is also my boss, hosted the party at his home. Isaac asked if he could pick me up and then casually tossed out that we could grab a drink together afterward. I only hesitated briefly when he asked because I was concerned about what others might think of us arriving together. It had nothing to do with him and more to do with fraternization within the workplace. Clearly, I got over that, as everyone knows we've been seeing each other since.

His eyes scan over my face before they come back to mine. The emotion in them is pouring out, and dread sinks to the bottom of my stomach. I feel horrible. He's anxious and sad, and apparently, I put that look there.

"Let me give you a few examples. At work, you never come and find me to ask me about my day."

"That's because I know you'll come find me," I answer quickly. It's become almost routine that he does, and I look forward to those moments.

The group at the table next to us laughs loudly, and my eyes cut to the noise before coming back to him.

Sheepishly, he says, "Well, it would have felt nice to find you in my doorway every now and then."

My frown deepens. He's right. I've never really sought him out. I've never had that uncontrollable urge to see him. He's always the one to come to me or to bring me treats. Why has it never occurred to me to do these things for him? This makes me feel selfish and ungrateful for his kindness even though I didn't mean for it to be this way.

He takes a deep breath. "The only time you've ever

asked me to do anything with you was Gasparilla. You asked if I would go to the parade with you. All the other times we've gotten together, it's because I asked you."

I did ask him to go with me to the parade, but surely, that can't be it.

"What do you mean? We have a routine. We always go to dinner on Tuesday and Friday nights. Sometimes Sunday, too."

"Yes, and call me crazy, but I would like to see you outside of those nights, too. Don't you want to see me?"

"I . . ." My face flushes, and heat rushes over me. "I thought that was what you wanted?"

He shakes his head and then continues.

"Maybe that was my fault. Maybe I should have asked for more, but back to the eggshells. I don't know what you want."

I lean forward. "Isaac, I'm sorry. I didn't know I was making you feel bad. That was never my intent."

"I know that, but, Sophie, I've also never been inside your townhouse. It's been months. When we get to your place and I walk you to the door tonight, were you planning on inviting me in?"

I wasn't. It didn't even occur to me to.

"See," he says, then runs his hand over his face.

I think about that time he invited me over for dinner. He lives in a condo downtown. It has great views of the city and the water, but he's never invited me back. Or now I'm wondering if maybe he was waiting to see if I would ask to go back?

Part of me feels like I've been tested and put on trial. I can't believe that was ever his intention, but it feels terrible knowing someone you think you're getting close to is waiting to see if you pass or fail.

"I'm sorry. Do you want to come in with me tonight?" I ask, feeling strange as I do. An image of Jonah flashes behind my eyes. I had zero hesitation about asking him inside. In fact, I couldn't wait to get him inside and all to myself. My stomach aches. Have I thought about being intimate with Isaac? Sure. But I wasn't in a rush to get there. I wanted to date, get to know him, and now I'm wondering if I hesitated because something was missing.

Something I refused to look at because I was too busy trying to settle into a routine of my new life and being happy to have a friend.

Or something, because I've never planned on staying. Of course, he doesn't know this, just my close friends, like Camille, but I can see how subconsciously I would have put up a wall and not allowed things to get more serious.

"Of course I do, but more than that, I wanted you to want me to come in, and up until now, you haven't, or you would have asked."

He's right. I'm thirty-three. At our age, we should know what we want, and as he's pointing out, I didn't want him, or things would have progressed faster than they have.

More guilt.

"I thought we were dating. I haven't dated in so long, actually really ever, and I've been enjoying all of our time together," I tell him. I thought we were on the same page. I thought he was enjoying getting to know me, too, but he's not wrong, and it has been months. Suddenly, I feel as if I have been leading him on. I didn't think I was, but maybe.

"I guess our definitions of dating are just different," he says sadly.

From the time I was twelve, I knew I wanted to be a doctor. I loved playing Operation and learning about the body. When I was sixteen, I ruptured my Achilles tendon during a soccer game. I've always loved sports, too, but soccer was mine. The rehabilitation was almost a year, and by that point, I had missed the window to be recruited by a college, but it was the surgeon who inspired me to study orthopedics.

She was amazing.

That's right, she. In a field of predominantly men, I met her, and my life was forever changed.

Since then, I've done nothing but focus on my studies and get to where I am today. Yes, I dated a few guys over the years, but no one specifically for any period. A guy for me, or a husband as some would say, wasn't the end goal. The white coat, the title of doctor, and achieving every goal I set for myself. In fact, when it comes to guys, this time with Isaac is the longest I've been with anyone. With schooling and training, there really wasn't a lot of free time, not that I would have given it to myself. I had something to prove. I never questioned that I was smarter or better than the others in my class or residency pool, but competition and jealousy are a potent combination, and along with making sure everyone knew why I was there, I went out of my way not to do anything to tarnish the work that I was doing or my reputation.

And then there was also my mother's death.

I was seventeen when she died of breast cancer. I never would have made it through to high school graduation without my father. We leaned on each other for support and comfort. We understood what each other was going through because we were both losing and then lost her. Our relationship strengthened and locked into place. After all, we were all each other had left. Together, our plan was always undergrad, medical school, residency, fellowship, and then return home.

To Minneapolis.

I have no interest in living permanently somewhere he isn't. He's my family, and I'm biding my time until a place opens up for me.

"Do you think about me?" He snaps me back to reality, his boyish features and insecurity pulling on my heart-strings.

I glance down at my food and back to him. My plate is still mostly full, but I've lost all of my appetite. "Of course I do," I tell him, and I mean it. I think about him all the time, but now that I'm being put on the spot, I realize I haven't thought about him past what we're doing on a day-to-day basis. I haven't been dreaming of long term, something I've done my whole life, and that is eye-opening and telling.

Once the residency was over, most of my colleagues moved on. Yes, I'm friends with Camille, Missy, Lexi, and a few others, but it was those colleagues who I spent most of my time with, and over the past two years, I really haven't gone out of my way to make any more. Did I know who Isaac was? Of course, I trained with his physician group, but it wasn't until I was offered the job that he made his move. He became my friend, and I've loved being friends with him.

Friends.

This word strikes a mental chord, and internally, I flinch. A heaviness settles on my heart as I realize I don't see him in my future. At least not in the way he wants.

"What do you think about?" he asks nervously.

"You're a nice guy, Isaac. You're kind, thoughtful, handsome." Heat floods my cheeks. "I really like you, and I enjoy spending time with you."

"A nice guy." He nods his head and lets out a deep sigh.

He's right.

I've thought to myself over and over about how we are casually dating, and now I see that's all my doing. He wasn't taking us slow. I wasn't moving us forward.

His eyes find mine, and they are clear and sharp. He's made a decision about how he wants to lead this—well, finish it—and I squeeze the napkin on my lap because I'm not sure I want to hear it.

"I don't think of you as nice. Don't get me wrong, you are, but I think of you as absolutely amazing and incredible. I'm crazy about you. I think about you so much, it's like I'm having an entire other relationship with you in my mind. We are not at the same place in this. I want to wrap you up in my arms and shout to the world that you are mine. But after months and months, I don't know if you are. Are you mine?" he asks, hopeful and pained at the same time.

This causes me to pause, and my mouth opens with the words I want to say to him, but they don't come.

What is wrong with me?

I adore him.

I know he needs a response from me. He's politely begging me to give him something, so I answer him honestly because we've always been truthful with each other, knowing it's not the answer he'll want to hear. Only now, I wonder if I've been lying to him and myself all this time, and a huge part of me hates myself as I tell him, "I thought I was."

Chapter 8
Jonah

"I can't believe you got a dog," Tyler says as he sits down with us at an outside table at a restaurant where we're eating lunch in Hyde Park Village.

We shouldn't be outside, but the weather is mild for May, and the skies are a bright blue. Even though this table is a bit secluded, we are out in the open for anyone to walk up and speak to us. Of course, Tyler is as subtle as a bull in a china shop, and all eyes are on him as he's wearing a Tarpons shirt, giving us away, and he flips his baseball hat around backward, which means now eyes are on both of us. But with the puppy, we can't be inside. When I'm out with Vivi, sometimes I'm recognized, but more often not. However, throw Tyler into the mix with his six-foot-seven large frame, and people almost always know who we are.

"I blame Reid for this. He's the one who's been pushing the idea," he says as he leans over and ruffles Vivi's hair while she sits on the ground and encourages the puppy to drink. She always swats at his hand and acts offended that he's messed her hair up, but secretly, I think she likes it.

"Yeah, well, it was time."

After two years, Vivi finally started to become friends with this one girl at school, who I found out was also in her dance class, but outside of that, she still kept to herself. She loves Izzy, loves on her whenever they're together, and I figured Reid was right and it was time for her to have a dog of her own to love on too. She used to be such an affectionate child. I'm hoping this will help bring some of that back or at least be an outlet for her to express herself. Plus, the timing works because we can train her over the summer.

"Don't get me wrong, I love dogs, and I think all kids should have one. We had one growing up. It was a Lab mix, probably with a pit bull since we got it from an animal shelter, but that dog was the best. A lot of my childhood memories have that dog in them, from hiking to holidays or just lying on the couch."

"I'm happy to hear you say that since what's mine is yours, and what's yours is mine." I smirk at him and pointedly look down at the puppy.

"Right!" He laughs as the server comes over to take his drink order. Although, I'm not kidding. He's around so much that it makes sense that he'll be helping out with the puppy too. And by helping, I mean walking her at night as his payment for eating my food.

"So why now?" he asks. But instead of answering, my

eyes widen and my brows rise like he should understand the obvious. In return, his brows pull down in confusion until it dawns on him what today is.

Today is Mother's Day, and I thought the distraction would be ideal after the week Vivi had at school. I understand why schools do "Moms and Muffins" and other such events, but these things are an awful reminder to her and other kids in her situation or one similar to what she doesn't have anymore.

So what did I do?

I let her skip school on Friday.

While all of the moms were coming in, I didn't force her to have to sit there and see it. Instead, we went and bought a puppy.

I'm a sucker, I know it, but I have the means to do what it takes to make her happy, and that's my single goal in life when it comes to her—happiness and to feel love.

"Why not?" I shrug. "Her ankle is healed, so Vivi can walk her, and since school is about to end for the year, they'll have all summer together."

Vivi's therapist told me that getting a dog would be great for her emotional growth. Oftentimes, with childhood grief, children can lock up their emotions and become withdrawn. Not that there's a wrong way to grieve because there isn't, but research shows that loving an animal allows them to emotionally be themselves without relying on another person. Of course, I immediately felt guilty for not giving her this sooner, but at the same time, I'm not sure either of us were ready. We both struggled through the change and only recently have seemed to settle.

"Seems like it might be working," Tyler says as we glance under the table where Vivi tucks the sleepy puppy up against her chest with a fabric sling. Camille taught her this. There's no way I could have.

"We bought this one from the same breeder as Reid, so send good vibes our way."

At this, Vivi pops up from under the table and takes her seat.

She finally looks at Tyler and decides to acknowledge him. "Hi, Uncle Tyler."

"What's up, squirt? I see you have a new friend there." He reaches over and gently pets the top of the puppy's head with his fingers.

"Yes. Her name is Molly." She looks down at the puppy with her eyes full of adoration.

"Ah, Molly is a good name. I once knew a girl named Molly. She had the best—owww! What was that for?" he growls as I've kicked him under the table.

"Neither of us wants to hear about any girls you used to know." I give him a flat look.

Vivi giggles, and my heart squeezes. I don't think I will ever get tired of that.

"Are you laughing because he kicked me?" he asks her like he's put out.

"Yes," she says, her grin growing larger.

"Happy to know that you find him inflicting pain on me is funny." He scowls.

She picks up her Sprite, takes a sip through a straw, and sets the glass back down. "Did Uncle Jonah tell you what I made for him this week?" she asks, almost shyly.

"Noooo," he draws out dramatically, giving me a fake exasperated glare.

"Pot holders. My teacher gave each of us a small loom, and we weaved them in class."

His eyes get large like this is the best gift idea he's ever heard of. "That's awesome! You know I love it when your uncle cooks. Your house is my favorite place to have dinner." He smirks at me.

She grins. "Can you guess what color they are?" she asks, running her hand over her forehead to push back some of her fine blond hair that has fallen in her face. Her face looks so much like John's, but Ashley's too.

"Black like his soul?" he teases.

"Bro, seriously? I don't have a black soul. Tell him, Wildflower."

She giggles again, and a breeze drifts over us, pushing that hair back into her face. She swipes it again, and this time, when she smiles, it's large and happy and shows her teeth. Well, almost all of her teeth. Earlier in the week, she lost an incisor on the top, and now she has a cute gap.

"No! I made them teal and white."

Tyler leans back in his chair and nods like he's so proud of her choice. "Ah, to match our team colors. Smart girl you are. Jonah, I think we have a fan for life."

I smile at Vivi, and she smiles back.

Tyler is so good for her. In every sense of the expression, he is the fun uncle. I'd like to think that I was at some point, bringing her presents and making her laugh, but now it's just different.

I wasn't surprised by the potholders. She always brings home art and homemade things from school for me, and I always go out of my way to make her feel like these things are special to me. Instead of shoving them into a drawer, we found a place for them on the counter next to the stove.

"I can make some for you, too," she says while looking at Tyler.

"Really? I'd love that. But only if you want to."

"What colors do you want?"

"I like all colors, so I'll let you decide," he tells her.

"Okay."

I lean over and whisper loudly, "Maybe black like his soul."

Her eyes sparkle, and Tyler just shakes his head.

"So tell me about your new puppy. Eaten any of Jonah's shoes? Chewed a hole in the couch?"

I want to remind him that we've only had her for three days. Besides, she's too young anyway.

"No! She's not going to do that. She's a good puppy," she says, hugging the caramel-colored fur ball. We got a mini goldendoodle. Where I might have preferred a large dog, I reminded myself that this one isn't mine, and smaller is better for her. "She sleeps a lot right now, but the books told us that would change soon. Hey, isn't that Dr. Sophie?" Vivi asks, and my heart leaps in my chest at just hearing her name.

"Where?" I turn, following her gaze.

"Right there." She points at a woman walking across the street toward the fountain that sits in the middle of the shops and away from us.

I find her instantly, and my heart rate picks up. She's wearing a sundress, flip-flops, and her hair is pulled into a ponytail. She has her purse on one shoulder and several bags on her other arm.

"You know what, I think you're right." I glance at Tyler, and he smirks at me knowingly. "I think I'll go say hi. I'll be right back."

Leaving the two of them at the table, I can feel their eyes on me as I jog to catch up to her. Nerves creep their way up my spine, but I ignore them because I'm not going to let this moment get away.

"Hey, Sophie, wait up," I call out to her to get her attention.

She turns, and surprise flits across her face before she shuts it down and gives me a small smile.

"Fancy meeting you here," I say to her and instantly want to punch myself in the face. Her face, on the other hand, her beautiful face, I want to stare at indefinitely. "How are you?"

"Oh, I'm good. How are you?"

I like her hair pulled back. Don't get me wrong, I like it however she wants to wear it, but this way, her face is on full display. Almond-shaped eyes that are a bright blue under the sun, freckles across the bridge of her nose and over her cheekbones, and it's then that I notice the small diamond studs in her earlobes, which are attached instead of floppy.

"We're good." I glance at the table where Vivi and Tyler are watching us. Vivi shyly raises her hand to wave, and Sophie smiles so big when she waves back. It's a strange feeling that overtakes you when someone does the smallest and simplest thing, but you know it makes your kid happy. It's gratitude and admiration.

"Out for lunch, I see," she says.

"Yes. Vivi got a new puppy, and we've made several trips to the dog boutique shop this weekend."

"A new puppy. Sounds exciting," she teases, but in a fun way.

I glance back at them. The server is dropping off Tyler's drink, and she's taking our order. Who knows what Tyler will get for me, but I'm not picky.

"It's something. Would you like to join us?"

Please say yes. Please say yes.

"Oh," she says, surprised, but then glances at her bags. "I can't today. I'm on a mission, but maybe another time." She looks at me hopefully. At least I think that's what I'm seeing. My stomach tells me it is, and they always say to go with your gut.

I want to ask her what kind of mission, but that really isn't any of my business, and I also want to press for when that "another time" can be. Is she just being polite, or would she like to see me again? It's with that thought I find the courage to ask what I've been regretting for a long time now.

"I'd like that," I tell her, wanting to make sure I get across that I'd really like to see her again. "I know I'm almost two and a half years late, but I really would like your number."

A blush tints her cheeks, turning them the softest shade of pink. "Sure," she tells me, and my heart soars.

Reaching into my pocket, I pull out my phone and open the messages screen. She gives me her number. I send her a text so she'll have mine as well, but when the notification goes through, her watch lights up on her arm holding the bags, and on the screen, it says, "Jonah cell."

She sees the confusion on my face, glances at her watch, and then her blush turns bright red all the way to the tips of her ears.

"You already have my number?"

Hope and dread are a strange combination. I love that she has my number, but how long has she had it? Has it been this whole time, and she just didn't reach out? Not that I blame her. I stood her up in the worst kind of way.

"I might have been very unprofessional and taken it from Vivi's chart when you were in the office. I was going to check in with you after the first appointment to see how she was doing and thank you for the roses, but I obviously didn't."

She looks away from me and out at the people walking by. I understand how this might have made her uncomfortable, but I freaking love that she did this. Maybe things aren't so cut-and-dried. She's seeing someone else, after all.

My heart sprouts wings, and it feels like it soars as maybe things are better looking for me than I thought.

"I would have liked that," I tell her, one side of my mouth lifting because I'm so happy. So freaking happy that I can't even hide it because maybe somewhere deep down she wants to talk to me too. Her eyes connect with mine and hold before skipping away.

You know how people say that the best friendships are the ones where even though you don't talk to them every day or even see them regularly, it's like no time has passed when you do? That's how I feel seeing her. I've seen her three times in the past three months, and today, it feels like there's been no time gap. I feel like I saw her last week, and we're just catching up. She feels like someone who is more, or at least someone who is meant to be more.

I don't know much about her—well, really anything—but if fate keeps pushing us together, I'm confident that will change.

"So I'll see you around?" she says.

"I hope so."

Chapter 9
Team Chat

Sully: Who did it?

Bryan: Did what?

Sully: The locker room

Reid: What happened now?

Sully: Oh, you didn't see? Let me
show you.

Sully: (Sends pic of Reid posing with a
football in high school. There are large
megaphones set on either side of him)

Titan: 😂

Darius: Damn, Jackson. What's wrong
with your face?

Reid: I had acne

Darius: Is that what you call that shit

Reid: Speechless

Sully: Titan, you're looking especially fetching in your photo too

Titan: What?

Sully: (Sends pic of high school Titan— he's posing holding a football, but one foot is propped up on a wooden box)

Titan: Bro

Jonah: 😂

Darius: Is he peacocking? 🤣

Sully: Oh, lookie, marketing has found all the high school photos hung up IN THE LOCKER ROOM

Titan: STFU

Darius: Rizz, fellas. Rizz

Reid: D, you sound like a thirteen year old talking like that

Jonah: That's because he is a thirteen year old

Bryan: Why didn't they pick college photos

Sully: (Sends link)

Sully: Because these are funny

Bryan: Funny for who?

Darius: Based on this pic, you're just lucky Lexi knew you then

Rico: Un-fucking-believeable. Who did this?

Miles: Where did these photos even come from? Pretty sure I made my mom burn these

Camden: OMG. This has to be a fucking joke

Sully: Nope.

Jonah: I think I look pretty good

Rico: Shut it, Dallmann

Tyler: Woo Wee! Suns out guns out, Superman

Camden: Can't hurt steel

Titan:

Darius: Rico, are you wearing a compression tank top?

Rico:

Rico: When I find out who did this . . .

Tyler: D, is that a Mohawk?

Darius: Watch it, Ty. Might have to start calling you Bieber

Tyler: Bieber Fever was a real thing. Just ask the ladies

Darius: Bro, you dumb

Sully: We can probably get the security footage

Rico: Tell me when and where

Ryder: Isn't this against the code?

Chapter 10
Sophie

Work has been awkward this week. It's safe to say I completely understand why companies enforce the "no fraternization" policy. And it isn't even just the strangeness between Isaac and me, it's the staff. I know he's not a gossip, but that doesn't mean the rest of them aren't, and it irritates me greatly.

I didn't work my ass off for all these years for people to stand around and talk about me. I feel I'm owed more respect than I've been given this week, which further makes me question what I'm doing with my life. Why haven't I been consistently looking to see if there are any openings back in Minneapolis? Not that I'm trying to run from my problems, but the goal has always been to get back home, and I haven't looked in at least six months. During the six months that I was sort of dating him.

Monday, I'm definitely taking the time to see if anything is posted, as well as reaching back out to my office contacts to see if there are any changes in staffing or if additional locations are being added. Lately, many practices have been expanding as large city markets grow. Take Tampa—last year, it was the eleventh fastest growing city in the US, and the only place for these newcomers to land is either north, south, or east. There have been mumblings from the senior physicians that it might be time for a north location as two new hospitals are going up. New locations mean they need more physicians.

While Minneapolis isn't growing as fast, it is a much larger metro area, and I'd like to believe that opportunities will be open—if not now, then soon.

And when I do go, I will definitely not date anyone I work with.

Parking my car in Camille's driveway, I stare up at her house and admire what she's accomplished. This house is a home with her handsome husband and her soon-to-be beautiful baby. I may love what I'm doing and am proud of how hard I worked to get where I am, but I'm thirty-three. A part of me recognizes what I'm missing.

"Sophie, stop with the pity party," I chastise myself and climb out of the car.

We're one week away from Camille's baby shower, and despite having the world's best party planner gifted to her by her mother, who is technically the host, she invited me over because she said she needed my help.

Of course I go, but what I didn't realize is we'd be food tasting.

So much food.

We're at her formal dining room table, which seats twelve. She had built this table from reclaimed pine that was found through salvaging rural farmlands for her business, Vintage Soul. There's a mixture of old doors and barns. It has a natural antique finish and was distressed by hand. The legs have been shaped to remind me of one of those hanging Christmas ornaments where the top bulb is large, the middle medium-sized, and then there's the smallest just before the pointy end. The chairs are stained the same color, but she's upholstered them with an ivory fabric. It's beautiful. And spread out in front of us are three different salads, baked salmon, baked chicken, and baked eggplant. There are four different pastas, at least twelve different canapés, and twelve different finger desserts.

"Why didn't you have Reid taste all of this with you?" I ask her as I stare at the plates in front of us. A server slips behind me and fills my glass with water. I feel like royalty being served in her house like this.

"I asked him, but he thought I would enjoy this more with you. We get to pick our favorites, whereas he would just pick it all." She smiles at me. The pregnancy glow on her is a real thing. I've teased her that she's having a boy because her skin is too flawless to be a girl. In which she laughs and says her baby loves her too much to suck away all her beauty.

"Well, tell him my stomach says thank you," I say in awe.

The chef steps up to our table and takes his time explaining each dish. When he's done, we dive in.

"How's work going?" she asks.

I let out a groan. "Terrible. Apparently, my six-figure student loan affords me the title of ungrateful heartbreaker instead of surgeon," I tell her bitterly.

"What?" she asks, coughing as if she almost choked and needs to clear her throat. "What do you mean?" she asks as she stares at me.

"The loyal office staff have clearly taken sides, and it's not mine." My lips pinch together, and then I let out a deep sigh. It's nice to be able to talk to someone about this.

"You've got to be kidding me?" she asks, her fork hanging in midair.

"I wish I was."

Natural light pours into the room from the large windows overlooking her back patio. Frequently, when I'm here, my eyes drift to where Jonah and I danced the night away and where he first kissed me. Has that fondness for the moment faded some over the years? Yes. But it was still there, and now it's come roaring back just like he has.

I was so embarrassed when he saw his name pop up on my watch. I look like a creeper stealing his phone number. It's completely unprofessional, but the confused look which morphed to a pleased look lessened some of the sting. He was happy that I have it. Now I just have to decide whether I'm going to work up the nerve to use it.

"Isn't that like breaking a lot of the company policies? You're a superior to them, and they're speaking negatively, in addition to spreading rumors about your character and personal life." She takes a bite of the eggplant, and her eyes briefly close in satisfaction.

"I know, and I'm actually surprised that Isaac is allowing this. He must know it's happening. The tension at the nurses' station is thick and frigid."

"You should say something to him," she says between bites.

"And make it even more awkward? No, I can handle this. Regardless of whether this dies down this week, I will be setting expectations."

I pick up three different canapés and place them on my plate. The first is a crostini with whipped ricotta, sliced prosciutto, and pickled peaches. The second is a seared scallop topped with a bacon jam, and the third is a perfectly cut piece of watermelon with basil, feta, and balsamic vinegar. I've died and gone to heaven, and there's still so much more.

"As you should. And for the record, I've thought a lot about what Isaac said, and I kind of don't disagree. Ever since I have known you, you've had a purpose, something that drove you. You've always been go go go, but now that seems to have shifted to stalling. And I'm not saying that's a bad thing. I know that you ultimately want to get back to Minneapolis, but I feel like we need to channel some energy into something new. A new project. A new hobby. Something. You have always liked to be busy. When was the last time you took a vacation?"

I laugh. "A vacation. What's a vacation?"

I don't even bother telling her that I agree with her. I

agree with her and Isaac. I do feel like I'm at a standstill, waiting for the next chapter of my life to start. But I do understand what she's saying.

"Exactly. You need a trip where you go somewhere and do nothing but maybe formulate a more streamlined plan for what you want to do next. You're the smartest person I know. You are brilliant at what you do, and we need to channel this more. Meanwhile, breathe in the fresh air, feel the sunshine on your skin, and relax."

"So you're saying you think I'm capable of world domination?" I ask as I slip the watermelon into my mouth, and my tongue rejoices.

She laughs. "Most definitely."

I chew and think about what she's said. Could I go on vacation? I'd be by myself, not that I mind. I just don't know what I would do. "It's not really in my nature to relax."

"But maybe it should be. You've spent so many years working toward this one goal, which you crushed, but maybe you need to figure out some new ones."

She's not wrong. I've floated in this in-between space long enough. Am I moving back to Minneapolis or am I staying? If I stay, for how long and do I want to continue working for this practice or go somewhere else? If it's somewhere else, the big question is where? And then why?

"Assuming I could even get the time off work, where do you suggest I go?"

"Wherever you want. But you could go to the beach house if you don't want to go far. We're not using it anytime soon, and if you go over Memorial Day weekend, you can take the long weekend and not take time off work or take the whole week. It makes no difference to me. Kiddie camps don't start that week anyway. How many injuries could there actually be?"

"You'd be surprised."

I do love their beach house. Last year, Camille decided to have a girls' weekend, and several of us went. The house sits directly on the beach on Anna Maria Island. It's not an overly large house, but they don't need it to be.

And now that she's planted the seed, excitement courses through me.

I've been in Florida for over six years and haven't spent nearly enough time at the beach.

"I suppose I could, if you're sure you don't mind."

She smiles, and it's so genuine. "I don't mind at all. No one is using it, and it's just sitting there begging for visitors."

"Memorial Day weekend isn't a bad idea either."

"Exactly, and it's after the shower." She winks. "But anytime after that works for us. You just tell me when, and I'll make sure the kitchen is stocked."

"Oh, there's no need for that. I'll bring my own food."

"You know I don't mind."

"But I do! You're letting me stay there. You don't need to feed me too. And yes, I find that ironic as you're feeding me now."

She laughs.

There's a knocking on the front door, followed by the

doorbell and then Izzy barking. Camille and I both look toward the foyer, which we can see through the entrance to the sitting room. My guess is they don't get a lot of unplanned visitors, but when the door automatically opens and Vivi runs in with her puppy on a leash trailing close behind, Camille's face lights up.

"Hi, gorgeous girl," Camille says, as she slowly rises out of her chair and then squats down to give the little girl a hug. She's wearing a supercute romper that's pink with white polka dots and I can't help but to wish they made it in my size.

"Hi, Ms. Camille." She gives her a small smile in return and then a big smile to Izzy who's jumped into the middle of the greeting. It's then she notices me and the excitement on her face slips a little at the sight of seeing someone she kind of knows, but really doesn't. "Hi, Ms. Sophie," she says, politely, but a little more quietly.

"Hi, Vivi." I smile back at her.

Will the resemblance to Jonah ever stop being so alarming that my breath catches. I can't even pinpoint exactly what it is, but it's there. And with that thought, my stomach drops as I realize where Vivi is, he's probably close behind.

And sure enough, he steps in and the front door closes.

Is it possible for my mouth to water and go dry at the same time?

This guy always looks so good.

The memory again of him busting me with his number has heat climbing up the back of my neck. Just my luck.

The only explanation I really have is that I wanted it because in an intangible way, it made me feel a little bit closer to him.

Vivi getting attention from Camille has the puppy beelining for me. She jumps on my leg with her tongue flopping out, and I can't help but to bend down and pet her. Izzy shoves her way in as well.

"Hey, Jonah," Camille says, but his gaze is locked on me and my stomach dips.

He's wearing his typical attire of nice athletic wear. Navy joggers, a white T-shirt, and white running shoes. His hair looks disorderly, windblown, perfect, and everything about him somehow feels familiar and inviting, but completely foreign at the same time.

"Hey, Camille," he eventually says back, his voice rolling over me like white noise. Comforting, perfect for my ears, and something I'd like to listen to every night before bed. "Hey, Sophie," he says, acknowledging me too. My breath catches at the sound of my name on his lips. His full lips that I know better than I should.

"What are you two up to today?" Camille asks, as the puppy has moved over to her now and is now jumping for more affection.

"We're selling candy bars," Vivi announces, as she holds up a box in her free hand that has her dance studio logo on it.

"Is that so?" Camille grins at Jonah like she knows how painful this is for him.

"It's for the recital costumes," he grumbles. "Apparently, it doesn't matter that I offered to pay for all of them, Kelli, the studio owner, thinks it's important for them to learn the art of fundraising at an early age."

I roll my lips between my teeth to keep from laughing.

"If I get ten people to buy all my candy, I'll get a special colored flower for my hair," Vivi says.

"Yep," he says, popping the p. "Ten."

I don't even think I know ten people, and definitely not if I exclude work colleagues.

"All right, let me get my purse," Camille tells her, and we move into the kitchen. "How many do you think I should buy for Mr. Reid?" she asks her.

"All of them," Jonah chimes in. "All under ten different names."

"Uncle Jonah, you know that's not how this works!" she chastises him.

My heart squeezes at the look that passes between the two of them. It's the first time I've heard her call him uncle and I think about how amazing it is that he fully stepped up to take care of and raise his brother's daughter.

Camille buys four. I grin because I don't know if she's buying them for herself or to actually share with Reid.

Vivi turns to me. "Would you like to buy one, Ms. Sophie?"

"Of course I would. Us girls have to stick together when it comes to beautiful hair accessories."

Vivi beams and Jonah gives me a look so full of appreciation and thankfulness that butterfly wings flutter inside my stomach.

"Which one should I get?" I ask her, pulling my phone from my back pocket. Apparently, it's no longer cash or check, it's pay and donate by QR code.

"I like the ones with the rice krispies in them, but Uncle Jonah likes the peanut butter."

"Peanut butter." My eyes flash to his and find warmth and fondness staring back at me. "I love peanut butter, too. I think I'll take two of those."

"You've made a great choice," she tells me, as she walks me through the purchase.

"Wildflower, what do you say?"

"Thank you," she says, smiling at Camille and me both.

Wildflower. What an interesting nickname.

Chapter 11
Jonah

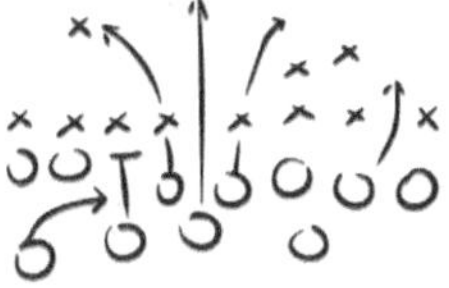

It's been two days since I last saw Sophie and I'm annoyed with myself about how much I think about her. It feels wrong and useless knowing she's with someone else, but I can't seem to stop. She will forever be my *the one who got away*, and for that alone I seem to be torturing myself. I have no one to blame but myself, but even if I did try to rewrite history, I'm not sure that I would or could have changed anything. That was such a horrible time in my life. Emotionally, I was spent with what I had, and to top it off, that was the year we lost the Super Bowl and Jack to an injury. At the time, Jack was a beloved starting wide receiver on our team. He was tackled in such a way that it blew out his knee to where he had to be carted off and it ended his career.

Everyone in that stadium felt the shock and horror of that injury. Some nights when I lie in bed I still see it play out from the replay on the jumbotron. Talk about my worst fear coming true.

But besides that, there is the absolute situation that Vivi and I are a package deal. A package that I think is amazing, but others might not see it that way. And reality is, Sophie and I had only spent one night together. There was no real foundation, we weren't even friends, I just really really liked her. From the moment I saw her, I wanted to know her, it's just too bad I didn't get the chance. Which has me turning full circle again. She's the one that got away.

Dating is hard. And whereas it wasn't scary before, now it is. I don't even know if I'm ready for it, but with the increasing thoughts of Sophie, even though I know she's unavailable, I might be getting closer. Or maybe it's just that I want to be close to her. Who knows. No one has piqued my interest in years, but her. Only her.

"I saw her on Saturday," I unconsciously blurt out to my friends, and then cringe. While I love my friends, they can be a bit meddlesome and gossipy. It's hard to keep secrets on a team like ours, everyone talks to everyone and everyone is up in everyone's business.

"Saw who?" Sully asks. His feet are propped up on the ottoman in front of him as we watch golf highlights on ESPN and eat barbecue. I put a pork shoulder on the smoker yesterday and let it slow cook all night and most of today. It makes the most delicious pulled pork, which is something that Vivi will eat if I leave the sauce off it.

I wasn't surprised that in addition to Tyler, Sully and

Camden made their way over after I mentioned it in the locker room.

"You know who," Tyler says, smirking at me and taking a bite of his sandwich. Add in some Publix baked beans, potato salad, mac and cheese for my mini, and a bag of chips, this is the perfect meal.

Yesterday, Tyler took Vivi and me out on the boat, and of course Vivi hit him up for a candy bar in which she innocently announced that she'd already sold some to Camille and Sophie. His eyes widened at this information, but I didn't engage. Even though he tried to coax it out of me, several times, in fact. That is until now.

"The hot doctor?" Sully asks, looking at me curiously.

Since our run-in back at Vivi's appointment, the guys have affectionately coined her the hot doctor. At first I was pissed and repeatedly told them to knock it off, but all that did was fuel them even more.

"Yep."

My heart rate picks up a little just mentioning her out loud and I glance out into the small backyard to find Vivi and Molly. It's been a week and I swear this dog is the playmate she's never had. The two of them are inseparable.

"And?" he probes, taking another bite of his sandwich.

I shrug. "She bought a candy bar from Vivi."

His face lights up and I can't help but to reciprocate and crack a smile of my own. Tyler's looking at me like he knows the answers to all the world's problems, but Camden says nothing. He's always been more of the "listen more and talk less" kind of guy.

"By the look on your face, I'm assuming she gave you more than just her money."

"No, but . . ." I don't know what to say. There really isn't anything.

"But what?" Camden chimes in, standing to go wander back into the kitchen for more food.

"They're trying to ask if you got her number." Tyler rolls his eyes.

"I do have her number," I tell them, already knowing how this conversation is going to go. And if Tyler opens his mouth to tell them that I've actually had it longer, I might just have to kill him.

"Have you texted her yet?" Sully asks.

I don't know why it's so hard to tell them this, but it is. "No."

The three of them look at each other, and then they look at me. I'm so uncomfortable, I want to kick each of them out of my house. I know I asked for this by blurting out that I saw her, but still.

"Why not? You should have texted her that night," Sully says, looking at me and pinning me with his knowing blue eyes.

The thing about Sully, he's a tank of a guy. To be a defensive tackle and on the line, you have to be. For all intents and purposes, his appearance makes him kind of scary, but when he looks at you with those clear blue eyes, it's almost calming. They give off kind vibes and instantly that scary shifts to big teddy bear.

"I know. I'm just not sure what to say."

"How old are you, five?" Camden asks. "Never mind, I take that back, even five-year-olds know how to talk to a pretty girl," he says, plopping back down on the couch with a full plate of food.

"Yeah, and word on the street is that you've seen her several times now," Sully says on the sly, meanwhile Tyler snickers.

My head jerks to look at him and he throws his hands up. "It wasn't me."

Everyone knows about my night from two years ago with Sophie, regardless of the fact that I told them nothing. I became an interest to them when I went from a recluse player to spinning her around the dance floor. Apparently, my actions made me an enigma to the teammates at the party and it was discussed at length.

"Darius?" It could be him; he is a busybody and a gossiper who overheard Tyler and me talking at the training facility.

"Nope." Sully's smirk stretches into a full-blown smile. He's enjoying this and I give him a look that lets him know I don't think this is funny. "It was Reid. He was mentioning it to Bryan and others overheard."

That makes more sense given the fact that Sophie and Camille are friends.

"What else did he say?" I ask him, but it's Camden who chimes in.

"I overheard this from Bryan. From what Lexi told him, after your little run-in at her office, she called Camille to find out all the scoop about you."

Did you hear the needle just scratch across the record to halt time? Because I swear I did and my jaw drops.

"She did?"

"Yep and that was a couple of weeks ago."

Not a couple. Now it was a lot. A lot of weeks ago we had that run-in at her office. Was this before or after I asked if I could see her again? Regret stings like an old wound that I waited so long to initiate another conversation with her. Then again, now she's seeing someone, so it's not like it would have mattered.

"And you're just now thinking to tell me this?" I ask him.

He shrugs. "Apparently, she thought Vivi was your daughter."

And with that, he just confirms every worry I've ever had. She didn't know about John, she didn't know how my life completely imploded, and all this time she thought I used her and ghosted her.

My heart sinks into my stomach.

I know I'm in the wrong here, I should have had someone reach out to her to let her know I wasn't coming. In the perfect world, she would have seen something or heard something, since we do have overlapping friends, and understood, but that's not what happened. I don't blame her for not coming to find me, if the roles were reversed, I certainly wouldn't.

I should probably answer him with something, but I have nothing to say.

Seeing my mood drop, he throws his hand across the

back of the couch and studies me before asking, "So what are you going to do about it?"

"What do you mean?"

"You like this girl," Camden states as if it was that simple.

"Yeah, well, she's got a boyfriend."

"How do you know?" His brows rise.

"Because, despite what you think, I actually did make a move. I asked her if I could see her again and she told me she was dating someone. Case closed."

"But is it really?" he asks suspiciously and I let out a deep sigh.

Maybe I could text her. I glance at my phone which is lying on the coffee table.

"Do it. Do it. Do it," Sully chants.

"You're a fucking idiot," I tell him, but I pick up my phone and pull up her name.

The text thread is obviously blank and it taunts me.

"Quit staring at it. It's just a text."

Tyler is watching me, staying quiet. He knows me the best and he knows not to push.

Sucking in a deep breath, I type the words and press send. My heart is pounding in my chest.

This reaction is so stupid. It's just a text. A text to a girl who I really like.

> Hey, it's Jonah. I just wanted to say thank you again for buying the candy bar.

"Did you hit send?" Sully asks.

I glare at him like he's suddenly annoying when he's anything but.

Tyler chuckles, but still he reaches over and pats me on the shoulder.

"This feels ridiculously like a therapy session."

"You still going to those?" Sully asks.

"No, I'm not. But Vivi still is. She's better for sure, but she's not quite there yet. And I'd like to think that by now I know what to do and what to say to make her happy, but I don't. She still has down days, and her therapist, I don't have the answers like she does, and I'm man enough to admit that."

"How often do you go?"

"We're down to once a month."

My phone vibrates in my hand and the screen lights up with Sophie's name.

Tyler sees it and smirks.

Of course. How could I tell her no.
Besides, peanut butter is my favorite.

"What did she say?" Sully asks.

"Nothing," I tell him. It's a stupid thing, but I like knowing something that is a favorite to her and I want to keep this to myself.

"She must have said something because you've got a stupid grin on your face."

I ignore them all.

I knew there was a reason I liked you. Great minds think alike.

Has she sold them all yet?

No. She's sold some to Camille, you, Tyler, Sully, and Camden. Next up, I'm unleashing her at the training facility. I don't think there will be anything left, but if there are, I'll cover it.

Personally, I'm traumatized from fundraisers. I was a Girl Scout and had to sell cookies.

Girl Scout you say. Cute little uniform and all?

It wasn't cute, but yes. The problem was, we were all Girl Scouts in my neighborhood and in the same troop. We were all trying to sell cookies to the same people, so it was stressful. I once had a little old lady tell me no, that the early bird gets the worm, and it wasn't me.

Stop.

See, traumatized.

So what you're saying is, you're a pro at this and next time you'll take Vivi out? Door to door?

Ha! Not a chance.

Chapter 12
Sophie

Walking up to Camille's house, I know I shouldn't be awed at the decorations for this party, but I already am as I stare at a large balloon arch that isn't an arch, but more like a piece of art. The balloons are in all different sizes and it's made up of silver, shades of green, and yellow. It's beautiful.

"Good afternoon," a gentleman in a tux says, as he opens the door for me.

"Hello there," I answer as I duck past him and into the foyer, which has exploded with green and white orchids. It's here where one staff member takes my gift from me and a server greets me holding a platter of white fizzy-looking drinks with mint.

I shouldn't be surprised she has a signature cocktail for the event, that's a very Camille thing to do.

Camille squeals when she sees me and she waddles

over to give me a hug. She looks radiant in a pale green dress that is skintight and hugging her belly perfectly.

"You have to come meet some people," she says, as she drags me into the living room. There are her friends from New York, Charlie, Ali and Leila who are both married to two brothers, her mother, and Reid's mother. Then there's Lexi, Meg, Missy, her friend Katie, and maybe ten more wives and girlfriends from the team. It's a nice-size group and I'm so happy for her.

It's then next to Lexi I see Vivi. She's watching me and I wave at her. She waves back and then slowly makes her way on over to stand next to me.

"Look how pretty you are today," I tell her as I take in her outfit. It's almost identical to Camille's and I love that she's gone out of her way to make this day special for her too.

"Thank you. I like your dress, too," she tells me.

The invitation said spring cocktail attire and I've known Camille long enough to know that means something different in the South.

"This old thing?" I pop my hip out. I'm wearing a coral-colored Lily Pulitzer dress that is tight on the top with spaghetti straps, but has a full flaring skirt that stops just before my knees. I have on gold jewelry and gold heels.

She giggles.

"Wanna play the games with me?" she asks, eyes big and hopeful.

"Sure, lead the way."

She takes my hand and my heart thuds in my chest. She's so sweet and she's so Jonah.

We spend the next thirty minutes or so guessing how many diapers are in the diaper cake, how many jellybeans are in the jar, filling in the blanks to classic nursery rhymes, filling out a card titled "Who Knows Mommy Best," and eating. Eating canapés that I've dreamed about since the tasting, lunch, cake, you name it, I'm stuffed. It was all so delicious.

We've just settled on the couch to watch Camille open presents when she leans over and curiously asks, "Uncle Jonah just said you were a doctor, but what kind of doctor are you?"

"An orthopedic doctor," I tell her.

"Orthopedic," she says more to herself and sounding out the letters.

While orthopedics covers all areas of the musculoskeletal system, such as, muscles, bones, joints, ligaments, and tendons, I make it easy on her when I say, "I'm a bone doctor."

"You like bones?" Her face is a little scrunched up like she doesn't understand.

"I do. I love them. They're so interesting. Take Ms. Camille's baby, when it's born, they'll have over three hundred bones, but by the time they're big like me and your uncle Jonah, there'll only be two hundred and six."

"What happens to them?" she asks.

"As you grow, they fuse to make you taller and stronger."

We then proceed to spend the next fifteen minutes talking about bones. Fortunately for me, it's a subject I could talk about endlessly, unfortunately for her, she's currently the recipient. But in the end she thinks about the things we've talked about and says, "I think I might like bones too."

"What else do you like?" I ask her.

She gives me a small smile as she says, "Ballet, Molly, dolphins, strawberries, baking, reading," shyly she pauses, "wildflowers."

Wildflowers.

Jonah called her Wildflower, there must be a story there.

"I love all of those things, too. Even the wildflowers. There's this one that grows here in Florida called a phlox. They are a mixture of pinks, purple, and white."

"I like pink."

"I can tell, look at your pretty fingernails."

She looks down at her hands. "Uncle Jonah painted them for me."

Be still my heart.

I already thought he was attractive, that's a given, but the more I hear of the little details like nicknames, painting her fingernails, going to the puppy boutique, he's starting to take on superhero qualities, which moves him to a whole new level.

"He did a good job."

"Thank you," comes a deep voice from behind us and my heart jolts.

She smiles at me and then turns to face him.

"Hi, Uncle Jonah," Vivi says, her face lighting up.

His gaze skips between the two of us, before it lands on her. Meanwhile, I can't tear mine off him. I don't know if he's coming from somewhere or if he dressed nicely to come inside, but he's wearing khaki pants that are molded to his thighs and a sage-green polo that is molded to his chest and arms.

"Hi, Wildflower. Having fun?"

She gets up to go to him, she jumps and he catches her. It's then I watch the two of them hug like they haven't seen each other in months. It's a tight, long loving hug, and my eyes prick at the sweetness and the devastation of her needing a hug like this. Obviously, I understand there's lingering trauma, but I never considered separation anxiety. Of course she worries that when he leaves her, she'll never see him again. My heart aches for them both. There's so much about what the two of them have had to deal with and overcome over the past two years, I feel nothing but admiration for him.

For her too.

She pulls back. "Yes, Ms. Sophie is teaching me about bones."

"Is she now?" His hazel eyes land back on me and I almost stutter, as he's half rendered me stupid by just one look, and I take a deep breath to pull myself together.

"Yes, she asked me what kind of doctor I was, which in turn led to a conversation about babies, her broken ankle, and how the foot has twenty-six bones."

"Babies?" He looks a little panicked.

I follow where his mind has gone and have to roll my lips between my teeth for a second to keep from laughing. "Yes, babies are born with over three hundred bones."

He looks back at her, she's watching him and he says, "That's a lot of bones. Try not to break any more of them, okay?"

She giggles.

"Why don't you go tell Ms. Camille thank you for inviting you, and that I'm here for you. Molly is in the car and we don't want her to get too hot."

"Okay."

He gently lets her down, she takes off, and Jonah and I end up staring at each other.

"So bones," he says, breaking the silence.

I shrug. "It's what I know."

He chuckles. "I'm certain you know a lot more than that. How was the party?" he asks, as he looks around. Now that the presents are opened, people have scattered into their own conversations and are all about the house.

"It was good, you know Camille. She's so happy today. I still can't get over them not finding out the gender of the baby. My type A personality can't handle that at all."

"Right. My brother and his wife found out that Vivi was a girl during one of their appointments. She instantly had an identity, became known to all of us as Vivianne and was a full-time member of the family before she was even born. Before that, I don't know, it was just different. She was just pregnant with a baby."

"Did they want a girl?"

He tucks his hands into his pants pockets. "They didn't care. Both of them were school teachers and loved all kids. John coached his high school's football team, so I think maybe he might have wanted a boy, but he was the best girl dad."

My heart aches at the past tense use when he speaks about them.

"Well, from what I've seen, you happen to be a pretty good girl uncle, too."

Jonah doesn't say anything, he just looks at me openly, a little pink hitting his cheeks.

"So I guess this is how it's going to be now," I say to him.

"What do you mean?"

"We went from not seeing each other at all, to running into each other all the time."

He hesitates, and then he says, "I hope so."

Butterflies dance their way around my stomach.

"You look beautiful, by the way," he says, his gaze traveling over me.

I glance down at the dress and smooth the skirt out. "Thank you."

"I'm ready," Vivi says as she moves to stand next to Jonah. She takes his hand, and his large one wraps around hers, covering it entirely.

"Okay, then," he says, looking at her and then at me.

Together the three of us walk toward the door. I'm not leaving, I'm just walking them out apparently.

The staff member that took my bag, hands Vivi a goodie bag that has her name on it. Her face lights up as she glances at the contents. While I'm certain she got the goodies everyone else is getting, her bag has a few more things stuffed inside.

"So I'll see you around?" he says.

And using his words from that day in Hyde Park Village, I tell him, "I hope so."

Chapter 13
Jonah

When I was first drafted out of college, Carolina took me in the fifth round. To say I was excited would be an understatement. While I do grasp how hard it is to stay on a team and be consistently a part of their fifty-three-man roster, naive me thought that didn't apply to me. I was dedicated, worked hard, and couldn't fathom that I wasn't in it until the end. With every team I've played on in my football career, I was with one team. There was my little league team, the Colts; my high school team, the Braves; and my college team, the Bulls. I wasn't one of those players who jumped around to find the best team, or entered into the portal in hopes to be seen by someone possibly better. When I commit, I commit.

And I committed to Carolina.

I bought into the leadership team, the words they spoke, the brand, the city, I even bought my first condo. I lived, breathed, and bled for Carolina, so when my agent and the coach sat me down to inform me that I was being traded, I was devastated.

All I could think about was, "What did I not do to make them believe in me like I believed in them?"

Stepping outside of myself, I understand these franchises are a business and I recognized that the move they were making was a good one for the team, but it didn't make me feel any better. It made me feel like my worth and commitment was devalued and it sent me spiraling.

So it was mid-season of my second year, the beginning of October and one month before the trade deadline that I packed my bags and moved to Tampa determined to be even better than I was before.

Every team has a culture, a vibe, and a motto or slogan, but at the time I was so focused on myself and proving to the team what I could do, that I overlooked the depth of ours. Everyone has heard of "Clear eyes, full hearts," or "Faith, family, and football," but for the Tarpons it's a little different, it's, "Victory starts in the heart."

The heart is where the most honest and pure emotions occur. Love, compassion, tenderness, devotion, faithfulness, all emotions that when they're not diluted with thoughts from the brain, speak to who we are. For both teams, I was trying to be an individual. An individual who showed up, worked hard, and was trying to keep my place. But it was when John died that I felt the heart—the heart of the team.

I loved my teammates in Carolina, we were great

friends, but here in Tampa the team is so much more, they're a family. I'd done nothing to receive the love and support that they all showered me with, but that's the thing about family, they never once ask for anything in return. It was freely given.

And once I succumbed to the true meaning of that phrase, everything changed. Victory became more than just winning games, which we still did, because the chemistry between us as the players changed too, but it was about how we chose to live our lives.

With each other.

For each other.

So I shouldn't be surprised by how many people show up for Vivi today, but I am.

"Bro, who's that woman standing over there," Sully asks, discreetly tilting his head toward the left side of the stage.

I follow his gaze to find the woman standing on the left side of the stage, wearing all black, and holding a clipboard.

"That's Kelli. She's the owner of the dance studio."

He nods his head, but doesn't say anything further. He just keeps his gaze locked on her and I can feel my brows rise in curiosity.

Sully is a guy's guy. He's all about the team. Leading the team, supporting the team, loving the team. He's probably been this way his whole life, and for some guys, that's enough. So I find it interesting he's asking about Kelli. He's never even hinted around about being interested in someone, but then again, neither have I.

Kelli, on the other hand, while she wouldn't let me pay for the costumes, she did accept my offer to rent the theater space tonight, and she picked Centro Austuriano, in Ybor City. It's an old theater from the early 1900s, and while her suggestion seemed great at the time, now that we're here and I look at how many of my teammates have shown up, I'm not so sure. The seats aren't all that accommodating for our large size. They're those old theater seats with the red velvety fabric you'd expect to find. Small, unforgiving when you sit in them, and the rows are close together.

"Do you want me to introduce her to you?" I ask him, and his face blanches.

"No. That's okay. I was just curious. I don't remember seeing her at the Christmas show."

"She was there, running around just like she is here."

"Huh," he says, still looking at her.

"Does Vivi have a solo?" Camden asks, walking up and joining our conversation.

"I don't think so. They're seven. She's in ballet two, that's one level up from beginner."

"Gotcha," he says, meanwhile Tyler's eyes light up and a mischievous smile creeps onto his face.

"Why do you look like this?" I ask him.

"Because you should look over your shoulder," he says.

Turning, I scan the people who are entering the room and that's when I spot Sophie. Her eyes meet mine, hold, and slowly I watch as she stands a little taller, takes a deep breath and then walks my way.

Tyler claps me on the shoulder, and both him and Camden leave me standing by myself.

"You're here?" I ask, completely shocked.

"I am. Vivi invited me at the shower."

I want to tell her that she didn't have to come, that I'm certain Vivi would have understood, but I don't. I will never deny her support and friendship, no matter who it's from.

"Well, thank you for coming."

I'm so happy she's here.

Behind her, I can see Tyler making everyone scoot over one seat. He's making room for her between us and he smirks at me.

"If you were hoping to blend in tonight"—she glances around the auditorium and then at the row of bulky players—"I'd say you failed."

I chuckle. I know we're a sight to see. "These parents are used to us. We might have been a little jarring at first, but two years in and we're just another family here for their dancer."

"I think that's amazing." She smiles back at me.

"Aren't you going to introduce us?" Tyler asks, all fake innocence.

I glance at the row of my friends and they are all staring at us, some more subtle than others, but most with blatant open curiosity.

"Sure." Heat climbs up the back of my neck. "Sophie, I

think you know some of the people here, but this is Tyler, Camden, Bryan and Lexi, Camille and Reid, Billy and Missy, Darius, Dylan, and Sully. Everyone, this is Dr. Sophie Black."

"Hey, Sophie," Camille calls out, her hands propped up on her very large stomach. The two friends smile at each other, and farther past her, Lexi and Missy wave.

Obviously, I know that she's friends with them. After all, I met her because of them, but I still find it strange that it took over two years for us to run into each other again.

"So why ballet?" she asks.

"It was the therapist's idea that she become involved in an activity. While it was important to let her grieve, he said it was also just as important to help her move on with her life. She needed outlets, things to look forward to that would surround her with others and keep her out of the house. We talked about gymnastics, soccer, and even swimming since she loves the water, but she was set on dance and ballet."

"That's good that she loves it."

"I think she does."

The lights flicker twice, alerting everyone it's time to take their seats. We sit down in the two tiny seats they'd left for us, and where I can see my friends struggling, I'm hit with the subtle scent of sweet and floral. It smells good. She smells so good that I want to lean into her space and bury my face against her neck.

I turn to look at her, and my heart flips in my stomach.

She's here, and she's so close, despite the fact that this is Vivi's night, I suddenly feel anxious.

"Listen, I'm not sure what you have planned after this, but we're all heading to Bern's for dessert."

I know she's dating someone, but if she knows more people will be there, like there are here tonight, maybe she'll come.

"Bern's Steak House?" She gives me this incredulous look.

"Well, yeah. Vivi likes the dessert room, so I made a reservation," I tell her like it's no big deal.

I understand why she's looking at me the way she is. I'm certain most grab something quick, but I want to celebrate Vivi in a way that makes her feel important and loved. And as it goes, her favorite dessert is from the most prestigious steak house in town. Can't fault the girl for good taste.

"As appealing as that sounds since I've never eaten there, I'm actually heading out of town after this and need to get on the road."

"Oh." My heart sinks. It's not like it would have been a date, or I'd get to spend a lot of individual time with her, as everyone is coming, but still. Call me greedy. Call me hopeful. Call me whatever you want. If I can get even a few more minutes with her, I'll take it. "Well, then you coming tonight means even more. Thank you."

Her eyes crinkle in the corners as she gives me a closed-mouth smile. A smile that really wants to draw my eyes to her lips, but I keep them locked on her.

"And if you ever find yourself hungry and craving a good steak and a glass of wine, I'd love to take you. You have my number," I tell her as the lights go out. I had to throw that out there. I want her to know that my invitation to take her out is still open.

Next to me, she crosses her legs so her foot rests up against the outside of my leg. I know I should move and give her more space, but honestly, the seats are too small to move anywhere, and I'll take any contact I can get.

Nerves race through me as the first group of little girls take the stage. The music is a famous piano medley that I should know but don't. I recognize the tune but not what it is, and as the piece escalates, so do my nerves. I want this to go well for Vivi. She's worked hard, and she loves it so much.

I can feel it when Sophie looks at me, but right now, I can only focus on the stage. I can only handle one large emotion at a time, and this moment is about Vivi. My hand tightens around the bouquet I'm holding. It's then that I glance down the row and realize all the guys on my team have brought her flowers. A lump rises up in my throat, and I have to swallow it down.

When Vivi's group takes the stage, I pull up my phone and start taking pictures. I know one of the other guys will get the recording, but I need one of her in the cutest little ballet outfit. They wear pale-blue leotards and tutus for this performance, with the standard pink tights and pink ballet shoes. Sure enough, all twelve little girls have their hair pulled back slick into a bun, with some royal-blue feathered thing sticking off their heads.

We're easy to spot in the crowd, as we're taller than most, and as they take their place, she finds me and gives me a small smile. She's easy to spot too as she's in the front row.

I wave, and her cheeks turn red. She then forgets about me as she finds Kelli at the foot of the stage.

The music starts, and the girls fluidly move, performing their routine.

These moments always feel so large for me, and I struggle with staying in the moment and the enormous amount of grief that threatens to take over. I'm so proud of her. I know what I'm feeling is what a parent feels for their child when they've worked hard for something, and you see them accomplishing their goals. But at the same time, that wave of grief always hits me because John will never see these moments. He will never see how brave, beautiful, kind, and smart she is.

My eyes blur for the unfairness that life afforded him, and Vivi too. While I would never be anywhere else but where my Wildflower is, if I could trade places with John, there'd be no hesitation.

I watch as she turns, bends, and changes formation. I don't know what it's called in the dance world, that's a football term, but it's essentially the same thing. She moves around the floor, ending where she started, and as the music drifts to a close, she folds herself into a final pose.

She was perfect.

And as the other parents quietly clap, our whole row erupts with enthusiastic but polite cheers. Chuckles echo around the theater, but all I can see is Vivi. Her smile now is large and bright, and I'm so full of love and pride, I take a deep breath in to push it down.

As they exit the stage, warmth slips over my hand. I glance down and see that Sophie has placed hers on top of mine. I didn't forget that she was sitting there. How could I? But I was fully invested in my tiny mini on the stage doing her thing.

I refrain from looking at her, as I need these emotions to be mine and mine alone, but I take a risk and flip my hand over to see what she'll do.

Without hesitation, she laces her fingers through mine, and if I hadn't already been on the verge of tears, this does it. I breathe in deep, let it go, and blink hard. While I have my friends, and they're here for both of us, at this moment it feels like she's finally here for me.

Chapter 14
Team Chat

Sully: Are we just going to ignore the elephant in the room, or are we going to talk about the hot doctor showing up for Vivi

Darius: Oh, when you said elephant, I thought you were talking about yourself

Titan: 😂

Sully: 🖕

Sully: You just wish you were my size so you could play on my side, the side that counts

Camden: Rethink that statement if you want to be in this chat

Darius: Yeah, what he said

Miles: I saw D eating all that bananas foster last night. He's trying to cross to the dark side

Darius: The fuck I am. Gotta protect the pocket.

Bryan: D, you know I love you

Reid: I knew she was coming

Bryan: Me too

Jonah: And neither of you thought to tell me?

Reid: And miss that look on your face when you saw her

Jonah: What look is that

Reid: (Sends GIF of a cat with its big blinking eyes)

Jonah: Oh, fuck off. I did not look like that

Tyler: You kind of did

Jonah: Brutus

Tyler: Just sayin'

Miles: Hot doctor fits her perfectly. She can wear her coat for me any day

Jonah: Don't talk about her

Tyler: Bro, that's just wrong

Sully: Too far, Miles

Miles: What? It's not like they're dating

Reid: Yet

Jonah: What's that supposed to mean?

Reid: (Send GIF of eating popcorn)

Chapter 15
Sophie

There's a feeling I get whenever I'm on this island. It's a place not far from home, but it makes me feel like I'm somewhere else entirely. The air is salty but breezy, the sky appears brighter, and as I stand on the deck this morning after completing a yoga workout and look out at the blue-green water edged with white sand, I can't help but wonder why it is that I've stayed away for so long.

Camille was right. I needed this.

It's quiet, except for the slow rolling of the tide against the shore, the rustling of the seagrass as it sways back and forth over the dunes, and the cawing of the seagulls. Not many people have found their way out yet this morning, and I've immensely enjoyed the peacefulness and the serenity of my surroundings. During my residency days, I read a study that talked about different ways to lower blood pressure. Did you know that all it takes is one minute and forty seconds of looking at an open body of water for a person's blood pressure to lower? Such a short amount of time has such a positive effect on the human body.

Gratitude sweeps over me that I've met such a generous soul. She didn't even think twice about offering me her house, and it's a house that I absolutely love. Then again, she has this unique decorating ability and could make a run-down shack or an igloo look appealing.

Grabbing my mat and rolling it, I walk back into the house and take in the details I've always loved. While the walls aren't stark white, they aren't fully cream either. They're painted just so that the interior feels bright and warm. Large windows face the water with sheer white curtains, the furniture in the living room is a soft caramel leather, and there are pops of color and beach decor like a pale-blue-seafoam-and-white swirl area rug, blue fabric chairs at the island, navy-and-white-striped pillows, and fish accents. The lamp bases are fish, fish artwork adorns the walls, and there's even a large glass fish on the dining room table filled with shells she's found.

I should collect some shells while I'm here. When I end up moving back to Minnesota, they will be a nice reminder of my time and friends here.

Friends.

All along the hallway wall to the upstairs bedrooms are pictures of Reid, Camille, their families, and their friends. Of course there is a recent one with the guys from the team in it. I shouldn't be surprised, but as I search for a smiling Jonah, my eyes lock on him when I find him.

I've always thought that Jonah Dallmann is the best-looking guy I've ever seen with his kind eyes, gentle smile, and spectacular body. But after seeing his vulnerability and love for Vivi last night, my attraction for him moved to a whole new level. There's something about seeing a guy who is head over heels in love with their child—after all, that is what she is now—and who wouldn't find that attractive?

I know what's happened to them both has left some deep scars, but as his eyes shined bright while staring at Vivi's every move, mine couldn't help but do the same. All those people were there for her last night, but I hope he realizes they were there for him too.

Gently, I touch the photo, then make my way to the shower. I have three whole days to myself where I don't have to think about work or what I want to do next with my life, assuming the Minneapolis dream doesn't turn out. Should I be using this free time to do just that? Probably. But there's sunshine, a brand-new book in my bag to read, and I just want to have food delivered while I sit back with my feet up.

Coming out of the bathroom, I round the corner as I head toward my room and run right into another person. A small person. It's so jarring to me that I screamed because I didn't expect someone else to be in the house.

Loudly.

And so does the little person. Or should I say little girl.

We are screaming at each other for a good couple of

seconds even though our brains have recognized who we're looking at.

The massive sound of thunder hits the stairs as Jonah heads our way, yelling for Vivi.

Like the train wreck that is about to happen, in slow motion, he rounds the corner with his features a mix between severe and terrified, snatches her up without even looking to see what the problem is, and his hand lands in the middle of my chest as he shoves me hard away from them. Hard enough that the wind is half knocked out of me, and I'm thrown backward. With a resounding thump, I ricochet off the floor twice.

"No!" Vivi yells at the same time I roll to my side, curl into a ball for self-preservation, and let out a noise that sounds like a whimper.

It's not like I think he's actually going to kick me, but what if he did? Fear does crazy things to people, and sometimes they can't see straight.

"Ms. Sophie," Vivi calls out, wholly distressed.

"Sophie?" Somewhere in the short span of me hearing her trying to get down out of Jonah's arms and me with my eyes squeezed shut, the red haze he saw clears, and he breathes out, "Sophie. Oh my God, are you okay? I'm so sorry."

Both of them are now squatting down next to me, and it's then I realize that I'm lying on the floor and remember I'm only wearing a small towel. The one that was wrapped around my head has half fallen off, and for all I know, my butt and other bits are hanging out for both of them to see.

So humiliating.

"I didn't expect for there to be anyone else here. What are you doing here?"

My eyes shoot to his, and I'm not sure what he sees, but he blanches.

"Please let me help you up," he says, putting his large, warm hands on me and lifting me to a sitting position.

I'm clutching the towel to my chest, and my legs are pressed together so tightly, but even still, this is so embarrassing. The towel on my head slides and falls off.

"I'm here because Camille gave me the house for the weekend. I told you last night I was going out of town. What are you doing here?"

I move to stand so I can pull the towel down. Vivi's eyes are so big as she stares at Jonah and me, while his expression is a mixture of confusion and awe. What he has to be awed over, I have no idea.

"Reid told us to take the house this week since they weren't coming this year, and it was available. Vivi loves the beach."

If I wasn't so mortified, I might actually stop and take the time to think about this, but I am, and I need him to stop looking at me.

Both of them.

"Do you mind?" I ask while picking up the extra towel off the floor, clutching it to me, and trying to shrink into myself so they both don't see anything I don't want them to see. Not that Jonah hasn't seen it before, but it's been a long time.

His cheeks flush red, and being more agile than a man his size should be, he jumps back and grabs Vivi.

"Right. We'll just be downstairs in the living room." At that, he spins and walks off with her tucked under his arm. Vivi looks back at me and grins.

Racing to my room, I pick up my phone and fire off a text to Camille.

Did you know that Vivi and Jonah were going to be at the beach house too?

I wait for a response, but nothing comes. No three dots, no call, no nothing. Silence.

I drop the phone on the bed and then myself, face-down, groaning into the comforter.

What are the odds that both of us end up here at the same time? Knowing all of our friends, I'm guessing pretty high.

Peeling myself off the bed, I get dressed, throwing on a pair of shorts and a tank top. I brush my hair, stop to look at myself once in the mirror, and then head back downstairs. Jonah is hauling Molly's crate inside, and next to the base of the stairs are their bags and a cooler.

"So," he says, dropping the crate and moving to the living room. His gaze follows me as he sits on the couch, and I sit in a chair opposite him. Vivi has Molly, who is running around and sniffing, checking things out.

"So," I answer, not really sure what I should be saying or really doing. Am I expected to leave now? I really don't want to, and the longer we stare at each other, the more my nerves kick into high gear.

He makes me nervous, and I don't know why. I wasn't nervous the night we were together, but maybe it's because so much time has passed, and I've thought about him a lot over the years. The reality of him vanished, but the memory became almost dreamlike. And now here he is, staring at me like he's happy to see me.

Vivi breaks the silence as she wiggles her way in front of me. "Do you want to go to the beach with us? Uncle Jonah promised to help me build a sandcastle but hates looking for shells. We could look for shells."

I glance at him to try to gauge if he's on board with this or if he wants me to leave. Do I want him to leave? No. Suddenly, with her invitation and his open expression, I think this weekend will turn into something completely different altogether.

"If it's okay with your uncle, I'd love to go," I tell her, and she smiles while squeezing the dog.

Jonah clears his throat and relaxes further into the couch with one arm thrown across the back. "I hope you'll stay the weekend too. The house is big enough, and Vivi would love the extra company," Jonah says.

"Just Vivi?" I tease, and as soon as the words are out of my mouth, my eyes widen in panic.

Why did I just say that? This is not how people talk in front of children, and she's sitting right there, looking back and forth between the two of us. Jonah's eyes widen too as he takes in my reaction, and then his lips press together in a suppressed grin. "I'd like to stay," I tell him.

His smile grows, and he lets out a deep exhale. "Good."

"Yay! I'm going to go change," Vivi tells us as she sets Molly down and runs off while Jonah and I continue to stare at each other.

His gaze slowly travels over me, and it feels like he's dragging a feather across my skin. My stomach tightens under his perusal, and then he frowns. His eyes linger on my shirt, turning heavy with remorse and guilt. "I really am sorry I shoved you. I heard her screaming, and I just reacted. Are you sure you're okay?"

I'd forgotten about that, and my hand involuntarily moves to the center of my chest. It's not sore, and neither is my tailbone, but my pride might be—after all, this is Jonah Dallmann.

"I'm good. No worries, no damage done, and I completely understand," I reassure him while standing. "But I'd better go put on a suit. I'd hate to keep her waiting."

A smile tips one corner of his mouth as he stands too. "I'd better go do the same. Oh, and, Sophie . . ."

"Yeah?"

"Not just Vivi," he says, his voice low and deep.

Heat flashes through my system.

Oh my.

That's how I ended up on the beach, under an easy shade that Jonah put up, sitting in a low-to-the-ground chair and watching them build a sandcastle with different-sized plastic buckets.

The view is so good, and I'm not talking about the water.

Jonah is shirtless with a hat and sunglasses on, and he's wearing a pink swimsuit that isn't long and baggie but medium length and the perfect size for his thighs. It should be a sin to look as good as he does. His arms are long and layered with muscles, and his abs look like they've been sculpted they are so perfect. I would say I'm envious of how fit he is, but I'm aware of how much work he puts into his body to get it to look that way, and well, no, thank you.

My eyes also find a tattoo that he didn't have before. It's not super large, but it's placed on his left rib cage, just under his heart. From what I can tell, it looks like stars, maybe a constellation permanently inked into his skin.

From my bag, my phone beeps, and I see it's Camille.

Oh, I might have heard that somewhere. I hope it's not a problem.

Remember what I said about her having a sweet soul? I take it back. She totally planned this.

Chapter 16
Jonah

o I even need to discuss my shock and freaking delight at finding Sophie here? I want to be mad at Reid about this, as Vivi and I have been looking forward to this beach week for what feels like months, but how can I? Vivi seems excited that she's here. She's someone else that will play with her, and me, well, it's going to be a rough few days of me trying to keep my tongue in my mouth and other parts calm as I stare at her in a bikini.

A tiny black bikini.

Damn.

I knew she looked good. I'd seen her before, but she's changed and toned more over the past couple of years. Her ass and her legs seem to go on for days, and her stomach and her arms are muscular to the point where I could drool. And don't get me started on the tiny triangle bikini top she's wearing. One little tug on the strings and the whole thing would fall off, and I know what's hiding underneath it.

My mouth waters.

It waters at the sight, and it waters thinking about all the places it's explored on this girl and wants to again.

Calm. I remind myself. Stay calm. The last thing I need to do is find myself in a lust-induced mental moment that has a visible effect below my waist to those around me. Namely Sophie. And well, Vivi too. I'm nowhere near ready to have any sort of conversation with her about boys and girls.

"How long are you planning on staying?" I ask her, taking the seat next to her. I've done my duty to Vivi for a bit. We built two sandcastles, and I chased waves with her. Now, I just want to sit here in the shade and talk to Sophie.

"Trying to get rid of me already, are you?" She smirks. Her face is half covered with a large pair of sunglasses, and I can't decide whether I like her wearing them or not. It's hard enough to be around her; add in staring into her eyes too, and I become a useless fool. But I do like how I feel when she looks at me. From the moment I met her, she's made me feel seen.

"No, not at all. Just trying to figure out your plans so we either join or work around each other."

At the thought of being here with her for a whole week, I can't decide if I'm in heaven or hell. How many times have I imagined being with her? And now that she's here, I feel like I'm living in some kind of dream.

Dream.

If I could smack myself for how stupid I sound, I would.

It's only been a couple of hours, and I'm already internally acting like an idiot.

She tilts her head, and I can tell she's eyeing me suspiciously from behind those dark lenses.

"I was planning to stay until Monday afternoon. I have to be back at work on Tuesday."

Monday afternoon. That means I basically get two more uninterrupted days with her.

"You good to hang with us, or were you looking for peace and quiet?"

She looks up and down the beach. Others are out here, but it's not as crowded as I would expect for a holiday weekend. At least not yet. The northern schools aren't out for a few more weeks, but this place will be packed once they are.

Her gaze comes back to Vivi, who's sitting just on the edge of the water, making a drip castle. "I'm good to hang." She smiles softly.

"I'm glad," I tell her, reaching into the cooler bag for a bottle of water. "Want one?" I ask, holding it out in her direction. I watch as her head lowers just the tiniest bit and then rises. Behind those sunglasses, her gaze travels from my hand, which is holding the bottle, and then slowly slides up my arm to my face. My heart rate picks up.

Staying unaffected is going to be harder than I thought.

"Sure. Thanks," she says.

I hand her a bottle and both of us sit in silence as we

drink them and watch Vivi. Digging around in the sand, she finds something she likes, and her whole face lights up. Jumping to her feet, she runs up to us under the tent.

"Look, Ms. Sophie, a purple butterfly."

In her hand, which she holds flat for us to see, there is a coquina clam shell. It's a tiny bivalve shell, and it's open, so it resembles the shape of a butterfly. They come in all different colors and patterns.

Sophie leans forward and acts like this is the best treasure Vivi could have ever found. "That's so pretty. How did you know these are my favorite shells?"

"I didn't. But now I do. I can find you some more."

"I would love that. We'll keep them, and then later, we can glue them to make a piece of art. What do you say?"

"Okay." Vivi gives her a small smile, and my heart squeezes. She turns to look at me, and she's so serious. "Uncle Jonah, can you go buy us some glue?"

I chuckle. "Of course. Who am I to stop artistic greatness?"

She gives me a small smile too and then runs back to her spot on the beach. She really does love the beach.

"You're very good with her," Sophie says, watching me. I don't say anything because I can't. Conversations about Vivi lead to me becoming emotional, and this is not the time or the place. Taking a sip of my water, the only response I can muster is, "Thanks."

Next to Vivi, a seagull lands. The two of them are facing off, and I can't help but grab my phone, zoom in, and take a picture. Sophie laughs next to me.

"Does she like to feed the seagulls?" she asks.

In turn, I give her a look of absolute horror. "Please tell me you're joking."

She shifts in her chair so she's angled more toward me. "Why would I joke about seagulls?"

"Maybe because they're disgusting," I tell her, frowning.

She laughs again, and it sounds so good.

"They are not," she teases.

"Yes, they are. Seagulls, pigeons, they're all one and the same. Rats with wings."

"Jonah, look at it." She waves her hand toward Vivi, who's gone back to shell hunting. Meanwhile, the seagull is just prancing around. "It's so pretty."

"Oh, I'm looking at it. It probably carries diseases and wants to eat Vivi's eyes."

This time, when she laughs, I can't help but chuckle along with her. Vivi pushes her hair out of her face and looks over at us through squinty eyes. The sun is bright. I need to get her a pair of sunglasses too. Even though we're only like fifteen feet away, Sophie waves, and Vivi waves back.

"As a kid, I used to love feeding the seagulls. They all come out of nowhere, and they sort of float in the air, just waiting to be given a treat. I also love the sounds they make. I associate the calls they make to vacation."

"That sounds like a great memory . . . for you."

She giggles again.

So her parents used to take her to the beach for vacations. I wonder how often they went? Were they visiting someone? Did they always go to the same place? If so, where? Come to think of it, I don't even know where she's from. And it's this thought that makes me sad. I want to know this girl. I wish I'd had the past two and a half years to get to know her. Instead, we're exactly the same as we were the night we met. Strangers.

Taking another sip of my water, I glance over at her. So beautiful. "You know, for as often as I think about you, I really don't know anything about you."

"You think about me?" she asks, surprised.

Behind our sunglasses, we stare at each other.

"Sophie." I state her name in a way that makes her know that not only am I serious but it should be obvious.

Her cheeks turn pink, and I'm certain it's not because of the heat.

"Yes, I think about you. But I'm not really sure what I'm even thinking. Obviously, I had no idea that you were a surgeon—which is incredible, by the way—but it's all the rest of your life that I don't know. I don't know where you're from, what your family is like, what religion you are, if you like sports or politics, what your favorite food is, or even what your hobbies are. We certainly weren't talking about life goals the night we met." I let out a deep, disappointed breath. "I don't know. I just find myself thinking about this amazing girl I met . . . and regret what it could have been."

Was that too much? I don't know. But it's the truth.

There's no sense in me denying that I want this girl. I've wanted her for a long time.

She stretches her legs out in front of her and digs her toes in the sand. I want to watch her, to see the expressions on her face as she thinks about what I've just said, but I can't. Being vulnerable is not something that feels good. Instead, I watch the water past Vivi. It's so blue green today, and the waves are just enough. There really isn't a prettier beach in the world.

"Italian. That's my favorite food."

Italian. With just this one tiny detail, I suddenly feel lighter and like I won the lottery. I know this reaction is stupid, but it's happening.

"Good to know," I tell her, trying to remain calm and remember every Italian place in Tampa I've ever been to so I can offer to take her.

"Actually"—she cuts off my thoughts—"to be more specific, it's pizza. Pizza is my favorite food. I love all kinds of pizza, but no anchovies."

This definitely narrows things down. Together, if she wanted, the three of us could make it a challenge to find the best pizza in the Tampa Bay area.

"No anchovies, noted."

She takes a sip of her water, too, and after a long moment, she says, "I think about you, too."

Heat rushes to the surface of my skin, the hair on the back of my neck stands up, and with this confession, if I was alone, I would fist-pump the air.

She. Thinks. About. Me. Too.

I turn to look at her and memorize the details of the side of her face. There's the line of her jaw, the shape of her nose, and the tiny diamond stud in her ear. She's so beautiful that it hurts to look at her.

"You want to know something funny?" she asks, turning to face me too.

I don't answer. I just keep looking at her. Tiny hairs are blowing around her face from the Gulf breeze, and even though we're in the shade, her freckles are getting darker.

"I don't really know much about me anymore, either." Sadness blankets each word, and I hate it. I also don't understand it.

"What do you mean?" I frown. This doesn't sound funny to me.

She sighs and peels the label off her water bottle. "This last year, I've kind of just gone through the motions. I've spent fourteen years trying to accomplish my goal, and now that I have, I don't know what to do with myself. I go to work and then go home. I'm not even where I thought I'd be."

I understand what she's saying about working for so long for one goal, but I don't understand not having that feeling like it can end. Playing football, it's a constant worry that I might somehow not make the active roster, but at the same time I thrive under the pressure of the push. I'm not sure what I'll do when that push is gone, like what she's talking about. I hate that she's experiencing this.

"What about Pilates? I thought you did that with

Camille several nights a week, and what happened with that guy you said you were seeing?"

"I do go to Pilates. I've been trying to find fun new things to do, but I'm not sure that it's working. As for Isaac . . ." Her toes dig into the sand again, and she lets out a harsh laugh. "He's a nice guy, but he wasn't the one for me."

My breath catches in my throat. Is she saying what I think she's saying?

"What was wrong with him?"

She glances at me. "Nothing. But according to him, I was using him as a place filler."

"A place filler for what?"

"Time," she says, shrugging one shoulder like I'm supposed to know what that means.

"That sounds stupid."

She lets out an incredulous laugh.

"But he was right. He became one of those things I just filled my time with, and nothing more."

"Did you want more with him?" Please say no.

"No." She looks away from me, I can't tell if it's because she feels ashamed to have led the guy on, or if it has something to do with me staring at her.

"So you're not seeing him anymore?"

She turns back to look at me. "No, I'm not."

Well then, this might be the best thing I've heard all day.

"Good."

Chapter 17
Sophie

We spent hours today on the beach watching Vivi play. She built sandcastles with Jonah, played catch with a foam football, snorkeled in the water, and we walked up and down the beach to collect shells. And while I had planned on spending this weekend by just bringing a towel down and lying out in the sun, past that I was uncertain. This however, became an amazing day and what I'm sure will be the start of an amazing weekend.

"Wildflower, you look sunkissed," Jonah tells her as he rubs some after-sun lotion on her arms.

"I feel sunkissed. I got a tan today," she says, sticking out her legs and looking at her golden skin. She's wearing another super cute romper. This one is navy-and-white striped. I can't help but wonder if Jonah takes her shopping for these clothes or if maybe Camille volunteers.

"You did," he tells her, kissing the top of her head, then placing the bottle on the coffee table.

Earlier, I told him he was doing a great job with her, and he really is. He's so attentive, and it's clear he adores her something fierce. He's giving me straight-up single-hot-dad vibes, and I swear my ovaries jump and rejoice. I'd like to blame it on my age, but it's just him.

For dinner, we decided to walk to the Beachside Café. Jonah offered to cook us dinner, but this was Vivi's idea. I've been here once before for brunch, and from what I remember, the food was amazing. As we make our way down the beach, Vivi is in the middle and she reaches for both of our hands. It's so innocent and so sweet, but over her head, Jonah and I lock eyes onto each other. The three of us are connected, and my heart stutters at how we look. Is his doing the same?

We look like a family.

A really beautiful family.

Vivi starts swinging our arms and humming, and Jonah's eyes drop to her. He seems surprised by her actions, but she doesn't seem fazed at all. It's like the three of us walk together all the time instead of this being the first time, and I can't help but wonder, could this be a glimpse of our future?

"Look, Uncle Jonah, dune sunflowers!" Vivi shouts. She lets go of his hand and points toward the sand dunes on our right. All three of us turn to look. The dunes on the island at this point aren't large, but they are beautiful and covered with seagrass. And sure enough, close to the ground, there are patches of shrubs that are covered with little yellow flowers with a dark center.

"I see them," he tells her, and she retakes his hand.

"Tomorrow, can we go hunt for wildflowers?" she asks, looking up at him with big eyes.

"Of course we can. We'll see if we find any new ones."

She smiles up at him, then looks at me.

"Do you want to come with us?"

"I'd love to go, but you need to tell me more about what we're going to be doing."

"Hunting for wildflowers!" she exclaims, like that should explain it all.

I glance over at Jonah.

"Wildflowers are our thing." He shrugs his shoulders. "When we have the chance, we go out exploring to see how many we can find. Vivi gets to pick one of each flower we find. Sometimes we make a bouquet, and other times we make a collage."

"Sounds fun. I take it you've done that here before?"

"Yep," Vivi chimes in. "Last time, we found four."

"That's amazing. I can't wait to see what we find tomorrow."

Vivi continues to swing our arms, and not so secretly, I take peeks at Jonah. What is it about this guy? Tonight, he's wearing a pale-blue T-shirt, khaki shorts, and he's carrying a pair of flip-flops. His hair was wet when he first came down the stairs, but now after being in the breeze it's dried. Just like Vivi, his skin is also sunkissed. He looks so good. Catching me looking at him, his mouth tips up on one side. It's not a big smile, but one that says, "I'm happy you're here, too."

"Ms. Sophie, this place has the best food."

"Do they?" I ask her, not bothering to tell her I've eaten here before. She's so excited to take me there.

"Yes." She looks up at me. "I love their lemonade, and for dessert, they have banana pudding with the cookies in it."

"Sounds delicious. What do you get for dinner?"

She thinks about this for a moment and then says, "Most of the time, I get the grilled cheese, but tonight, I think I want fried shrimp."

"I'm allergic to shrimp," I tell her, and at this tidbit, Jonah looks over at me. Since his confession about not really knowing me, I've noticed that all day he's been soaking up anything new I tell him about me. I'd be lying if I said I wasn't doing the same. I just leave out the part where I've basically internet stalked him since he reappeared in my life and know quite a few details about him. But these, I learned today.

Jonah's favorite food is tacos. Even though he grew up in Boston and loves lobster rolls and clam chowder, he says he's a sucker for a good taco. He admitted to trying tacos in every city he's played in. While sometimes there's free time to venture out, other times he has them delivered to the hotel.

His favorite movie is *Cinderella Man*. He saw this in the theater with his brother. It was the first "adult" movie he remembers letting him see, and for a time when he was a kid, he wanted to be a boxer.

He loves the smell of sunblock, he's never met a potato chip he doesn't like, and aside from hating seagulls and pigeons, it turns out he really doesn't like birds in general. When I asked him why, he mentioned a duck biting him once and the Canadian geese taking over Boston.

I laughed thinking he's being ridiculous, but hey, he's allowed to feel however he wants.

"Does that mean I can't get them?" Vivi asks, frowning.

"Nope, you can still get them. It just means I can't eat them," I tell her, tightening my hand on hers. "Or give you a big kiss on the lips."

"What happens to you if you eat them?" Both of them are looking at me now.

"My lips swell up real big, I break out in hives, and I look funny."

She tilts her head. "I don't think I have anything like that. There's a boy in my class who can't eat nuts. Because of this, we aren't allowed to have anything with nuts in the room. Not even a peanut butter and jelly sandwich."

"Well, I think it's definitely better to be safe than sorry, don't you?"

"I guess so." She shrugs. "But I do like peanut butter."

"Just like your uncle," I goad her and Jonah smiles.

It's just after six when we walk into the restaurant, a bell rings over the door. Sunset isn't for almost two more hours, so we've beaten the crowd.

"Hi, y'all. Grab a seat anywhere and I'll be right over,"

says an older woman who is smiling from ear to ear. She pushes her way through the swinging door that leads into the kitchen and disappears.

Vivi picks a table in the front of the restaurant, close to the window so we can see out.

"Can I sit beside you?" Vivi asks.

"Of course," I tell her, and Jonah scoffs.

"I see how it is. You girls have to stick together and all that, right?" He's teasing her, and she giggles. Meanwhile, Jonah sits across from me, and butterflies swarm in my stomach. It was different sitting next to him on the beach. We could look out at the water there, but here, we're facing each other.

"I just love repeat customers. How are you, Ms. Vivi?" the lady asks, and Vivi brightens at being remembered.

"I'm good," she tells her, giving her a small smile.

The lady turns to look at me. "I see we brought a friend."

"This is Ms. Sophie," Vivi declares, proud to introduce me and my heart swells at how sweet she is.

"Hi, Ms. Sophie," she says, giving me a wink. "Everyone around here calls me Aunt Ella, so if you need anything, just holler."

"She has a shrimp allergy," Jonah blurts and Aunt Ella and I both swing our gaze his way. He looks so serious and so concerned, and Aunt Ella just pats him on the shoulder.

"Got it. No shellfish near your girl here."

The fact that he just made this known, to make sure nothing happens to me, my heart sighs and I swoon on the inside. I know I shouldn't compare, but Isaac never did this.

We give her our drink order, and watch as she walks away.

"So, Vivi." I shift in my chair to look down at her. "I want to tell you how much I loved your performance on Friday night. You did so good."

Her cheeks turn pink. "Thank you. I love ballet," she says, as she pushes her menu around the table.

"I remember from when you were in my office. I kind of figured that out when we first met."

Vivi's cheeks turn pink.

"What made you fall in love with ballet?"

"My mom loved ballet," she says, so matter-of-factly.

"She did?" Somehow this wasn't the answer I was expecting or I wouldn't have asked and opened this door.

"Yes, she took me to see *The Nutcracker* before she . . ." She doesn't say the word, but we all know, before she died. Vivi glances down at the table, sadness washing over her. I feel that sadness too. Even after all these years it sometimes creeps up on me, and my heart aches knowing she'll go through life feeling this too.

"Hey." I put my hand on her back and she looks up at me. Giving her a small smile, I tell her, "I love that you share ballet as one of your favorite things. That's so special. My mom loved the opera, but me not so much. All that high-pitched singing hurts my ears." I hold my hand out and try to recreate some type of sound that you would expect to hear from a singer, only I sound like a dying cat. Vivi's sadness recedes, and she lets out a little laugh.

"What about you, Jonah? What's something that you loved or hated?"

"Hmm," he says, tapping his chin. "Okay, I have two for you, one of each. I spent most of my time with your dad"—he looks at Vivi—"and you might remember this, but he loved parades. I don't know why, either. Every year, when I was a kid, he used to drag me to the South Boston St. Patrick's Day parade. It's so crowded, the bagpipes are so loud, and well, I kind of hated it."

"He took me to that parade," Vivi says, eyes wide as Jonah talks about her dad. I can't help but wonder how often do they talk about them?

"I'm not surprised at all. I'm not sure that your mom liked going either, but your dad was all, 'It's a tradition!'"

"I have some green beads from that parade in my jewelry box."

"You have a lot of beads in your jewelry box."

"You're the one who took me to the Gasparilla parade this year."

"Well, now you know why. I know if your dad was here, he would probably dress up like a pirate, and embarrass us all while trying to talk with a pirate accent, but he'd make sure we went every year because he loved parades."

"Can we go again next year?" she asks, looking at him with big eyes.

"We can go every year," he tells her, a promise laced in his words.

Jonah and Vivi stare at each other, both lost in their own memories.

"What about the thing you love?" I ask.

"I'm almost embarrassed to admit this," he says, glancing at me, while rubbing the back of his neck.

A smile stretches across my face. "Oh, now you have to tell us."

He looks back at Vivi. "Your dad liked country music, and it kind of rubbed off on me."

I bark out a laugh. "That's your dark secret? That you love country music?"

"Listen, Bostononians don't listen to country music."

"That's not true at all! People everywhere listen to country music. Boo, I was expecting something juicy," I taunt him.

Vivi giggles.

"I wouldn't say it's well received in the locker room either."

"Boo," I say again, chastising him. "Lame."

"Whatever, yours was opera."

I stick my hand out again and sing the note.

This time Vivi laughs out loud.

"Well, now you have to tell us something that you love," he says, sitting back in his chair and smirking.

What is something that I love?

"Hmm, you already know that I love bones, if I had to pick something else, it might be baking."

Vivi's face lights up. "I love baking, too!"

"I have a bit of a sweet tooth and think it's fun to bake cakes, cupcakes, cookies, pies, you name it."

"I love cupcakes and cookies."

"That's because you're a smart girl," I tell her.

"Uncle Jonah doesn't like them." She smirks, totally pleased with herself for outing him.

I turn to face him directly. "How is that even possible?"

He holds up his arm, pushes up his sleeve, and bends his arm to ninety degrees, popping up his bicep. "Rock solid," he says, and I just shake my head at him. When Vivi lets out an exaggerated sigh, I take it this is not the first time she's seen him do this.

"What are your plans for the rest of the week?" I ask, changing the subject.

"Looks like tomorrow we're going wildflower hunting. We'll go for a bike ride. We'll take the golf cart for some ice cream. On Monday, we're going to the aquarium. One day, we'll wander through the boutiques, and I'll let her do some shopping, and we might go to a movie."

"So all the good beach stuff." I nod at Vivi, and she nods back.

"That's right," Jonah says. "Nothing but the good stuff for my girl here."

"Well, I'm glad I get to be here for some of it," I tell them.

"Me too," Vivi says, wrapping her arms around mine and leans into me for a quick hug.

Tears prick my eyes, and I turn and give her a full hug instead.

Chapter 18
Jonah

Watching Sophie with Vivi is like the sweetest torture. It's been two days, and Vivi has essentially become Sophie's shadow. I get it; she's new, but I genuinely think she likes her. Other than Camille, Lexi, and maybe Kelli, to a certain extent, she hasn't connected with anyone else this way. Not even her teachers.

Of course, over the past two years, I've thought about what it would be like if I ever brought someone home to meet Vivi, but I never expected it to be like this. I thought it would be awkward or hard, but Sophie's slipped right in like she's always been here. Only, I can't decide if this is a good thing, or if I am allowing Vivi to set herself up to be hurt.

Do I want Sophie in our lives? Without a doubt. Wanting her has never been the problem. Where I'm concerned is that Sophie might not want us in return. We are a package deal. An insta family, and that might not be what she had in mind when she thought about having a family of her own. Do I think we're worth it? Absolutely. I just have to make sure Sophie thinks so too before I let all of this go any further. I can't have Vivi losing someone else she loves. Is that inevitable? Yes. But not yet.

Not today.

Mostly, today was another repeat of yesterday.

This morning, I left Vivi with Sophie and went to the store to buy us groceries and glue for the rest of the week. After I got back, we went to the beach, built sandcastles, and then came in for lunch. In the afternoon, some clouds rolled in, so we skipped the water and went back out to do some wildflower hunting. Vivi chased the seagulls away for me, and once, when Vivi wasn't looking, I reached over and gently grasped Sophie's hand. She seemed surprised at first, but then her fingers wrapped around mine.

For dinner, I grilled some steaks. Afterward, we started a puzzle, and now Vivi and I are out taking Molly for a walk.

"Maybe we should buy our own house here, what do you think?" I ask her. Molly's grown a lot over the past month and along with her size, so has her energy. She pulls on the leash and Vivi jerks forward. I'm already thinking we might need to have someone come to the house to train her.

"Really?" she asks, excitement evident in her tone.

I look up and down Reid's street. Each house is similar sized, and while some are lower to the ground, most are on stilts. I can't imagine owning a home here and it not being on stilts. With storm surge and who knows what else, it seems like flooding could be a real possibility.

"Why not? We like it here. I think we'll come more often if we have our own place."

"Will it be on the beach?" she asks, with hopeful big blue eyes, and then she jerks again as Molly is pulling her toward a mailbox to sniff. This particular mailbox is shaped like a wooden pelican. I don't hate it.

"Probably not." I internally laugh at what that would cost and what we cannot afford. I mean, I could swing it, but I don't want to add that extra pressure on us should my career suddenly end. Also, I'd have to consider renting it out and I don't want to do that. I want this to be another home for just us. "We can look, but if it's not, it'll still be walkable. You know the island is small."

"Can I help you pick it out?" Molly has decided there's nothing interesting at the mailbox and has moved along the road's edge to the neighbor's yard. These roads are sandy, gravelly, and I imagine in the summer scorching hot.

"Of course. That's why we're talking about it. It's not my house. It'll be our house."

She takes a moment to think about this.

"Do you think Ms. Sophie will come stay with us at the new house?"

Wouldn't that be another dream come true? If Sophie and I actually turn into a thing, maybe she'll want to pick the house out with us. I certainly won't be able to decorate it. I would let her and Vivi do whatever they want.

"I suppose we could ask her when the time is right."

"I think you should take her on a date."

Her statement catches me off guard, and my brows rise as I look down at her.

"What do you know about dates?"

She smiles up at me, while swinging my hand which is wrapped around her free one. When we're outside like this, I always make sure she's holding my hand and on the inside of me. Away from the road. Safety first.

"That's what grown-ups do. They go out and have dinner together."

That's what her parents were doing, out having dinner. I wonder if she's associating the two. I hope not. There will come a day when I do go out to dinner with someone, hopefully Sophie, and I don't want her to live in fear that I won't come home.

"Well, I'll have you know I already asked her and she said no."

A frown drops onto her face, as she tries to understand. I can see how in the mind of a seven-year-old, who thinks her uncle is awesome, that it doesn't make sense that someone would say no to me.

"Why?" She looks at me curiously. She also looks offended, and I have to try hard not to grin at her reaction.

"At the time she had a boyfriend," I tell her.

"No, she doesn't," Vivi declares like it's a fact, not picking up that I said, "had," as in past tense.

"Why do you say that?" I ask her, curious about what she knows and I don't. Molly starts circling, letting us know she's about to be finished, and I'm glad. I'm ready to get back inside.

"I heard her at the baby shower, she was talking to Ms. Lexi."

Oh, to have been a fly on the wall at this shower. Ex-boyfriends, recitals, and bones, they seemed to have talked about it all.

"What did she say?" I ask, probing her for more details.

"Ms. Lexi asked her about some guy named Isaac and she said, 'There is no more Isaac.' That's the guy, right?"

"Yeah, that was his name."

No more Isaac. I know Sophie told me this, but it feels really good to hear it confirmed, without worry that there will be a relapse. She said it was over, and I feel pretty strongly that she's telling me the truth.

"So you don't want to ask her again?" She looks up at me like she's confused.

"You like Ms. Sophie that much?" I ask, my heart thumping at her answer, even though I already know it.

"Yes. And she's so pretty."

"She is pretty." So pretty I find it hard not to stare at her. "I'll think about it."

"Good," she says. "Do you think she'll make cupcakes with me?"

I bend down to take care of Molly's business and tell her, "I'll make cupcakes with you."

"I know, but she said she likes to bake, and I don't know who she bakes for. Maybe she would think it would be fun to bake with me."

My sweet girl. She's worried that Sophie doesn't have any friends to bake with. If it wasn't so sweet, I would laugh.

"I'm not sure. You should ask her, then."

We haven't even made it to the garage yet before Vivi takes off running through the door.

"Ms. Sophie! Where are you?" Vivi yells.

"I'm right here," she calls out.

"Hold up there, Wildflower. You have to give Molly her treat first, then you can go play. We can't forget our responsibilities."

"Oh, yeah," she says, running toward the direction of the kitchen where we have the snacks on the counter. Molly follows and sits nicely when Vivi tells her to. After that, we both find Sophie in the living room in her chair with her legs curled under her. She's looking at her phone, and my heart trips in my chest as she smiles at us. I still can't believe that she's here.

I take a seat on the couch and Vivi moves to stand in front of Sophic. Sophie lays down her phone to give her full attention.

"Do you want to make cupcakes?" Vivi asks, practically jumping up and down with excitement.

Sophie looks surprised at the question, but then she looks at me to make sure it's okay, and I nod.

"Sure!" she says, returning Vivi's enthusiasm. "You know I love them."

Sophie climbs out of the chair, and as the two of them

make their way into the kitchen, Vivi says, "Uncle Jonah can watch."

Sophie looks over her shoulder, and her eyes collide with mine. She gives me a small smile, and my heart thumps hard.

"First, we have to make sure Ms. Camille has everything we need," Sophie says as they enter the kitchen.

"Don't worry, Uncle Jonah got it all yesterday at the store."

"Did he now?" She looks at me again as I make my way over to the island and take a seat to watch them.

"Well, I think my version of cupcakes might be different from yours. Mine come from a box."

"There's nothing wrong with that. Everything needed in one place."

I watch as she moves around the kitchen, finding all of the ingredients needed to go with my box cupcakes: eggs, milk, oil, spray oil, and the can of icing.

"Ms. Sophie, what flavor is your favorite?" Vivi asks, looking up at her with such fondness that half of me feels moved, but the other half of me hears alarm bells going off.

Sophie looks at the box and then goes back to Vivi. "I'm thinking strawberry cupcakes are my favorite."

"Mine too!" Vivi grins.

The Vivi from March when she first met Sophie differs from the Vivi she is today. Yes, she's seen Sophie a few times, but certainly those few interactions can't be what's causing this change in her. Is it the dog? Is it that more time has passed and life is moving forward? I don't know, but seeing more of this side come out of her over the past couple of days makes my soul sigh in relief. I promised John to take care of her, and I really am doing my best.

Sophie turns on the oven, Vivi drags over a chair so she can stand on it, and I watch as they follow the instructions to mix this batter. Grabbing my phone, I tell them to smile. Vivi holds up the mixing spatula, and Sophie wraps her arm around her. Staring at the two of them through the screen as I take the picture, I know without a doubt that I want this—her. I just need to figure out a way to make it happen.

They keep stirring, and my emotions stir with them.

"Do you think it's done?" Sophie asks her.

"Uncle Jonah, you should taste it," she says to me. Then she looks at Sophie. "He never lets me taste the batter. He says raw eggs are bad for little girls." And then for the first time, I watch Vivi roll her eyes.

"Well, that was mean," I tell her as I get up and walk around the island. "I don't roll my eyes at you."

She says nothing but looks at Sophie to see her reaction.

"Your uncle loves you, and he's not wrong. Sometimes those eggs can make you sick."

"None of my friends have ever gotten sick," she counters.

"Not that you know of," Sophie says, backing me up. "And maybe keep the eye rolling for just your room so he can't see you. You can roll your eyes a hundred times there, and he'll never know. A girl's room is her safe place." She winks at Vivi.

That was actually great advice. As she gets older, gestures will happen, and words will want to be said, but if she's in her room, then that's her neutral zone.

Sophie sticks her finger into the batter and then tastes it.

"How does it taste?" I ask.

"You should try it," Sophie says to me at the same time as Vivi says, "It has to be delicious."

So I do. Taking one from Sophie's playbook, I grab Sophie's hand, stick that same finger back in the batter, and then bring it to my mouth to suck it off.

Sophie gasps as our eyes lock, and Vivi squeals.

"Uncle Jonah, you're supposed to use your own finger!"

"Maybe, but Ms. Sophie's tastes so much better than mine." I grin.

And then just to prove a point, I dip her finger back into the batter and bring it to Sophie's mouth. She opens instantly, then wraps her lips around her finger and slowly pulls it out.

"Definitely better on you," I tell her.

Chapter 19
Sophie

When Jonah said we were going on a trip to the aquarium, he neglected to tell me that he'd booked a half-day private adventure full of fun for just the two of them that became the three of us. Well, I'm guessing it was for the two of them, but he added me, and no one questioned it. I've lived in Florida all these years and haven't been to one aquarium.

"Ms. Sophie, do you see that one?" Vivi whisper-shouts as if she's afraid to startle the manatees.

"I do," I tell her as I carefully turn my kayak so I can take a closer look.

The day full of fun started with a behind-the-scenes aquarium tour while the biologist started their morning rounds. The science lover in me soaked up all of the details as they talked about their resident sharks, where we watched a feeding, the live coral reefs, and the stingrays that we were able to touch. After a quick snack, we headed outside to the kayaks.

Kayaks that I didn't know we were paddling in.

Now, I've never given much thought about whether I'm an outdoorsy person, but I'm thinking I'm not. I go to Pilates. I do yoga at home. Granted, I haven't had many opportunities over the past couple of years to go hiking, camping, or kayaking, but now that I'm out on the water, I'm thinking I could be. The fresh air is nice, and I love being in the sun. Kayaking, however, is not as easy as people make it seem. The kayak wobbles, and the current pulls with the tide.

"You okay over there?" Jonah asks. He's been amused by me since the moment we walked outside and they handed us our life jackets.

"Yep. I got it," I tell him. There's no way I'm letting him see me fail at this, even if I'm still reeling over how kind he's been today. Well, not just today but for the past three days. And don't get me started on his hands. Hands like his should be outlawed.

The first real time he touched me was on our wildflower hunting trip. Vivi was so absorbed in running around that she completely missed the affection and sparks flying between us. Since then, it's like his need to touch me has increased by the hour. It's little things, too, like tucking loose hair behind my ear, putting sunblock on my shoulders and back, helping me into the car, and his hand brushing against mine as we walk next to each other. And that stunt he pulled with my finger and the cupcake batter,

I went to bed dreaming about how warm his mouth and tongue were and how dilated his eyes became.

Even now, he ignores my willfulness of effort and reaches his long arm over to grab me by the arm to pull my kayak close.

"Thanks," I tell him, blushing at how he's looking at me and the large warm imprint he's left on my skin.

This guided kayak tour has taken us out into Sarasota Bay. We've gone over shallow seagrass beds where we've looked for fish, and we've gone out into more open water where we looked for dolphins, manatees, and birds. I knew that Vivi had a love of dolphins, but this, watching as she squeals with full delight when one pops up not too far from her and Jonah, who are in a tandem kayak, is something else.

Just then, a pair of fins pops up next to us, and she gasps.

"Did you see it?" She turns to look at me with bright eyes.

"I did!" I may be in my thirties, but I'm not immune to the wonders of being near a dolphin. In many ways, this feels like a once-in-a-lifetime thing, and I'm very grateful to be tagging along.

"Uncle Jonah, you have to get its picture," she says, forcefully patting his leg.

"I'll try, but you have to sit still, or we'll be swimming with this dolphin."

She whips around to look at him. "Can we? Can we swim with the dolphins?"

I laugh, and he shoots me a look.

"No can do, kiddo," the guide says. "These dolphins are wild animals, and this water is their home. It's not nice to just go into someone's home. Think of your house—you see people who walk on the sidewalk outside, and that's normal, just like we are on top of the water. But if those strangers were to walk inside your home, it would be scary. If we were to go into the water, it would scare the dolphins too."

"Okay," she says, looking slightly disappointed.

Jonah, who looks like a nerdy tourist, pulls out his plastic protective phone carrier that he has looped around his neck. The carrier seals, so should it get wet or if he dropped his phone, it would stay dry. Carefully, he takes his phone out, and we wait.

"How many bones does a dolphin have?" I ask the guide. Vivi perks up and grins at me.

"A dolphin has about three hundred bones."

"Just like we do!" she says excitedly.

"Yes," he tells her. "What doesn't have bones are sharks."

"Why not?" she asks. "They look the same. One's just meaner than the other."

"Their skeleton is made of cartilage. It's soft and flexible. Your nose and your ear are made of cartilage. See how flexible it is?" The guide bends his ear a few times, and Vivi does it too.

It's right about this time that the dolphin pops back up. Vivi shouts with glee, and Jonah grins, meaning he got the picture. I wonder if he angled it in a way where he got Vivi and the dolphin. She will love it.

"How about you pass your phone over to me, and I'll get a family picture of the three of you," the guide says.

Without missing a beat or correcting him, Jonah says, "That would be great. Thank you."

Very swiftly and competently, the guide moves his kayak to grab the phone and then backs away to get the three of us in the photo.

Jonah pulls me right next to them so our kayaks are lined up.

"Smile!" he says, and we do.

This moment with them is captured, and I love it.

The guide hands Jonah back his phone, and he smiles as he looks at the picture.

"Will you send it to me?" I ask, and an emotion quickly passes over his hazel eyes before his smile grows even more. "Of course."

"All right, folks, it's time for us to make our way back to the aquarium. We have one more stop to make before our fun day ends, and that's the Marine Mammal Research and Rehabilitation Center. There, I'd like to introduce you to my friends Cash, Brutis, and Sunny, our resident green sea turtles."

"Oh, sea turtles!" Vivi squeals.

Chapter 20
Jonah

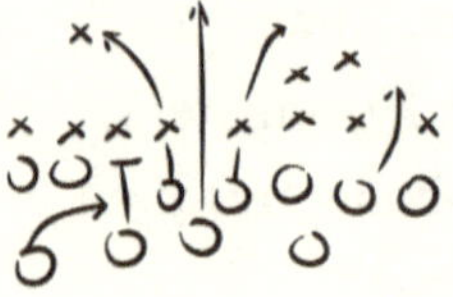

Once we get back to the house, all three of us part ways and go to our respective rooms. Molly needs tending, and we each need a shower and, well, maybe a few moments to decompress, too.

Today couldn't have gone any better. Vivi's continued to smile more than I've seen her smile in the past two years combined. I don't know if she thinks of Sophie as a playmate or if she's just so comfortable around her that she feels she can fully relax and be herself. All of this makes me wonder again, what is it that she's not getting from me, that she is from Sophie? Is it that there are two of us? Or is it that she's a woman? My gut says this is it. After all, little girls would tend to be more attached to a woman than their single uncle. I try not to let this upset me. It is what it is.

For dinner, the three of us eat some homemade pizzas, and afterward, we watch a movie in the living room. The sun sets so late here during the summer. While I would prefer Vivi to be heading to bed soon, I did promise her a trip to Bean Point, and I already know she's going to hold me to it. As the credits roll, Vivi pops up and looks at me.

"Is it time? Can we go now?"

With that excitement in her voice, how could I ever tell her no? I glance out the window. There's only a tiny tint of light left, and mostly, the sky has turned to night. By the time we get there, it'll be completely dark out.

"I suppose so. Go put Molly in her crate."

She leaps off the couch, startling Molly as she scoops her up.

"Where are you going?" Sophie asks, confused. She mentioned earlier that after the movie, she was going to head out and go home, but selfishly, I want her to stay longer. Maybe this will pique her curiosity enough.

"I think you should stay tonight and head back tomorrow morning," I tell her. She's curled up on the other end of the couch. For the movie, I sat on one end, she was on the other, and Vivi sat between us. She sprawled out like kids do, and the scene was so domestic, my heart pinched.

She studies me for a moment. "I'll have to head back pretty early. I have surgeries scheduled."

"Yeah, but heading up to Bean Point to look at the stars with us will be worth it. We won't be there for long. I promise you'll get your beauty sleep," I tease.

She doesn't take the bait and instead looks at me curiously. "Stargazing?"

"Yes. Vivi and I love to look at the stars."

Her eyes briefly drop to my rib cage, and I know she's thinking about the tattoo I added since the last time I saw her.

"I can't remember the last time I looked at the stars. When I was a kid, we used to go outside and look for the northern lights."

"Can't say I've ever seen that, but I bet Vivi would love it."

"She certainly would."

Silence falls between us as she thinks about her schedule and what it would mean tomorrow if she stays here the extra night. One of the things I've learned about Sophie over the past couple of days is that she is not a spontaneous person in her everyday life. She likes to plan, she likes a routine, and she doesn't like the uncertainty of what's happening next. I'm kicking myself now for not mentioning this sooner, but I kind of wanted it to be a surprise, and I really want her to stay. Who knows when I'll see her again after she leaves, but I'm hopeful she'll say yes if I ask her out again.

"Okay, I'll stay," she says, and I just smile.

"Okay, guys, let's go," Vivi yells as she bounds down the stairs.

"Did you get a blanket?" I ask her.

"Oh, right."

She runs to the laundry room, where Camille keeps beach blankets and towels, and returns with the largest one she could find.

"Alright." I look at Sophie as she stands. "You ready?"

"Sure." She grins.

Vivi takes off for the garage, and the two of us follow. It's not a quick walk to the Point, so we load up onto the golf cart and head out. There are hardly any clouds out tonight, making it perfect to see the stars.

Bean Point is the northernmost tip of Anna Maria Island. It's where Tampa Bay meets the Gulf of Mexico. While the beach is beautiful and it's a great place to watch the sunset or to stargaze, it's not a place to swim. Rip currents can be fierce, as well as the sea life.

"It's so dark here," Sophie says as we park the golf cart and walk the tree-lined trail leading us right where we want to be.

Vivi has slipped her hand into Sophie's and I pull out my phone and turn on the flashlight so we can see.

"You'll appreciate the darkness once we're down there," I tell her.

Soon, we hit the boardwalk bridge that opens up the view of the Point and takes us to the beach. The sand here is crisp white, cool, and deep, and the sound of the water is hypnotic. I don't know what it is about the water here versus the Atlantic Ocean in Boston, but it's just different. It feels calmer and not as fierce, which makes it easy to see why people love Florida west coast beaches.

"I've never been to this part of the island," Sophie says.

"You're going to love it," Vivi tells her.

We've paused to take in the view in front of us. The stars are striking in the night sky, and the moon has made it bright enough so we can see our surroundings. The white of the sand against the dark water makes the curve of the Point visible, and you feel like you're standing on top of the world. But the half dozen fishermen lined up in front of us, spaced out about ten feet apart, cause us to pause.

"What are they fishing for?" Sophie asks.

"Sharks."

She turns to me, shocked. "Really?"

"Yep. The currents here create the perfect pathway for them to go in and out of the bay. Bull sharks can tolerate salt water and fresh water, so the environment here is perfect."

"Wow. Why are they using glow sticks on their lines?"

"They use the green ones because the bright hue attracts fish and sharks."

"Do people eat bull sharks?"

"Yes. Here in Florida, this is legal fishing to keep the populations manageable, and if you hit up any mom-and-pop seafood restaurant near the coast, they probably have shark nuggets on their menu."

Sophie frowns. "I'm not sure I would like that."

"You never know until you try it. Come on, let's head over there, away from these guys."

"But, Uncle Jonah, I want to see a shark," Vivi says.

"You just saw one at the aquarium."

"But this is different."

I can't argue with her there. But we are not sticking around these guys out here at night. I don't know them, and quite frankly, people who wrangle sharks at night might not be my kind of people.

"Why do you know so much about this?" Sophie asks.

"Tyler likes to fish. He loves to talk about all the different species here and the different ways to catch them."

"Where is he from?"

"Originally, I think Jacksonville."

"So he grew up fishing?"

"Yes."

After finding a suitable spot, Sophie helps me spread out the large blanket, and we each settle in and lie down. Vivi is between us, her head right at about shoulder height for both of us.

"It's so peaceful out here," Sophie says as a breeze blows over us. "The last time I looked at the stars, I was in high school. We used to stay up late to see the northern lights. Do you know what those are?" she asks Vivi.

"No. What are they?" Vivi asks.

"They're streaks of blue-greenish lights that swirl through the night sky, almost like a river in the sky."

"Can we see that here?" Vivi turns to look at Sophie, eyes wide.

Sophie looks down at her. "No. The light gravitates toward the North and South Pole. You'll learn all about it soon in your science class."

"Okay," she says, accepting that answer.

"Vivi, what do you see?" I ask her.

"The summer triangle. It's right there. Do you see it,

Sophie?" Between us, I can feel Vivi turning to look at her again.

"I'm not sure. Why don't you point out what I'm supposed to see?"

Vivi scoots a little closer to Sophie and points at the sky. "That bright one right there is called Vega. It's the brightest one. Do you see it?"

"I do," Sophie says, a little animatedly for Vivi's sake, and it has me turning to look at her, too. The profile of her face with her hair scattered all over the blanket—she's so beautiful it hurts.

"What's next?" Sophie asks her.

Vivi's arm slides a little until she's pointing at another star, but I can't seem to look at the stars anymore. I just want to look at the two of them. Mainly Sophie.

"And then the last one is there." Her arm slides again.

"How did you know how to find this constellation?" she asks.

"Uncle Jonah uses an app."

Sophie turns to look at me, her brows raised in question. "An app?"

"Yep." I slide my phone from my pocket and open SkyView. I hold it up to the sky, it reads the stars in the sky and then draws the constellation to identify it for us. At this moment, there is Ursa Major and Ursa Minor.

"That's really neat," Sophie tells us.

"When Uncle Jonah travels, he sends me the stars so I can see that we're looking at the same ones."

"I love that," she says.

"Ms. Sophie?" Vivi asks.

"Yes, darling."

"Do you have a mom?"

Shock and then sadness slip over Sophie's features as she thinks about how to best answer her question. We both understand what she's asking and why. I just hope Sophie phrases it in a way that might bring her some peace of mind.

"Yes. Although she passed away a long time ago."

Vivi's quiet as she thinks about this. I know kids see things more in black and white. Either you have something or you don't, but for Vivi, I know Sophie wants her to see she still has a mom. She's just not here anymore.

"How old were you when she died?"

"I was seventeen."

Sophie catches me looking at her. This is something else I didn't know about her, but now I do. I know she can see the sorrow that has taken over my face. I don't feel pity for her. I'm just sad for what she experienced and what she lost.

"How did she die?" Vivi asks.

"She got cancer."

"Oh."

"Yeah, it all happened pretty quick."

Vivi rolls onto her side and looks at Sophie. Sophie rolls to match her, and the two of them stare at each other. It's taking everything in me not to reach over and pull them both in close.

"My mom died quick, too."

"I heard," she tells her, and then Sophie brushes a few pieces of hair off Vivi's face and tucks them behind her ear. "Why don't you tell me three things about your mom?"

"My mom liked to sing and dance. She always had music playing and would dance while she cooked."

"That's so fun," Sophie tells her. "Now I know where you get all of your dancing talent from."

She giggles. "But she didn't sing very good. My dad used to make fun of her, but she didn't care."

"As she shouldn't have. I love that your mom used to sing because it made her happy. You should always do the things that make you happy, no matter what anyone else thinks. Okay, tell me something else."

"She used to braid my hair."

I stop breathing, and my chest aches. I remember her hair always being styled, but I didn't know this was something she thought about. She never mentioned it.

"Do you know how to braid hair?" she asks Sophie.

"Well, it hasn't been something I've ever really needed to do, but I will practice so I can braid yours next time I see you. How about that?"

"I like a fishtail braid."

"Why doesn't that surprise me? You do like dolphins."

"I do. My stuffed dolphin, her name is Coral. My mom bought her for me."

"That might be the best name I've ever heard for a dolphin."

"There's a real one named Coral at the aquarium. My mom took me to see her once."

She looks over Vivi's head. "Which aquarium?"

"Clearwater," I answer, my voice rough.

She looks back at Vivi. "Oh, I've heard that's a nice aquarium. They used to have a dolphin named Winter."

"I saw the movie. The first one and the second."

"Of course you did. Kind of cool what they did for his tail, huh?"

"Yes."

"When that movie came out, I might have looked up on the internet to see if their tail has bones in it, and it does not."

"You like bones a lot."

"I do."

"Their tails kind of go like this." Vivi raises her arm in the air and waves it back and forth.

"Just like the guy at the aquarium told us today. Cartilage is bendy. Okay, you owe me one more thing about your mom."

Vivi lowers her arm as she thinks about this.

"Her name was Ashley Lynn Dallmann."

"Ashley is a really pretty name."

"It's my favorite name."

"I think that would make your mom very happy."

Vivi smiles, then she scoots a little closer to Sophie. Sophie, doing what comes naturally, starts running her hand up and down Vivi's back.

Chapter 21
Sophie

After getting Vivi to bed, Jonah finds me slipping into the hot tub on the back porch. My head tilts a little as he opens the sliding glass door and makes his way outside to join me.

"How's the water?" he asks, his eyes roaming over what he can see.

"Perfect. You should get in," I tell him, hoping he will.

He's not wearing a swimsuit, but he has on athletic shorts. Not that I would mind him dropping both and just climbing in with me. Without hesitation, he reaches behind his head, grabs his T-shirt to pull it off, and tosses it onto one of the lounge chairs. Leaving on the shorts, he carefully swings one leg over the edge and climbs in. He slides over so he's closer to me and not on the other side. The whirling of the jets replaces the sound of the water lapping on the shore.

"I really do love it down here," I tell him after he

settles, and I look out at the water. Tonight was a night I will never forget. As I lay under the stars with the two of them and Vivi curled up against me, she's quickly secured a place in my heart. It really is devastating for everyone. Obviously for Vivi but for Ashley too. She will never see what this amazing little girl has become or what she'll grow up to be. I know it's the same for Jonah's brother, John, but from one person who lost their mother to another, I understand.

"We do too. Especially Vivi. We've actually talked about maybe buying a place here so we can come more often."

I turn back to look at him and laugh. Steam floats around him, starting to make his skin glisten. No guy should look as good as he does. It's a crime for all other guys in the world.

"What?" he asks, one side of his mouth tipping up into a grin.

"Not many people just say, 'Wanna buy a beach house tomorrow?' and then do it."

"I'm not going to apologize for working hard for what I have," he says, flicking water my way.

"You absolutely shouldn't. You're living the dream of so many who wish to play a professional sport." I flick some water back.

"Don't think it was easy to get here because it wasn't."

"Oh, I'm not saying that. I'm very aware of how dedi-cated and hard you all work."

I spent an entire year studying just pediatrics and

sports medicine. I know without a doubt on the adult level and at the high-performing level that he is, the work on his body to keep it healthy and at its full potential is intense.

"I do love it, though," he says as he hesitates, then brings his eyes to mine. "Thank you for talking to Vivi tonight. Sometimes she opens up to me, but not a whole lot. It's good for her to talk about things, and I appreciate how you handle her. It means a lot to me."

"Jonah, she's incredible, and I know I've said this before, but you really are doing a wonderful job with her."

He ducks his head to break eye contact and brings his hands to the water's surface. Dragging them back and forth, he collects his thoughts as the water flows through his fingers. Eventually, his eyes return to mine.

"Every day, it still feels surreal. She was never meant to be mine, and then one day, she was."

My nose stings as my eyes burn.

"One day, she was," I agree with him. Nothing I say will make him feel any differently about this situation. He feels loss, he feels scared, he feels overwhelmed, but beyond all that, he feels love for this little girl. All she needs from him is love, and she'll turn out just fine.

"Tell me about this." My hand drifts his way, and under the water, my fingertips brush the constellation he has tattooed on his side.

"It's Gemini. Although the word means twins in Latin, which John and I are not, it also represents brotherly love. It has other meanings as well, but my brother . . ." He thinks about him and swallows hard. "He was a high school science teacher, and he loved astronomy. The stars were his thing."

The stars were his thing. So much his thing that he wanted them permanently branded on his body. Oh, Jonah. Sometimes I have to remind myself that it isn't just Vivi who experienced the loss; it's him too. He's lost so many people in his life.

"That's why you take Vivi stargazing."

"Yes. It's stupid, but it makes me feel closer to him, and by talking about the stars, I'm still giving a piece of him to Vivi."

"It's not stupid. Not at all. It's incredible. Stars, parades, ballet, sea animals, the things I don't know, I would say you're giving a lot of them to her."

He drops his gaze and looks down at his hands. He's flipped them over and is cupping the water before he spreads his fingers, and it falls through. "Most days, I feel like I'm failing her in every way."

"Why would you think that?" I turn to face him, and our knees brush.

"I'm not what she needs. She's different from how she was when they were alive, and I just feel like . . . I'm not enough." He lets out a deep sigh. His honesty and the vulnerability make me want to wrap him up in my arms.

"Jonah, that's just not true." Reaching over, I place my hand on top of his. "And of course she's different. Who would be the same after that?"

"You don't understand. I wasn't ready for this. I was barely getting by myself. That year, I had been released from Carolina. I was working so hard to make this my team, for them to want me past the one-year mark, and then John died. I mean, I'm not so far removed from reality to say that although I was twenty-four, in many ways, I was still a kid myself.

"I'd worked so hard for so long to get where I was, I rarely stopped for fun. I didn't have the young professional experience that most have in their twenties. Yes, I had money, but all good things must come to an end at some point, and I was trying to be responsible. That night with you, my actions were so far out of my day-to-day character, yet of all the days and nights over the past couple of years, I remember that night with you the most."

"That night was very out of character for me too, and I also remember it as if it were yesterday."

Turning his hand over, he laces our fingers together. His hand is so much larger than mine, and I love it.

"I don't know what I'm doing. I feel so in over my head." He runs his other hand through his hair. The water forces it to stick up straight and be unruly. His hair, his expressive eyes, and the slightly dejected frown on his face are almost too much, and the need to comfort him is fierce.

"Every night, I lie in bed, stare at the ceiling, and wonder if I'm doing enough for her. Am I making her life worse or better? Am I disappointing them? When we stare up at the stars, I can't help but wonder if wherever they are, can they see the same stars too?"

Grief is such a heavy emotion. There's no timeline for how long it lingers or how often it rears its ugly head.

People cope in so many different ways. I just hope that, through all the chaos and change, he's had his moments, too.

"I thought about you over the years. A lot. I was sitting in front of your place on New Year's Day when I called my uncle back, and he told me about John. For a split second, I thought about running back inside to you, but I couldn't. I had to go. And going to Vivi was such a hard thing to do, but also the easiest. As much as everything overwhelmed me, I had to be numb at the same time. I had things to do and people who needed me. Funny enough, who I needed was you. I don't know why, but you were all I wanted."

He needed me. He wanted me. My eyes now blur with an unmistakable heartache that I didn't get to be there for him. I would have, too.

"Oh, Jonah. I wish you would have come back inside or at least called me."

He shakes his head. "We had just met. I couldn't bring you into the tragedy of my life. It didn't feel right. So instead, I played our night together over and over and over in my mind. From the dancing, to our first kiss under the fireworks, to what it felt like hearing your laughter and the other sounds you made. Those tiny moments gave me light when I was drowning in the dark."

I don't say anything, not that he expects me to, but he sees my eyes are glassy with emotion. I would have been there for him. I could have helped him. Shame ripples through me that I wasn't woman enough to seek him out and ask why he didn't show. They say pride is the killer of all good things, and my pride cost Jonah the good that he needed, as well as two years when we might have been together.

"How long has it been since you and that guy ended?" he randomly asks.

"Probably a month."

"Good."

"Good?" I laugh.

"Yes, because I want to hug you equally as much as I want to kiss you," he says, his eyes lingering on my lips.

My gaze travels up his broad chest, across the tanned skin of his Adam's apple, and over the sharp defining line of his jaw and the fullness of his lips until my eyes find his. His are roaming my face, like he's memorizing the tiny details he doesn't yet know. They pause on my mouth and then lock on to mine. His hazel to my blue. At this moment, I want to drown in him, as heat races down my spine and butterflies take flight in my stomach. No one has ever looked at me the way Jonah Dallmann is. The way he does.

Scooting closer, I unconsciously lift my hand to push the fallen hair back off his face, but he captures my hand and flattens it to his cheek, his eyes briefly closing at the connection.

"So why don't you do both?" I whisper.

Laying his forehead against mine, he lets out a deep exhale and wraps his arms around me until we're pressed together.

"I know this probably sounds completely wild to you, but I missed you."

Surprisingly, this doesn't sound crazy to me at all, and I feel nothing but truth and honesty when I tell him, "I missed you, too."

We had something that night. I knew it then, and I know it now. I had convinced myself that I had made it all up, that these feelings were one-sided, and it turns out they weren't. As I hear him say these words, the disappointment I'd felt over how things ended between us drifts away. I know why he didn't show up that day, but tragedy aside, I wasn't really sure how he felt about me. I only knew how I felt about him. And with that, his mouth lands on mine.

Many times over the past two years, I've thought about what it felt like to be kissed by Jonah. It isn't simple, and although some of his kisses are sweet and tender, after that night, that's not how I would normally describe them. They're consuming. A whole-body encounter. Which is what I'm experiencing now.

Large hands have wrapped around my head, and his fingers have tangled in my hair. He's angled me how he wants me. His lips are full and soft as they coax mine open, and his tongue tastes delicious as it dips inside to refamiliarize mine with his.

Good gracious. This man undoes me.

Time passes as Jonah takes this moment to thoroughly kiss me and make up for the loss of the past two years. He sucks my tongue into his mouth; he bites my bottom lip and then licks it to wipe away the sting, and he breathes air into my lungs. I try to think back to the last time I made out with someone just for the sake of kissing them, and it turns out it was with him.

It was only ever him.

He pulls me through the water by my waist until I float over his lap and straddle him. Just like the night we met. Yes, the water is warm, but I feel like his skin is even warmer. His hands roam over my hips, butt, and back, and everything below my waist tightens as he shifts me closer, and his hardness settles perfectly between my legs.

No one in this world has a more perfect body than Jonah Dallmann, and I take advantage by tracing the hills and valleys of his stomach, running my fingers over the individual bumps of his spine, and flat handing his broad shoulders and upper arms.

From here, his hands slide up my thighs, and his thumbs dip into the crease of where my legs meet my body. They're so close to touching me intimately that I exhale harshly against his damp lips.

He pulls back just a little, and his eyes find mine. I'm mentally shouting the word yes at him, and by the way his mouth twitches on one side, my message is received. I want to be close to him, as close as possible. His hands then shift and both of those thumbs rub straight down the middle of me.

I've died and am floating away.

I don't know what it is about Jonah. Never in my life have I ever wanted someone the way I want him. I crave the nearness and the connection with him to the point it makes me feel crazy. His skin and the way it feels and smells, the roughness of his cheek against mine, his arms when they wrap around me, and his hands when they're on me. I want it all, and I'm almost embarrassed to say, all the time. Physically, I want to grab him and never let go. Emotionally, even though I know something is there, I'm doing my best to push that aside. I can't think about that now. I don't want to think about that now. After all, what good will it do if I end up leaving?

Chapter 22
Jonah

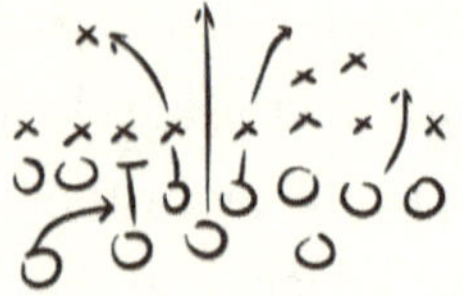

I didn't think I could get any harder until a noise leaves Sophie that's so full of want and satisfaction as I run my fingers over her. She's so perfect, and at this moment, so mine, I feel like I have wanted her for forever, and I'm not slowing down unless she tells me to.

Leaning forward, she sneaks her tongue out and traces my bottom lip before she sinks it into my mouth to rub against mine. Being given the green light, I move her bathing suit bottom over and dip one finger inside while my thumb continues making circles. She pushes down on my hand, and I add a second finger.

Her hand lowers between us, and she pulls on the string that ties my shorts. It comes undone, and she slips her hand inside.

"Sophie," I groan, but she doesn't stop. Her hand wraps around me and then slides up and down. It feels so good I can barely breathe. "Go slow. I haven't been with anyone since you."

"I haven't either," she whispers against my lips.

I pull back to look at her. "No Isaac?"

"Nope. That was part of the problem. Apparently, I didn't want him, and it took him pointing it out for me to realize he was right."

"Do you want this? Me?" I ask her even though I already know the answer.

"More than I know how to articulate."

No more words need to be said as she frees me from my shorts. I lift her, she lines us up, and with our eyes locked on each other, I lower her down. Inch by inch until she's fully seated.

Both of us moan at the sensation, and as the fullness overtakes her, her eyes squeeze shut, and she tips her head back in bliss. She's so tight and warm around me, the feeling is indescribable.

Needing to see and taste all of her, I lean forward, move one triangle of her top away, and suck almost her whole breast into my mouth.

"Jonah," she moans as she tentatively rocks her hips. "You feel so good."

"You feel and taste so good," I tell her as I run my tongue from the right side to the left, pushing the fabric on the other side out of the way too.

Sophie arches her back and continues to rock her hips at a pace that isn't fast or slow. It's just right for us to live in the moment and enjoy each other.

Wanting her chest completely bare to me, I pull the strings on her back and then drag the top over her head. It lands somewhere in the water next to us as I sit up straighter and pull her against me. Chest to chest.

"Do you have any idea how hard it's been for me to see you in this tiny bikini all weekend?" I mumble against her lips.

Her eyes find mine, she smiles, then she squeezes me with her inner muscles.

"Yep, I can definitely feel how hard it's been," she teases.

"I want this. I want you," I tell her, hoping she understands what I'm actually saying, but instead of acknowledging the words, she leans forward and captures my lips with hers.

What would it take? What would I have to do to make her, me, the three of us a real thing? All she has to do is name it, and I'm in.

Wrapping my arms tighter around her, she tips her head back until the ends of her hair skim the water. She's so beautiful, just the sight of her like this is a dream come true.

At some point, my eyes slip shut, my face falls into the curve of her neck, and my hands are spread across her back, holding on. The feeling and the rhythm of her rocking in my lap is so good, the base of my spine tingles.

"Soph," I mutter against her skin.

"I'm there," she whispers, and together, we both fall over the edge. She's clinging to me, I'm clinging to her, and

I'm certain she can feel my heart pounding as I can hers. Eventually, every muscle in her relaxes, and her head falls to my shoulder. Having her in my arms is all I want. This feeling, it's euphoria and contentment. It's friendship and love. There is no one else I want to do this with, and if I'm lucky, I'll be able to convince her of the same. Am I getting ahead of myself? Probably. Will I take it slow for her? Absolutely. I already messed this up once; I'm not going to do it again.

Sophie lets out a loud, pleased sigh, then pulls back to look at me. Her eyes are so blue and so clear. With both of her hands, she pushes my hair back off my face and my forehead and leans down to sweetly brush her lips against mine.

"Thank you," she says, and a chuckle escapes me.

"Pretty sure I should be saying that to you. That was . . . unexpected but incredible."

"Incredible, huh?" she teases.

To play her game from earlier, instead of answering, my dick, which is still inside her, twitches.

She laughs.

"Your hair is shorter from when we first met," she says as she runs her fingers through it again.

"And yours is longer," I tell her, lifting my hands so I can do the same. Hers is half wet and half dry, but all completely sexy. "Should we get out?" I'm trying to be cognizant of her sleep schedule. I know she has to get up early and has a long day tomorrow, and I did promise her beauty sleep.

"Only if you agree to sleep with me tonight," she mumbles, her lips kissing the corner of my mouth.

"Can't live without me already?" I tease, and a grin stretches across her face.

"Something like that."

Running my hands up her thighs and over her hips, I shift her until she's standing in the middle of the hot tub. Her gorgeous rack is eye level, and my stomach clenches. Needing to taste her one more time, I lean forward and suck her nipple into my mouth. A moan escapes her, and then her fingers are back in my hair.

"You better stop that, or we won't be heading upstairs."

With that, I stand and pull off my shorts.

"Well then, looks like I'm not the only one ready for round two," she says, her eyes falling below my waist.

She shimmies out of her bottoms and tosses them along with her top onto the deck. I will never tire of seeing this girl naked, and definitely not in the moonlight with her tan lines on full display.

Grabbing her around the waist, I haul her up against me and hug her. How is it that one person can make me feel so good?

"You know, I think they planned this," she says to me as we climb out and dry off with the towels she brought out.

"Probably. I wouldn't put it past Reid. He knew I was happy to run into you again."

"How happy?" she asks, turning to walk backward into the house while giving me mischievous eyes.

"Very happy," I tell her, fully on board with wherever she's taking us.

"Maybe you should show me just how happy." She sways her hips.

"You want my tongue or my cock?" Her eyes widen at my bluntness, then drop to below my waist again.

"Hmm," she says like she's actually thinking about this while still walking backward toward the stairs. "I think both."

"Done."

I drop the towel and she turns to sprint up the stairs. Turns out, she's not going to be getting much sleep after all.

Sometime early in the morning, the alarm on her phone goes off. She slides out of my bed, and I follow. She turns toward her room, and I make my way down to the kitchen. Dropping a pod into the K-cup machine, I make her a coffee to go.

Walking her to her car, I watch as she tosses her bag into the back seat and turns to face me. Even at five in the morning, with no makeup on and her hair just barely brushed, I still think she's the most beautiful woman.

"So I'm glad our friends were meddlesome, and we ended up here at the same time. Thank you for deciding to stay. It goes without saying that I had a great time, but I know that Vivi did too. It means a lot to me how kind you were to her."

She drops her gaze for a second and smiles at the ground.

"I'm glad this weekend turned out this way, too," she says, her eyes again finding mine.

Sucking up my nerves, I go with my gut and my heart, and ask this question again. "I know we've gone about this a little backward, but will you have dinner with me next weekend after we get back?"

After a short pause, her eyes start to crinkle in the corners, her lips turn up into a small smile, and she says, "Yes."

Chapter 23
Sophie

The drive into the office goes quicker than I expected. One minute, I was leaving the island, and then the next, I was pulling up to our building in South Tampa. Some pediatric groups are attached to a hospital, and the scheduled surgeries are performed there, but ours take place on the first floor of our building in a state-of-the-art surgery center.

The sun is finally rising, and the eastern horizon glows orange, ending one of the best nights I've ever had in my whole life. And yes, that includes the night we met. Was I going to stay? No. But I broke out of my comfort zone, weighed the risks and the rewards, and boy, was I rewarded. Three times.

Jonah surprised me this weekend. I mean, I already knew he was doing a great job at being Vivi's guardian, but it goes past that. He goes out of his way to give her not only all the care and love she needs but also memories and tributes to his brother and sister-in-law. He's not just passing the days with her; he's trying to enrich them in a way they are a part of the things she does and the traditions they're trying to make.

I try to visualize Jonah at the Gasparilla children's parade, and a smile slips onto my face. I can just see them now—Vivi on top of his shoulders, both dressed in some sort of pirate gear, and standing next to the parade route so Vivi can catch beads thrown her way. If he had to pick a parade, this one is definitely iconic.

And don't get me started on the stars. He mentioned both of them were teachers, and John loved science. I wish I had asked him what his major was in college. What subject does he love? What would he do or be if he wasn't playing football? Then again, I guess we have time.

"Good morning, Dr. Black," Laurie, one of the group physician assistants, says when I climb out of my car. I pulled in just after her, and she's waiting for me.

Laurie was already with the practice when I joined, and her skills are very comprehensive. I find I'm lucky that she's fallen onto my rotation more times than not. She's about my age and my go-to first assistant in the operating room when it comes to shoulder and knee arthroscopies, and open and closed fracture internal fixations. She's my height, and when we're standing next to each other and working, it's like I'm a double with two sets of hands. Words don't even need to be said. She anticipates what I need and want without me even having to ask.

"Good morning." I smile at her as we head inside. Of

all the people throughout the practice that gossiped about Isaac and me after the fact, to my knowledge, Laurie wasn't one of them. She already had my respect on a professional level, but she gained it on the personal too.

While the waiting room for family members is nice enough, once we pass through the restricted area doors, I'm met with fluorescent lights and antiseptic, and my heart smiles. My father has never understood my love of the medical setting, but I imagine if you are a baker and walk into a bakery or a librarian and walk into a library, it's the same thing.

"For it being so early in the morning, you look like you're glowing. Nice weekend?" Laurie asks, wiggling her brows at me.

Heat rises into my cheeks. She sees it, and her eyes shine back in delight. "Very. I spent the past three days at the beach. That glow is my new tan." I hold out my arm between us.

"You went to the beach?" she asks, her gaze shifting to one of curiosity.

"I did. Does that surprise you?"

"Kind of, yeah."

I'm a little bit taken aback by her answer, and by the time we reach the surgeon's office and I settle in, I can't hold back anymore.

"Why does me going to the beach surprise you?"

Laurie sits at her station pulling up this morning's schedule and charts when her eyes pop over to me.

"I guess it's just in the time that I've known you, you've

never taken any kind of vacation. I've heard you mention Pilates and your dad, but not much else."

She's not wrong. I've never been a spontaneous person. I like a plan. I like to research, organize, and I guess in a way be in control. But outside of my personality, I have been here for two years, and other than taking a few quick trips home to see my dad and a girls' weekend with Camille, I haven't done anything else. My fellowship year, I was way too busy worrying about my board certification exam, and well, this past year, I agree with Isaac when he said I was just passing time. My life has been on hold. I haven't been living it.

"I guess I haven't, but I think I'm ready to change that."

She nods like she understands me. "My friends and I get together at least twice a month to go to whatever festival is happening in Curtis Hixon Park. It doesn't matter what it is, from a margarita festival to a macaroni and cheese festival or a sports viewing party. I'd love for you to join us."

"I'd love to go. Just text me when. Thank you for inviting me."

Look at that, I'm making a new friend.

"Great. This weekend is Mimosaland and an R&B music festival."

"Because nothing screams mimosas more than an R&B concert." I laugh.

She shrugs. "Ehh, we've learned to just go with it."

"Sounds fun."

"And maybe you'll tell me more about that 'glowing tan' you got." She wiggles her brows.

My cheeks flush again, and I look away from her. Look at that. It's only Tuesday, and I've already made plans for Friday and Sunday this weekend.

Opening up the schedule, I run over the surgeries and see that they are back-to-back all day. First up, a tibial shaft fracture. I scan the X-rays, hoping that I can do a closed reduction, where I realign the broken bones without cutting into the skin, but I don't think it's possible. This one is an unstable displaced fracture. Set it, pin it, cast it.

From there, I review each case and set a tentative game plan. Just as I'm finishing, my watch thumps against my arm with an incoming text. Seeing it's from Jonah, I pull my phone from my bag.

> Thinking of you. I hope you have a good day.

There's no way I can keep a smile off my face. He makes me happy. The kind of happy where I feel like twirling with my arms spread wide, and I'm not a twirling girl. I instantly reply.

> Thank you. I'm missing the sunshine already.

More like I'm missing being with the two of them, but the beach was nice too.

"Don't think I don't notice you smiling over there," Laurie says, eyeing me suspiciously.

My smile grows even wider.

It's interesting how fate keeps throwing us together. I know this past weekend was because of our friends, but before that, the timing seems to be on point to be anything other than fate. I can't speak for him or Vivi, but for me, I wasn't in this place that I am now.

You could always come back.

What I wouldn't give to head back down there after work today. But the drive is just a tad too long to commute, and I know he and Vivi have a week full of fun things already planned.

Tempting, but I can't. Duty calls. Make sure you both wear extra sunscreen.

I may be in orthopedics, but that doesn't change the fact that I know the long-term damage caused by overexposure and burns from the sun.

You know I will.

Thank you for the amazing weekend.

I hope we can do it again sometime.

I heart the comment and then set my phone down to get back to work. It's then I check my email and find one from MCOSC, Minneapolis Children's Orthopedic and Scoliosis Center.

My heart rate picks up, and I click it open.

It's from the office administrator to Dr. Leville. She's informed me that they have received my interest in joining their practice, and she would like me to call her at my earliest convenience to schedule an interview.

Oh no.

And just like that, Mistress Fate has me wondering what she's doing now.

I've dreamed of this moment. I've lain in bed for years and thought about what it would feel like to finally get the opportunity to go home. I expected to feel so much excitement. After all, this is the next step in my dream of returning home, my plan, but I don't. At all. Instead, I feel confused in a way that I don't know what to do with myself. Dreams and plans are these giant-pie-in-the-sky endgame goals. They're the things people work toward while still living their life, like a life where you meet people who might be changing you. Where you melt over the sweetest smile and little hands wrapped around yours, as well as big hands that know just how to touch you to set your world on fire. I know three days with them shouldn't weigh on any decision I'm trying to make about my future, but somehow, I find it does.

Chapter 24
Jonah

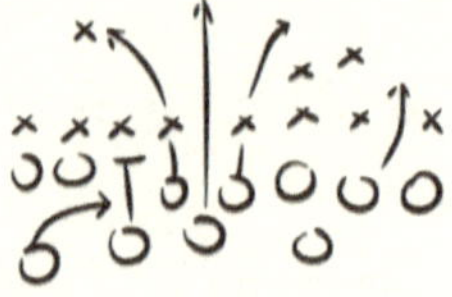

Being back at the training facility feels a little bit like going back to work. Don't get me wrong, I love playing football, and if I could it for the rest of my life, I would, but this feeling has more to do with just rolling off an amazing vacation and trying to get into the swing of things.

Last week, my body was thanking me for the reprieve. Today, it's cursing me for the drills I'm putting it through. We've been at it for only two hours, and I'm exhausted.

Vivi and I had planned on coming home today, but when Bryan texted that a bunch of the guys were getting together to prepare for the upcoming minicamp, I couldn't say no. Well, I could, but I didn't want to. Full team practice starts in a month, and I need to make sure I'm as ready as I can be. Vivi was okay heading out a day early, so we packed up yesterday and came home. She's spending some time at Camille's this morning while I'm here, on a Sunday, sweating my ass off.

"You're looking mighty tan there," Sully says as we convene around the water station. A water station in our new practice facility. The organization went all out on this one with three natural-grass practice fields, a ten-thousand-square-foot new weight room, three hydrotherapy pools, a turf outdoor field, a new outdoor cooling trailer that is set at twenty degrees to quickly lower core body temperature, and more.

His tone has me pausing the green Gatorade bottle I've just lifted, and my eyes shoot to his. He's smirking, and it doesn't take a genius to know what he's talking about. I glance around at our group. Sully, Tyler, Reid, Bryan, and Camden are all watching me.

All of them knew I was taking Vivi away for the week, but only one person knew that Sophie would be joining us. My gaze swings to Reid, and he gives me a half-apologetic shrug.

"Really?" I ask, shaking my head, sweat dripping down next to my ear.

"You know nothing stays a secret around here," he says.

"Well, maybe this could have. I'm still processing." I swallow some water, toss the bottle, and then grab an unused towel off the bench to run over my face. Now that I'm thinking about it, if they all knew, then I'm surprised they waited two hours to ask me.

"Process through talking to your favorite people," Camden says, grinning from ear to ear. Camden is the quietest of our group and also the fastest. While he's really good at football, he's also wicked smart. It doesn't surprise me that he used the word "process" since he processes everything. Somewhere along the way, he earned the nickname Superman because he's all buttoned up with his glasses on during the day, but then when duty calls and he steps into his uniform, beware.

"You're definitely not my favorite people," I say as I look at each of them. One whole wall of the new facility is windows, so the light streaming in is natural and bright.

"Lies," Tyler chimes in from where he's standing to my left. "Football is family, and family is football," he says all innocently, and I want to remind him that some families hate each other.

I feel circled. They've each taken a spot around me, placing me in the middle, and I want to laugh. This is what wolves do with their prey. Maybe they're playing for the wrong team and should be heading to Washington.

I look each one of them in the eye, toss the towel, pull off my gloves, and throw them to the ground. I tilt my head from side to side to crack my neck and then look at Reid first.

"You ready?" There's no humor in my tone, only seriousness.

"For what?" he asks, suddenly skeptical of me.

"To fight," I tell him point-blank, pushing my hair back off my forehead so I can see.

His brows shoot up, and his jaw drops. "What are you talking about?"

I turn in a circle and hold my hands out, looking at each one of them.

"You've got me surrounded, and while you might think it's fun to gossip like girls, I'd prefer to throw down like men." I lace my fingers and then stretch my arms out in front of me so they can crack.

"Well, this is going to be fun," Sully says. Bro has at least fifty pounds on me, and while they don't know I'm messing around with them, the thought that Sully would actually fight me is terrifying. I might be quick, but tackling guys is literally his job.

"Don't you have somewhere else you need to be? Go harass your own people." By people, I mean the defensive line.

"Nope, I think I'll stay right here and enjoy the show." He laughs.

"Bro, for real?" Tyler asks, eyeing me like I've suddenly become unhinged and shifting his weight.

I lock eyes with him and pause for dramatic effect.

"Nah, I'm just kidding." I ease out of my stance and crack a grin. "Had you going there, didn't I?" I smile victoriously, and all five of them groan as the tenseness releases.

"You're an idiot," Reid says.

"Me? Y'all literally surrounded me to ask me about a girl. Don't you have other things to talk about?"

Collectively, they all say, "No."

"What about him? After all, he's the one about to have a baby." I point at Reid.

"We talked to him all week. We're caught up. Baby is

measuring six pounds and is the size of a head of lettuce," Tyler says.

"Really? Lettuce?" I glance at Reid and think about that for a second. What would it be like to walk around with a head of lettuce in my stomach? Weird, that's for sure.

"Listen," he says, pulling my attention back to him. "We're just all happy for you and want to know how it went."

"Well, she didn't leave. She stayed the weekend. So that's something."

"Did you have a good time? What did you do? Was it awkward or were sparks flying?" Sully asks.

I think of all of us in this group. Sully is always the one most curious about the relationships his friends have. He cheers us all on and will lend an ear if we need one, but when it comes to him, I've never known him to date anyone. He'd make someone so happy too. He's the type of guy who's present and thoughtful. Well, lightning will strike one day, and I look forward to it.

"First off, Vivi was with us. So no sparks." At least none that I'm going to tell them about. "And second, we did beach things. We hung out, built sandcastles, ate food, that kind of stuff."

"Beach things. Is that why your fingernails are painted pink?" Camden asks, and the guys chuckle.

I hold out my hand and look to see that yep, they're still painted. I completely forgot about that.

"Why don't you stop by sometime? I'm sure you won't

walk away unscathed either once Vivi gets her hands on you."

"Don't you remember that time she put little ponytails all over Tyler's head with the colorful rubber bands?" Sully chimes in. "You've got plenty of hair for that."

Camden frowns.

"Well, I think a beach trip sounds awesome," Bryan says. "I can't remember the last time Lexi and I went to the beach."

"Yeah, but you just took that trip to Napa where you ate and drank in luxury down the California coast. You can't really complain," Reid says.

"I'm not complaining. I'm just saying it sounds nice. Me. Her in a tiny bikini." His eyes glaze over.

"Doesn't your brother-in-law now live in Key West?" Camden asks, and Bryan nods. "You could visit him there. I hear there are some beautiful coral reefs to explore."

"Key West is home to North America's only living coral barrier reef. We studied them in my ecology of marine environments class, and then I snorkeled them. Top-ten experience right there," Tyler tells us.

Camden nods, agreeing with him when Sully claps his hands.

"You're getting off track. Focus." He turns to me. "So are you in love?" he asks in a teasing voice.

My expression drops to one of a blank stare. "It was three days."

"Three days seems like it's not really accurate, given the situation between the two of you. Besides, does it matter? My best friend told his now wife that he loved her after six days," Tyler says.

I've heard him talk a lot about Lance over the years, although I've yet to meet him. Good dude from everything he's said.

"Six days?" Camden chimes in, his face one of disgust. "How is that even possible?"

"When you know, you know." Tyler shrugs.

"Well, I don't know." Actually, I do. There's definitely love there for her. Has been since the night we met. Whether or not it's endearing love or a forever kind of love is yet to be seen. "Y'all forget, I just had one night with her before, and there wasn't a lot of talking going on. When Vivi had her appointment, that's when I learned her last name is Black, and she's a freaking surgeon. At the beach, she talked about her dad and how she's from Minnesota and allergic to shrimp. I literally know nothing about this girl, and she knows nothing about me."

"But you had a good time?" Reid studies me.

"I did."

One of the best weekends of my life.

"What did my girl think about her being there?" Tyler asks. I love that he's always thinking about Vivi.

"Oh, she was on cloud nine. Sophie was another person to play with, and they did all the girly things."

"Except paint nails, apparently," Camden blurts out, his gaze falling to my hands.

"Well, that has to be a bonus that they get along so well," Reid says.

"But what happens if we don't work out? I can't help the ball of anxiousness that sits in the pit of my stomach at the possibility of her losing someone else she cares about."

"You might not have known Sophie for two years, but I have. She's chill and not going anywhere. Even if y'all don't work out, she'll still be coming to our house, and Vivi will see her. She's nice, and knowing what she knows, she would never leave her hanging," he tells me.

"Right, and she works with kids, so you know she loves them," Sully volunteers.

I do know this, but here's the thing. Other than building sandcastles, I had all the time in the world to think about this, her, us, and I know what's best for Vivi, and even me, is not to play games. As great as it would be to have a little fun with Sophie, Lord knows she brings me to my knees. I'm not looking for someone who wants a friends-with-benefits situation. That gets messy, and inevitably, feelings get hurt. And no matter what, those feelings can not be Vivi's.

"I'm seeing her again tonight. Reid, can Vivi hang for a bit?"

"Of course," he says. Vivi is really easy. She talks to Camille, plays with Izzy, and watches movies or colors. She's even become a bit of a bookworm and will sit on the couch and read. Unless she's somehow miraculously in their way, you wouldn't even know she was visiting.

"I'll take her tonight," Tyler says.

"You sure?"

"Absolutely. Just let me know when you want her home."

I nod and clap him on the shoulder. "Thanks."

"Big night out on the town?" Sully asks.

"Nope. I'm bringing her back to my place. I thought about it, but I need her to see my life, our life. That way she can form her own decisions about whether this/we are something she wants."

"All or nothing, huh? I didn't see that coming," Tyler says.

I shrug my shoulders.

I didn't either. After all, I've done nothing but fantasize about this girl for years. But now that she's finally here, and reality is setting in, given the cards Vivi has already been dealt in life, I'm not sure there's another way. They say parenting is about making tough choices for our kids, and they weren't wrong.

Chapter 25
Sophie

Right at six thirty, Jonah knocks on the door. It's been almost a week since I've seen him, and I'm way more nervous than I should be. Did we talk all week? Yes. But only through text messages, and those were more along the lines of, "How was your day?" and "What did you and Vivi do today?" There were no deep and serious discussions. I'm not even sure I really got to know him more than I do.

Smoothing down the skirt to my dress, I open the door, and there he is.

I'm immediately hit with his clean and delicious smell, and I breathe in as his frame fills the doorway. His eyes find mine, and he smiles so big. It's easy to see that it's genuine, and he's happy to see me. With that smile, the butterflies in my stomach enthusiastically flap their wings like they're waving. They're happy to see him too.

It's quite possible I'll be in big trouble when it comes to this guy. Especially since he's not part of the plan.

"Wow, you look beautiful," he says, his eyes quickly dragging over the length of me before he steps forward, leans in, and kisses me on the cheek. His lips are warm, his cheek is soft, and my eyes fall shut at the sensation.

His smell intensifies to where I can now recognize notes of fabric softener, vanilla, and coconut. It's the same smell from the beach and the perfect pheromone concoction to make me want to bury my face against his chest and breathe him in indefinitely.

"You don't look so bad yourself," I tell him, taking in his date attire of dark slacks and a button-down with the sleeves rolled up.

"I'm kind of having a moment," he says almost quietly, his cheeks tinting red.

"What do you mean?" I ask, my eyes searching his hazel ones that are so unique and so pretty. There are flecks of gold and patches of green—so many colors I could never pick a favorite.

"This place. Your door." He shakes his head. "You have no idea how many times I wanted to stop here and knock just to see if you still lived here."

"I wish you would have," I whisper, feeling a longing for the time lost that we could have had together.

Regret slips over his features, and I can't have that, so I run my hand down his arm and take his hand.

"Doesn't matter. You're here now." I smile up at him, and his gaze dips to my lips.

Does he want to kiss me?

God, I hope so.

Clearing his throat, he takes a step back and asks, "You all set?"

"Yep," I tell him, moving out of the front door to lock it.

Slipping my hand into his, I lace our fingers together as we walk toward his SUV. For it being June, the evening is mild and not humid. I almost wonder if we're going to be sitting outside?

"As far as date nights go, while there are a lot of places that I'd love to take you, there's only one place that means the most to me. You in?" he asks as he opens my door.

"Of course. Now you have me even more excited."

He winks as he closes the door and makes his way around to the driver's side. That one little movement takes my butterflies from flapping to somersaulting. He might have had a moment on the doorstep, but I'm kind of having one now. I'm about to go on a date with Jonah Dallmann. In a way, it doesn't even feel like last weekend happened. This, now, feels foreign and brand new.

Slipping into the car, he turns it on and then shifts to look at me. His gaze is so open and so clear, the line of his jaw is smooth, and his skin is golden from the week in the sun. Add in the blond hair, wide shoulders, and impressive frame; he's so striking that he could be a Nordic king. How good he looks should be illegal.

"Thank you," he says, reaching over to again take my hand. His is so much larger than mine, and goose bumps race down my back as his thumb starts rubbing from the inside of my wrist down into my palm.

"For what?"

He blinks. "For saying yes to tonight."

A smile stretches across my face. As if there's anywhere else I'd be.

As he pulls away from the curb, a comfortable silence wraps around us as he drives, and we cross the bridge that leads to Davis Islands. We pass the shops and restaurants, make a few turns, and then pull up to a house and park on the street. It's not a small house, but it's not a large one either. The two-story white house almost looks Mediterranean with the clay pot roof, and I know instantly it has to be his house.

He lets out a sigh as he turns off the engine and faces me.

"I thought about taking you somewhere trendy or elegant, fun, I don't know just different, but the thing is, this is my life now. Vivi is my life. We spend a lot of time at home, and I thought I would bring you here so you can see what our life looks like and let me cook you dinner. She's out with Tyler at the moment, so it'll be just us, but he'll bring her back later. Then maybe the three of us can walk a few streets over so she can show you her favorite ice cream place. I know this isn't the most romantic, but you'll be able to decide sooner rather than later if this is something that you want. If we are something that you want."

Instead of answering, I just watch him for a few

moments. That comfortable silence from just a few moments ago turns heavy. One of his hands holds the wheel, and I hear the squeak of the leather as he tightens his grip. His lips purse together in a straight line, and he breathes in slowly through his nose, his nostrils flaring. He's nervous, and I find it endearing because I'm nervous too. It makes sense that he would bring me here, and it also makes sense that he's stating his intentions or concerns early. I appreciate that he's not here to play games, but it goes both ways.

"How do you know that I'm what you want?" I ask, feeling a little uneasy.

He hesitates and tilts his head. "I guess I'm trying to figure that out too."

"Okay. Then I'm glad you brought me here." I smile at him, and he gives me a small smile back.

Getting out of the car, he meets me as I slide out. While we only live a few miles away from each other, the air here somehow feels and smells different. Yes, we're surrounded by water, and maybe that's it, but as we walk up the sidewalk and I glance around at the other houses of his neighbors, it's the smell of grass, salt, the oak trees, and summer that makes this feel like home.

A home.

I don't know what I expected about where Jonah lived. Maybe part of me still occupies the mindset of guys his age having bachelor pads, but this is anything but.

With his hand on my lower back, we walk inside

together, and internally, I stutter as I need to take a moment. Jonah is years younger than me, yet standing here in his foyer, it feels the other way around. This is adulting. This is at a whole different level than I am, and I feel a mixture of pride for him and, in a way, inadequacy. At the present, my life is far from ever looking like this. I'm the walking stereotype of medical school loans and second-hand furniture. This house is straight out of a *Restoration Hardware* magazine.

"Jonah, your home is beautiful," I tell him, as I basically do a three-sixty to take it all in.

He swallows, looks around to maybe see what I see, and then looks over at me. "Thank you. I can't take all of the credit, though. I had some help."

He might have had some help, but this isn't a showroom. It's a home. There are shoe baskets by the door, dog toys on the floor, and a small table I can see in the living room next to the kitchen for artwork. Yes, the furniture, lighting, and decor are stunning, but it's more than that.

"Camille does have an amazing eye, doesn't she?" I say to him, trying not to make him feel uncomfortable.

He tosses his keys into a bowl on the console by the door. "I basically gave her an unlimited budget, and this is what she came up with."

The home is made up of warm tones. Beiges, different shades of green and wood, black wrought-iron accents for the light fixtures and the stair railing, and light. The home is bright and airy.

"Well, she also knows you well enough to know what you like and what you don't like. So although she may have pulled it all together, it's still you. Where did you live when we first met?"

"In a condo downtown. There's one building where a lot of the team lives. Makes it easy for commuting to the facility."

"I think that is more of what I expected even though I knew you lived on Davis Islands from what Camille told me. This is just so much more."

"I needed to give Vivi a home. This house was available and move-in ready, so I bought it. I didn't want Vivi to have to go from her house, to the condo, and then another house. She was already dealing with so much."

I turn to face him. "You're a good man. I hope you know that."

He shrugs but looks relieved at my quick assessment.

"Can I get you a glass of wine?" he asks, changing the subject and moving toward the kitchen. In this house, the kitchen, dining, and living room is one great room. The furniture is laid out in a way that it all feels separate, yet the whole space is open.

"Yes, I'd love one," I tell him as I walk around the living room and look at the pictures. There are a lot of his brother, his sister-in-law, and Vivi together. My heart aches at the thoughtfulness of him keeping them out so she can see them and remember her parents. I know firsthand how memories fade, except for the ones in the photos.

It's then my gaze travels over the wall of windows leading to a back porch and the backyard.

"You have a pool." I'm surprised, but I don't know why. It seems like most people in Florida have a pool.

"Yes, and I'm glad," he says as he pops a cork and pours us each a glass. "Vivi loves to swim. The only thing it's missing is a hot tub. I've contemplated buying one and building a small deck for it."

He also has a large wooden playground.

So . . . domestic.

So . . . perfect.

He then surprises me even more by pulling a small charcuterie board out of the refrigerator he's wrapped in plastic to keep fresh. He places it on the large island, and I move to join him.

"So fancy." I smile, and he blushes a little, sliding my glass over to me.

"Vivi wanted to help. She picked out these flowers for you too, so you'll have to take them home with you tonight."

"She's so sweet. She could have been here tonight with us. I don't want you to ever think that I don't want her around."

"I don't think that. I just wanted to spend time with you. Alone. I want to get to know you better, and sometimes kids can be a truth buffer. The conversation stays light because of the little ears."

"I understand completely. We actually get sensitivity

training on how to talk to the parents and how to talk to our tiny patients."

"I should say that surprises me, but after the past two years, it doesn't."

Picking up the glass of wine, I take a sip and am met with a burst of flavors.

"Mmm, this is good."

"Thanks. Camden on the team recommended it. He's more savvy when it comes to things like wine." Jonah picks up his glass, and his brows rise as he swallows, agreeing with me.

"Well, tell him he has good taste."

He smiles. "Nah, that will just make his head bigger than it already is. You should have seen the look on his face when I asked for a suggestion in the first place." He loves talking about his friends. To be in the situation he found himself in and to be surrounded by so much support. I'm happy he has his teammates. He's lucky. "So tell me, what have you been up to for say . . . ever?" he asks, grabbing a piece of cheese and tossing it into his mouth.

I laugh. "Well, the past twenty-seven years of it, I have been in school."

He grimaces, and this makes me laugh even more.

"Did you always know that you wanted to be a doctor?"

"Yes." I then tell him the story that sealed my fate. "What about you? Have you always wanted to play football?"

"I have. My dad left us when we were fairly young, so John kind of filled that role. He was older, and I always thought he was the coolest. He loved football, so of course I did too, and this was a way for me to spend time with him. He would have been happy for me no matter what I ended up doing in life, but once football became my dream, it became his too. I wouldn't be where I am today without him."

"I feel that way about my dad too."

"You mentioned he's in Minnesota?"

"Yep, Minneapolis."

"You never wanted to move back there to be with him?"

This would be the time to tell him about the interview, to let him know that it is a real possibility, but I can't find the words for some reason. As the expression goes, "Don't borrow tomorrow's troubles today," and that's what this is. All I know for sure is that I have an interview. Nothing more. I guess when I have something to discuss with him, we'll do it then, but for now, I just want to be here with him.

"That was always the plan."

"And it's not now?" he asks, tilting his head a little to study me.

I think about how to best answer this.

"I certainly haven't closed that door. My dad, he's my family. But for now, I'm working here and living here."

His eyes drop down to the food as he thinks about this, and then he nods his head at whatever conclusion he comes to.

"I understand that. Football isn't forever. My plan was always to find my way back to Boston to be with John and Ashley."

Which makes me wonder, if I did end up back in Minneapolis, and we became a more permanent thing, would he eventually come with me?

"Boston is cold." I frown at him, just thinking about how many times we'd watch the news and hear about those frigid nor'easters.

He laughs. "As if Minnesota isn't."

"True, but I don't think it's the same. Our Midwestern snow is different from your violent windy snow." I pick up a grape and plop it into my mouth.

"Living in the South, I can say I've gotten used to not being in snow."

"That makes two of us. Speaking of, I know it's last minute, but I'm flying home next weekend to visit with my dad," I tell him, feeling really nervous for no reason. Well, maybe I have a reason. As much as I'm trying to convince myself that I'm living in the moment, a tiny part of me feels guilty. I firmly stand in the camp that lying by omission is still lying. I just can't think about that right now.

"Oh, really?" he asks, looking at me in a way that makes me feel like he's looking through me.

"A flight opportunity popped up, so I'm going. It's just an overnight trip, but I haven't seen him since Christmas." And it did just pop up, all of this is true.

"Well, that's good. Are you excited?"

My stomach dips. I should be excited, but instead, I'm

feeling kind of numb toward it. "I am." After all, that is the correct answer to give him.

"Do you want a ride to the airport? I can take you," he offers because he's a thoughtful guy like that.

"No, it's okay. I don't mind driving, but thank you."

"If you change your mind, just let me know."

Time passes as we talk, snack, and laugh. We've found ourselves sitting on the barstools at the island, with the platter between us, and he's right—a night for just the two of us was needed. At least for a few hours. Eventually, he pulls a casserole dish covered in foil from the refrigerator and places it in the oven. It's nice to watch him move around his kitchen and be in his space. How many meals has he cooked here? How many meals has he burned?

"What are we having?" I ask, smiling, dropping my shoes to the floor to get more comfortable.

"Lasagna," he says, proud of himself.

"And you made it yourself?"

He shrugs. "I mean, I didn't make the noodles or anything, but I did the rest. I've gotten pretty good at making one-pot dishes and casseroles. Easy to heat after school and easy to clean."

"I guess I've never really thought about it. I'm one person, so food is simple. If I make anything like this, I just portion it out for multiple meals. How often do you eat dinner together?"

"Pretty much every night unless I'm on the road. Tyler is usually here too. He eats more food than I do, so we never have any leftovers."

I met Tyler briefly at the recital, but other than that, I don't know him.

"What does Vivi do when you're on the road?"

"One of the coaches has a daughter in college here. During the season, she picks her up after school, takes her to dance, that kind of stuff, and then she sleeps over or she takes her to Camille's."

"She's worked for you for two years now?"

"Yeah. I pay her well. But I only have one more year with her, then she'll graduate and move on to something else."

"Do you ever worry about being let go or traded to another team?"

"Every day. I've already been traded once, so I know what it feels like, but my contract has a few restrictions. Vivi and I have talked about it several times. If it does happen, I don't want it to be a shock to her. But we'll see where I'm at in my career at that point. Who knows, maybe I'll just retire."

"Where do you see yourself living after you retire?"

"Honestly, we haven't gotten that far. We were in survival mode the first year, and then this past year, it's been about settling in and healing." He looks away from me and toward the living room. "It's been hard for Vivi."

"That makes me sad," I tell him, feeling the lingering grief on him that sometimes accompanies conversations about his brother.

He runs his hand through his hair, lets out a deep sigh, then looks at me again. He's so handsome.

"It's okay. She's had a lot more good days than bad, and slowly, I've been seeing her old self peek out, so we're getting there."

"Anything I can do?" I lean over and place my hand on his thigh.

"Nope. Just be you." He gives me a lopsided smile and then covers my hand with his.

Chapter 26
Team Chat

Sully: Rico, is there someone outside just sitting in your car?

Rico: Wouldn't you like to know . . .

Sully: Seriously, I just pulled into the training facility, and there's someone in your car

Camden: Why didn't you tell security?

Sully: Hang on, I'm about to

Miles: Bro, she definitely belongs to Rico

Titan: 😂

Sully: What do you mean?

Miles: Just what I said

Sully: Rico, you can't bring strange women to the facility and leave them in your car while you work out. Especially not this early in the morning

Ryder: Is this part of the code?

Titan: 😂

Sully: FFS. Have you not read the handbook yet?

Darius: You're assuming he can read

Dylan: Ah, yeah! Just pulled in. Rico, you got Tammy a new shirt

Rico: Damn straight. Needed her repping her man. #2 baby

Ryder: I can read

Darius: I'm going to quiz you next time I see you

Ryder: Gotta catch me first

Sully: Who is Tammy?

Rico: My passenger princess

Sully: Explain, or I'm calling security

Rico: Bro. Chill.

Titan: 😂

Miles: Tammy is his blow-up doll

Sully: The fuck you need a blow-up
doll for

Dylan: She's equipped to handle all his
needs

Sully: OMG

Darius: Oh, I can catch your ass no
problem, Rookie

Camden: My money's on Ryder

Sully: People. Rico needs an
intervention. Focus.

Rico: Bro

Darius: Seriously, Cam. I'll remember this

Camden: I'm just stating a fact. Look at
his 40 to yours

Titan: 😂

Dylan: You misspelled intervention. It's traffic violation

Rico: The law doesn't state it has to be a living being. All it says is occupant, and Tammy occupies. She keeps me company

Dylan: Suuuure, she keeps you company

Sully: You bought a blow-up doll to drive in the HOV lane?

Rico: Gets me here quicker. Jealous you didn't think of it?

Sully: Something is seriously wrong with you. You need help

Rico: If by help you mean head, hell yeah

Dylan: Tammy can do that too

Sully: For fuck's sake

Chapter 27
Jonah

The moment Sophie opens the door, I shuffle her back inside and up against the wall next to it, slamming it shut without even letting her say hello.

"What are you doing?" She laughs, her eyes wide with happiness.

"This," I tell her, crowding her space and bending down to crush my mouth against hers. While I did kiss her good night last night, it was more of a first-date kind of kiss, since Vivi was in the car. As it turns out, after I left, that kiss wasn't enough for me. It's all I've thought about, she's all I've thought about after what I consider the best date of my life, and now here I am eighteen hours later ready to devour her. She's wearing strawberry-flavored lip gloss, and my tongue rejoices as it licks it clean off her.

"I can't stop thinking about kissing you, and I just couldn't wait any longer."

She grins against my lips. "Well, who am I to deny you," she says as she lifts on her toes and wraps her arms around my neck. Pulling me closer, Sophie kisses me back, matching my intensity.

Pushing her against the wall, I move my mouth to her ear, her neck, and then lower. I cup both of her boobs, pushing them up and lick my way across her skin at the edge of her shirt, dip my tongue down in the valley and then drop to my knees.

Sophie groans as her head tilts back, and she arches her back. My hands drag down her sternum to her waist, where I momentarily lay my forehead to just be near her.

"Jonah," she says, her voice slightly breathy, and I can one hundred percent listen to her say my name like that over and over. The door is closed, and not that I think anyone from the sidewalk out front can hear us, but they might, and her sounds are for my ears only.

Lifting her shirt, I suck on her stomach and dip my tongue into her belly button, as my hands find their way under her skirt. It's loose and flowy, and I have no problems sliding them up the back of her legs and ass, which feel so good. Her hip bones are sharp under my thumbs, and her underwear are wet as I skim my fingers down the middle. Without asking or waiting another second, I pull them off.

I have to taste her.

I need to taste her.

Lifting her skirt so it's out of the way, she spreads her legs just the perfect distance for me to lean forward and drag my tongue over her. Her fingers sink into my hair, and as I glance up at her, I see her eyes are squeezed shut. I already know this isn't going to take long.

"Sophie," I call her name, and her head drops as her eyes open and look at me. They are dilated and heated. There's a blush on her cheeks, and her chest rises and falls at a rapid rate. "I want you to watch me."

"I don't know if I can," she whispers.

Lifting one of her legs, I place it over my shoulder and rub my thumb against her. She closes her eyes for just a second, and then they pop open again to find me. Leaning forward, I suck her into my mouth while sinking two fingers in, one at a time. She's soft, warm, and tight, and I could do this for the rest of my life and die a happy man.

I love the taste, the smell, and the feel of her. Hell, I already know that's not the only thing I'm starting to love. It's too soon to talk about what that might mean, but time doesn't change the facts. After last night, if this girl wants me, she's got me. I don't need any more time to figure it out. I'm not sure I ever needed the time. I just knew deep down that she's the one for me.

It doesn't take long before I feel her start to shake. I hear the change in her breathing, and then she pulls so hard on my hair, making my eyes water. From her thighs all the way to her face, she flushes red. She's beautiful.

Dropping her leg, I gently put her back together, then lick my lips before dragging them across my arm to dry them and standing.

"Hi," I say to her.

"Hi," she says back, eyes sparkling and sated. "Thank you for that. It was . . . well, you know . . ." She blushes again.

"I wanted to do that last night but thought it was best to hold off until date number two," I tell her, adjusting her shirt and settling my hand on her waist.

She giggles. "I certainly wouldn't have complained," she says shyly.

"Are you ready to go?"

"I'm not sure. Am I?" she asks, her tone edged with an unexpected wonder.

I laugh.

"Yes. Vivi should be done with her dance camp in a few minutes, and I don't want to leave her there too long."

"Vivi," she whispers, her eyes growing large with panic.

"She'll be fine. She loves it there," I reassure her, my fingers tightening around her. My hands are so large, just one of them wraps around half of her.

"Okay." She reaches between us, runs her hand down over me, and gently squeezes. I was hard before, but now with her hand on me, I'm like steel.

"Seems not fair," she says quietly, and with my other hand, I wrap it around her face and tilt her head back. Tiny freckles, long eyelashes, and perfect lips stare up at me.

"Fair is you sneaking over to my house later tonight after Vivi has gone to bed to keep me company." I brush my lips against hers and take in the closeness of this moment.

She smiles. "And when is bedtime?" She runs her hand up and down me again.

"Eight," I barely get out.

"I'll keep that in mind," she teases as she kisses me one more time, then releases me. Stepping away, she turns to look in the mirror over her couch. She smoothes down her skirt and fixes her ponytail while I glance around. Everything looks exactly like I remember it, from the couch to the vintage skeleton posters on her walls. Which also now makes sense. She was a doctor, and I had no idea.

"Is Vivi excited to go out for pizza tonight?" she asks, pulling me from my memories.

I can't help but chuckle. "Prepare yourself. I'm not sure you can handle what we've planned."

She grins. "And what is that?" she asks, picking up her purse and moving us out the door so she can lock it.

"A pizzapalooza."

She smiles up at me, and my chest constricts. "A what?"

"You heard me. Vivi had an idea, and I just let her run with it." Wrapping my hand around her ponytail, I run the strands through my fingers. Her hair is so soft, just like all of her. Her lips, her skin, that sweet spot between her legs. Internally, I groan at how perfect she is.

"What's on the agenda for our pizzapalooza?" She grins at the silliness of it.

She's intrigued, and I'm pleased. Vivi will be excited.

"I'm going to let Vivi tell you, but just so you know, she made a poster."

"A poster?" She laughs.

"Yep." I slip my fingers between hers, and we walk to the car just like last night.

"Well, I officially love our pizzapalooza date." She smiles.

Everything in South Tampa is fairly close, so it only takes a few minutes to get to the dance studio, and Vivi is waiting for us just inside the door when we arrive. She's never this eager to see me, and although I know Sophie would never do anything to hurt her, I can't help the wave of wariness that rushes over me. Parenting is strange. I never realized how much on the defense one plays. I'm constantly looking for things that could hurt her or make her unhappy.

"Ms. Sophie!" Vivi's eyes light up, and even though she remains conservative with her emotions, her happiness is written all over her face.

"Hi, sweetheart," Sophie says, opening her arms to hug her.

The two of them embrace, and I have his overwhelming urge to wrap my arms around both of them and say, "Mine."

"How come you never greet me like that?" I ask her.

"Because I see you every day," she states, like that should be obvious.

"You just saw her last night," I point out, arguing with the seven-year-old.

"Uncle Jonah, it's just different," she states, like I should know better.

"I guess so. I'm chopped liver."

She giggles. "Gross."

"So we're not putting that on our pizza?" I ask as I grab her bag. She slips her hand into Sophie's as we walk outside.

"No!" she says, looking up at Sophie. "Did he tell you?"

"Nope. He just said you planned something for us, and I can't wait to see what it is."

I scoff. "Wildflower, I told you I wouldn't tell her."

"Well, I didn't know. You tell Uncle Tyler everything."

I glance at Sophie and shake my head. "Not everything."

Sophie grins as Vivi races to the back of the Tahoe to open the trunk.

"Ms. Sophie, you have to see what we made this morning!"

"I'm so excited," she tells her.

"I didn't make it. This was all you," I tell them both.

Vivi pulls out the poster and shows her it's a large chart. There are spots for twenty pizza places down the left-hand side, and then across the top are columns to rate for crust, sauce, cheese, restaurant decor, overall, and total. She's labeled the scale from one through ten, with ten being the greatest.

"It's to help us find the best pizza place in Tampa!" she says, bouncing on her toes.

"This is the best idea ever," Sophie tells her, looking at the poster in awe. Vivi has even colored little slices of pizza around the edge.

"I agree. It means I'm guaranteed at least twenty pizza dates with you."

Sophie hears what I'm saying without saying it—that I'm excited to spend more time with her. That I want to spend a lot of time with her.

"So where are we going first?"

"Santoro's Pizzeria."

"Never heard of it."

"Exactly."

Chapter 28
Sophie

During the flight to Minneapolis, I think about Jonah and Vivi when I should have focused on interview questions. Three nights this week, we got together to go eat pizza, and they were three of the best nights ever. We told stories, we laughed, and we stuffed our faces. I was in heaven.

For years, I have known that I was going to work with kids. I love kids; otherwise, I never would have chosen them as my profession, but I can honestly say that I've never really given much thought to my own kids. Did I think I would have them one day? Yes. Of course. But that is where my vision ended. Graduate med school. Get a job back in Minneapolis. Get married. Have a family. That was basically the order I had planned for my life. When I met Mr. Right, it didn't matter. But not once in my dream did it occur to me that Mr. Right might not want to live in Minneapolis, or that he might already have a child.

And Vivi, I don't even know how to talk about her without my heart feeling like it's going to explode. She is so beautiful and sweet, hardworking and kind, and most of all, I think she's brave. Whether we're fifty or five, losing our loved ones is hard. It takes a lot of inner strength not to drown in the sadness and just keep going. And that's what she's doing. I know it's been hard for her. Jonah and I have talked about it, but she's doing it every day, and I'm so proud of her. I didn't expect to find them, and I certainly didn't expect to be falling in love with them.

I've thought a lot about what would have happened if Jonah and I became a thing two years ago. Would that have changed my dreams, or would they still be the same? I've never not considered ultimately ending up where my dad is. If there was no Vivi, would we have done the long-distance thing, or would I have stayed with him, knowing I'd end up with him? I don't know. The shoulda, coulda, woulda, and what-ifs don't really matter because that's not where we are, but I think about them because I feel like they would guide me on how I should navigate this. Am I putting the cart before the horse? Absolutely, but there's not just me to consider or him. There's her too.

The plane lands, and I stare out at the familiar landscape. How many times have I made this trip over the years? And if I move here, how many times will I be making it in reverse to get to Tampa? It's crazy because I have been looking forward to this moment for what feels like my whole life, and now that it's here, I feel uneasy.

Off. Like something is out of place, missing, or I forgot something.

I also feel guilty for not telling Jonah the true reason for coming. While I'm seeing my dad, he was not the real reason for coming here. I told a half-truth, and it feels wrong.

I know Jonah would be happy for me; it's just we haven't had the talk yet. Then again, I don't know if we will. We're kind of just falling into this life together, and if it was anyone else but me, this wouldn't be an issue. But it is. It's hard for me to wrap my head around the fact that it's only been a few weeks because it feels so much longer. If I'm being honest with myself, it feels like years.

My mind drifts to Vivi and the first time I met her in my office. The first time I saw him in over two years. Really, what are the odds? Of all the orthopedic rooms in Tampa, how did they end up in mine? Then there's the running into them in Hyde Park Village, the baby shower with her, her recital, and then our amazing weekend at the beach. It was so easy for the three of us to become one unit. There were no awkward moments and no getting-to-know-you phase—we just were. And don't get me started on her poster. She was so proud and excited to show it to me. She wants me around, and she wants me to be a part of their life.

As I exit security and walk into the center concourse, I immediately find my dad. He's smiling from ear to ear, wearing his typical attire of jeans and a Minnesota Twins T-shirt, and he's so familiar to me that my eyes sting.

"Hi, sweetheart," he says as I walk straight to him, and he wraps me in his arms. "It's so good to see you." His familiar scent of Old Spice surrounds me, and just for this split second, every fear, every worry, every plan slips away. It's just me and him like it's always been.

"Ah, Dad, I missed you," I tell him, and I mean it. I hate that it's been so long. It seems like the more time passes, the fewer times we get together.

But then my mind shifts because I also miss the two I left behind. It hasn't even been a day yet since I've seen them, but I could be back there with them now, spending the day with them, exploring something new. Instead, I'm here, following my dreams.

At least this is what I keep telling myself.

"I can't believe you're here," he says. "Are you excited?" He looks me over from head to toe. He's looking thinner, and I'm almost tempted to ask him why, but I don't.

"I am," I tell him while smiling when I'm weirdly not. My heart is just not into it.

"Well, I'm excited too. Just the thought of finally having you back home where I get to see you more often, we're almost there. After all these years, I have a good feeling about this." He wraps his arm around my shoulders, and we walk toward the parking garage. "How was the flight?"

"Quick and easy," I tell him, not really wanting to talk about anything more.

Eventually, we find ourselves standing in front of a brand-new, big black truck. When I make a comment about it, he just shrugs and says it was time. For years, he drove the same one and never talked about getting anything new. I thought he loved it, but now I'm starting to wonder if he was keeping his money to help me out through school.

We climb in and take off.

June in the north is such a pretty month. Most of the humidity hasn't settled in yet, so the highs are in the low eighties, and the lows are in the sixties. I crack my window and breathe in the cool air. The grass and the trees are different here. A hint of clover is in the air, and it feels nostalgic. When I came home during college, my eyes would water with happiness and a sense of relief over this smell. Now, it feels more like a childhood memory than a present one.

"Thanks for offering your truck today. I'm not sure how long I'll be there. If you want, I can grab a rideshare."

The two partners interviewing me were gracious enough to offer me a Saturday interview. As they both know, once schedules are locked and surgeries are booked, it's hard for someone like us to just take a day off, so I'm meeting them at two o'clock this afternoon.

"Don't be ridiculous." He glances at me like I'm crazy. "This baby is all yours."

"But what if you need it?" I ask, looking around. I've never driven a truck quite like this before, and it's almost intimidating.

"I have another one."

"Oh, you kept your old truck. That makes sense; you loved it."

I'm glad. I loved it, too. I feel like there's a lot of change, and I need a bit of stability. Jonah, Vivi, unexpected emotions, jobs, possible changes, potentially moving, having to say goodbye, him losing weight, new trucks, uncertainty . . . everything feels like it's leaning on an edge about to fall. One strong gust and over I go.

"No, I traded it in for this one. I was spending more money on fixing it than it was worth."

I turn to face him. I'm confused. "So you bought a second car?"

He glances at me but smiles to himself. His cheeks shade a little red, and I feel like I'm having an out-of-body experience. My dad doesn't blush. What is going on here?

"We have much to talk about," he says like it's some deep, insightful enlightenment.

"What do you mean? We talk all the time." And we do. Every day through text and at least once a week on the phone, sometimes more if the Vikings or the Twins are winning.

"Yes, we do, but now that you're here in person, I have some exciting news to share with you."

His eyes twinkle. Like actually twinkle.

My subdued, laid-back, nothing-fazes-him father must be under a spell.

"Like what?" I ask, anxious to hear if he won the lottery or something.

That blush spreads, and the tips of his ears turn pink. I feel like I'm in some alternate universe where my dad's personality has suddenly been swapped with someone else's.

He holds his breath for a second and then slowly lets it out. "I met someone."

Whoosh goes that gust as it slams into me and knocks me over.

"What?" I'm shocked.

Leaving one hand on the wheel, he rubs the back of his neck with the other. "I wanted to wait until we got home so you could meet her, but clearly, that didn't work out as planned."

Meet her. That means she must be there. At. Our. House. He was going to spring her on me without warning?

Oh my God.

"How? When? Where?" I fire off.

"At the gym of all places and just before Christmas."

I feel my jaw drop as I'm momentarily at a loss for words.

"You joined the gym?" I've never seen him work out a day in my life. He used to go for walks with my mom, but that was it.

"Well, yeah. I'm not getting any younger, and the doctor told me I needed to do more strength training."

That explains the weight loss, especially if his muscles are getting leaner and stronger.

"I understand why you need to work out, but before

Christmas? Why didn't you tell me then? Or any day since then?" My heart twinges with a feeling of betrayal.

The truck slows and then turns. He glances at me again and then looks out at the road. Our home is in Falcon Heights, not too far from the airport, and with each minute that passes, I know we're getting closer to her. Heat flashes under my skin. It's not that I don't want my dad to date, or that I've never considered what it would feel like when he did, but it's just always been us.

And now it's not.

"Because we had just started dating. I didn't even know if it was going to become something."

"But when were you going to tell me? If I hadn't come here, she would still be a secret to me. This person who apparently means so much to you."

And yes, I do hear myself and the irony, but the difference is Jonah and I haven't been together that long. They've been together for over six months.

"I had actually already planned on telling you. Chrissy —" His tone is all affectionate just saying her name, and I have to cut him off.

"Chrissy?" I look at him like he has two heads. My mother's name was Valerie, and I've never heard another woman's name cross his lips like this.

He smiles at me. "That's her name. It's actually Christine, but she's gone by Chrissy since she was a girl."

"Chrissy," I whisper again, just wanting to pass her name over my lips too.

"Yeah," he says, quietly too. "She's very excited to meet you. Nervous, but excited."

How bizarre that this woman is nervous to meet me. I mean, I guess I would be too in her shoes. After all, she's heard about me for months, and I'm just now hearing about her. Suddenly, it dawns on me that I'm the Vivi in this situation.

I almost laugh.

I'm happy for him, I am. I'm just shocked. For so long, I've worried about him being alone, but it turns out he's not. I didn't even know he wanted to date or was looking to date. Not that I necessarily want to think about him dating, that's kind of gross, but I want him to be happy, and it looks like he is.

"You really like this woman, huh?" I ask, seeing him in a bit of a different light. A light that makes him all glowy and, dare I say, reborn.

"I do. I really hope you like her, too." He glances at me quickly again and then back to the road. "Because I kind of want to marry her."

Mic drop.

Chapter 29
Jonah and Sophie

MY DAD JUST TOLD ME HE'S GOING TO GET MARRIED!

Wait, I'm confused. Do we not like the bride-to-be?

We don't know her! He kept her a secret.

Scandalous.

Ugh . . .

* * *

So did you meet her?

Yes.

Do we hate her?

No.

What's she like?

Perfect. She baked me a chocolate cake and made him laugh. He doesn't laugh, he chuckles.

Sounds nice.

It was.

* * *

Tell me something fun you did today.

Why, miss us?

Yes.

Well, that makes me feel good. We miss you too. We had breakfast with Tyler, and then he took us out on his boat. There's a small island he knows about that has a lot of birds, including two flamingos. (Sends a picture of Vivi with the flamingos in the background.)

Wow! What are they doing there?

Don't know.

What time is your flight back tonight?

Departs at 6:50.

We're headed to Bryan's at 6.

You're gone all week?

Yes, but don't make plans for next weekend.

Why?

Because you're mine.

Yours, huh?

Yes.

Anything particular planned?

I'll be in a tux, preferably you're in a nice dress.

Sounds fancy.

I suppose it is.

I seem to remember liking you in a tux.

I wouldn't be disappointed if you wore that dress.

You just liked being able to get underneath said dress.

I do like what's under the dress . . . you.

Chapter 30
Jonah

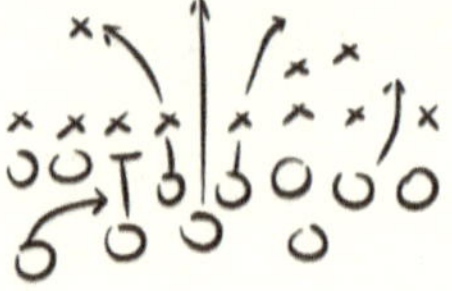

Every year, in late June or early July, individuals of professional football teams start hosting mini-camps. It's a time for key members who work closely together to train and bond as the new season approaches, and this is our week.

This is the third year in a row that Bryan has hosted a minicamp at his house out in the country, at least that's where we tell him it is. When actually, it's just about two hours north of Tampa. He and his wife, Lexi, have their home in Tampa on the river and this old large Southern home that they inherited. Apparently, they grew up together here, and it's such a one-eighty from how I was raised that I'm continually shocked at how different we are when I come here. The property is huge, a little hilly, and it's surrounded by fields and orchards. It's beautiful, it's peaceful, and I can see why they keep this place as their offseason home.

I'm sure you're wondering where we all sleep. Bryan rents a couple of high-end RVs, has them set on his property, and this gives each of us our own space at night. We start early each day, help him around the property with whatever needs to be done, run routes and drills critiquing each other as we go, and we eat all of Lexi's food. She's famous for her pies, and Vivi loves helping her bake them. To her, this is a weeklong vacation where Lexi takes her to ride horses and teaches her how to garden, but for me, it's work, work, work.

And I love it.

The smell of clean air and fresh-cut grass, the humidity and the whole body sweat that comes with it, and the guys, I'll remember these specific days for the rest of my life.

But needless to say, I haven't seen Sophie in a bit. She got back late Sunday night, but Vivi and I had already headed out to settle in at Bryan's. Typically, we do this week closer to the start of the season in July, but Camille is thirty-eight and a half weeks, and Reid refused to come if it was planned for later. As it turns out, he was right, and late this morning we got the call. Whereas he left immediately, the rest of us helped clean up and then decided to head back early to meet our newest team member.

Just thinking about Sophie has me laughing at her text messages all week. Her trip home turned out to be an interesting one, and I love that she reached out to tell me about it. I know her relationship with her dad is tight and special, and I can only hope that this is how I'll be with Vivi one day too.

Camden quietly laughs at something Reid says, and it pulls me from my thoughts. I'm certain this hospital has never seen so many random guys standing in their hallway at one time, but they don't understand that we're tight. If I've learned anything from these guys over the past couple of years, we celebrate together on and off the field, and these moments matter more than football. While everyone is being polite and keeping their voices down, we are a sight to behold, and it's funny.

Hearing the whoosh of the elevator doors opening, I glance over and see Sophie step off. My heart stutters in my chest at just the sight of her. She's come straight from work and still has her green scrubs on, and a scrub cap wrapped around her head. I've only seen her dressed this way one other time, and it adds a whole new layer to my level of attraction for her. Damn, she looks good. So good that a stutter causes my chest to seize up, and I stop breathing.

That is until she turns. Her eyes immediately connect with mine, and she smiles.

I fall for her all over again.

This feeling, I know without a shadow of a doubt it will happen over and over again.

As she makes her way to us, I feel someone clap me on the shoulder, but I have no idea who it is. Don't care either. I leave the group and meet her halfway.

"Hi," she says, smiling up at me. Her cheeks are pink, her eyes are bright and happy, and I don't even care who's watching. I wrap my hands around her face, bend down, and kiss her. It's not an indecent kiss, but with her lips pressed firmly to mine, I feel like the part of me that's been missing has returned, and I'm whole. A few low whistles echo down the hallway, but again, I don't care. Her hands land on my rib cage as she rises on her toes. It turns out I think she needed this just as much as I did.

Pulling back, she lets out a contented sigh.

"Hi," I say back, tucking a loose piece of hair behind her ear and under the cap.

"I'm so excited," she says, her hands slipping as she lowers back down and tightening on my waist. The heat from them fuses through my shirt onto my skin, and at this moment, I wish more than anything we were at home so I could feel more than just her hands.

"I waited for you," I tell her, soaking in all of the details of her face. Not that I know much about makeup, but it looks like she's only wearing mascara and lip gloss, and I love it. Clear skin, lots of freckles, and her sky-blue eyes.

"What?" She jerks back a little. "You didn't have to do that."

"I know, but I wanted us to meet her together."

Her smile turns soft, tender, and I swipe my thumb back and forth across her cheek.

"Well, let's go, then," she says, bouncing a little.

"All right. Let's go." I can't help but smile at her. Sometimes it still feels surreal that she's in front of me. How did I get so lucky?

Dropping my hands, she takes one and wraps hers

around it. Together, we walk through the guys, who are all staring silently at us, and to Camille's door.

"So that's how it is?" Sully grins at us. "Jonah, my boy, you've been holding back some details," he teases, and I shake my head. He can be insufferable sometimes, but he has a heart of gold and means well.

Meanwhile, she acknowledges him with a smile but more or less ignores every other person in the hallway. She's on a mission, and it's not to be social at the moment.

Knocking on the door to let them know we're coming in, Sophie opens it and pokes her head into the crack.

"Sophie," Camille says, and I can hear the emotion in her voice. "Come in. Come in."

Sophie slips through the door, and I follow.

The room is a standard single room. Camille lies on her bed. It has a padded rocking chair, a couch that I'm assuming doubles as a bed, and then the clear baby bassinet that's been pushed up next to Camille. In the room is Mrs. Jackson, Reid's mother; Nate, his brother; and a former Tarpons player named Jack with his wife, Meg. Jack is retired now, and they live in Charleston, but like I've learned with this team, once you're family, you're always family.

"I'm so sorry I wasn't here sooner. I saw Jonah's texts once I was out of surgery, and I came right over," Sophie says as she makes her way to Camille's bed to hug her.

"No worries at all. I'm just so glad you're here."

"Are you feeling okay?" she asks.

"I feel great," Camille says, and she looks great too for

just having pushed out a baby. "I'm on some cocktail of drugs that is working perfectly."

"Well, make sure you take it easy and don't overdo it," Sophie says as she runs her hand over Camille's arm.

"Do you see this crew?" She laughs. "I seem to remember Reid's exact words were, 'You can just sit there and look pretty. We'll take it from here.'"

Everyone in the room chuckles. I glance at Reid, and he's staring at Camille like she hung the moon.

"Hey, Meg, it's nice to see you," Sophie says as she walks across the room to give her a hug.

"You too," she says. "I was hoping we'd run into each other while here."

I had no idea that these two knew each other. Did they meet years ago, or was it sometime recently? This just further makes me question how did Sophie not know about John's accident? It's bizarre that no one ever said anything.

Nate rises from the couch and walks over to hand the baby off to Sophie. He moves slowly, nervous about waking and dropping her, but Sophie dashes to the sink to wash and dry her hands first.

"Sophie, I'd like for you to meet my daughter, Claire," Camille says.

Claire, after Camille's sister. I don't know much about that story, but I do know Claire is Camille's twin.

"Claire," she whispers with reverence, her eyes welling with tears as she takes her from Nate. "She must be so proud."

"I haven't told her yet, but I will," Camille says, the two of them sharing a quiet moment.

Everyone watches as Sophie looks down at the baby and wonder lights up her face. I step closer so I can see her, and I'm not surprised at all that Reid and Camille had the most gorgeous baby. Both of them are good looking, but this baby has his dark hair, the sweetest little nose and lips, and when she opens her eyes, they are very blue. They've wrapped her in a thin light pink blanket, and she has on a matching pink hat.

"She's so beautiful." Sophie slowly begins to sway her hips from side to side.

"Why do all women do that?" Camden asks from behind me. Apparently, a few more of the guys have made their way into the room as well.

Sully backhands him in the chest, but it's at this moment Sophie looks up and locks eyes with me. Her smile is so large, and in a way, so intimate. I can feel everyone in the room looking at the two of us.

Of course I smile back. How could I not? The most beautiful girl in the world is looking at me, and I would be lying if I said her holding that baby wasn't giving me caveman vibes.

"For the record, I feel like I got skipped in the line here," Camden says, and Sully groans next to him.

"What? I've been patient," he says.

"Bro." I shoot him a look that says knock it off, but Sophie just ignores him.

"Aren't you just the sweetest?" she says to Claire as she

walks over to Camille's bed, lays her down at the foot of it, and unwraps her. Claire lets out some little catlike noise as Sophie runs her fingers over her arms, hands, legs, feet, and then her spine. She gives Camille a smile and then wraps her back up. "Perfect."

What's perfect is how calm I feel watching her pick up Claire and love on her some more.

Calm watching her and knowing without a doubt I'm staring at my future. I'm almost twenty-seven, and although my and Vivi's lives both got thrown off course for a bit, I feel like we're finally finding our way. Most people at my age have some idea about what they want their life to look like, yet I really never got that far. It was work hard, get drafted, be traded, work hard again, the accident, learn to heal. But seeing Sophie here, among my friends, among our friends, and holding a baby, is shifting pieces inside me.

Shifting because I want this with her.

Only her.

It feels so good, and it just feels so right.

"Where's Vivi?" she asks as if she's suddenly realized Vivi's not here.

"Downstairs with Lexi getting a drink. I told her you were coming, so she won't be gone long."

"Okay, good. I miss her," she says, and those three words land at a place deep inside me. She then shifts to hand me Claire, and I take her.

The last baby that I held was Vivi, and that feels like a lifetime ago and yesterday. I once heard the expression,

"The days are long, but the years are short," and it couldn't be any more accurate. It's hard to believe that Vivi was ever this small.

Around us are quiet conversations, but at this moment, it's just me and Sophie.

"Do you want kids one day?" I ask her.

"I always saw myself having a family. As for the specifics, I didn't get that far."

"Same. It was always something I thought I'd have one day, but definitely wasn't something I was thinking about. Still haven't really. With Vivi, we've just been surviving."

"You two seem to be doing all right to me," she says, watching me in return. Her words slide into my chest. I really am trying to do my best.

"Jonah, time's up," Camden says, making his way in front of us.

"Maybe you should sit down for this," I tell him.

"Why? It's like you don't even know me. When have you ever seen me drop anything? That's the difference between a running back and a wide receiver." He smirks, and everyone in the room groans.

But without saying more, Camden moves over to the rocking chair and sits down. I follow, gently handing Claire off to him, and then move back to Sophie's side.

"What are you doing tonight?" I ask her. Her last text this morning didn't imply she had plans, but you never know.

"Nothing. Why?" she asks, looking up at me curiously but also with an excited anticipation that I might want to see her. I love when she gets like this, but she should know by now that I always want to see her.

"Do you want to have dinner with us?" I run my hand down her back and let it settle at the bottom.

She looks down and then frowns. "I didn't bring a change of clothes."

"That's okay. Clothes are optional," I whisper so only she can hear me, and her cheeks turn pink. "We can order in. I don't really have anything fresh to eat since we've been gone."

"Ordering in sounds good to me."

"Did I hear you say you're going to order food?" Tyler asks. The door is now open to the hallway so everyone can see inside, and unbeknownst to me, he's moved next to us.

I shoot him a look, and he grins. Sophie turns around to look at him too, but he just smiles even bigger at her.

"I'll have whatever you're having," he tells me, and I let out a sigh.

"Yeah, me too," Sully says.

I look at each of the guys, and they're all staring at me. While I would love that alone time with her, we'll get it after they leave and Vivi goes to bed. Vivi loves it when they all come over.

"Fine. Jack, do you and Meg want to come over too?"

"Yes," Meg says, smiling at Sophie.

"Mrs. Jackson? Nate?" I ask both of them as they are in the room and that makes them a part of the conversation.

"Oh, that's okay, dear. Thank you for including us too,

but I want to stay here for a little while longer and then just head back to the house."

"Well, if you change your mind, just let us know." I turn to Sophie. "Do you want pizza, Mexican, or Thai?" Her opinion on what we eat is the only one that matters to me.

"Do you even need to ask?" She laughs.

No, I guess I don't.

Chapter 31
Sophie

Over the past couple of years, the annual children's hospital gala has become one of my favorite events. I had no idea Jonah had tickets. Somehow, I had completely missed that it was coming up, and my jaw dropped when he told me where we were going. The money the gala raises for research and children in need is incredible. It's one of these events that always fills my heart and makes me incredibly proud to be in the healthcare industry.

"Wow," I whisper to Jonah as we walk into the hotel ballroom. "Someone did an exceptional job. It's beautiful in here." I gawk at the elegance and ambience.

"You're beautiful," he tells me, and I find him not looking at the decorations at all. "I know I told you this when I picked you up, but, Sophie, you are stunning tonight."

His words make my insides shiver. It's not even that he

gave me a nice compliment, which he does frequently; it's that I feel good, and I'm proud to be here with him tonight.

Looking down, I fluff out the chiffon. It's a gold strapless, figure-shaping gown with gold foil roses inlaid as a pattern, and it has a chiffon layer that is loose and waterfalls down over the dress. I found it in an upscale vintage dress shop and couldn't say no. I also know that Jonah loves me in gold and silver from the night we met, so this gold dress was perfect.

"Thank you," I tell him, and as I reach over to squeeze his hand, a ball of fire goes whooshing by our heads. I laugh, and Jonah frowns at the guy, pulling me closer to him.

This year, the theme is "A Night at the Circus," and they have outdone themselves. From red fabric sweeping from the ceiling to create a big-top experience, the gold, white, and black accents to all of the individual performers strategically placed around the ballroom. There are acrobats on silks, knife throwers, a tightrope walker, dancers, jugglers, musicians, a few animals, clowns, and fireblowers. The costumes are gorgeous, and I already know this will be a great night.

"Shall we go get a drink?" he asks.

"Absolutely, and then let's go browse the silent auction before they call us to sit down for dinner."

They advertised that the silent auction would have more than two hundred and fifty items. I love to bid on things even though I never win, but I'll help raise the price, which ultimately results in more donated money.

As we start walking toward the bar, I look around the room and spot a few people I know. Several are here from my practice, including Isaac; there are colleagues I worked with at the hospital and of course the residents who were a year behind me. I love that so many people are here for this.

"Sir," a server says, approaching Jonah. He's holding a tray of fun drinks, which he says are a rose sangria. We grab two, and off we go.

"These taste so good," I hum as I take another sip.

"It's a little sweet for me," he says.

"Of course you would say that. You do realize some of the most delicious things in the world are sweet," I mock him for his strict diet. Yes, he eats pizza and lasagna, but in general, what he eats on a day-to-day basis is all healthy.

"Can't argue with you there. I happen to think you are the sweetest."

"Look at you, pulling out all the charisma tonight."

He smirks as he looks down at me. His jaw is freshly shaved, making the line above the dark cut of his jacket appear even more pronounced. Seeing him in this tux is definitely doing something for me.

"Have you ever won anything at one of these?" I ask him as we approach the first table.

"Nope. I've never bid on anything," he says, tucking the hand not holding his drink into his pants pocket. He looks so debonair. Some men look uncomfortable in a tuxedo, but not Jonah. He owns this look.

I glance at him. "Really?"

"Nope. I'm not someone who collects things, and anything that I might want like hockey tickets or a weekend at someone's house in Aspen, I can just get whenever I want."

"But you're missing the point. Everyone in here can do those things, but these items are donated so all the money goes to charity."

He shrugs. "I get that, but I donate money during the 'open call' portion of the night. Isn't that the same thing?"

"I guess, but tonight, we're going shopping."

He chuckles.

All around the perimeter of the ballroom are the items. I know they also had them listed on a website where people not in attendance can bid. Security is also strategically placed around the room.

"Oh, Jonah, look at this one." It's an overnight birthday party in the Florida aquarium.

He's quiet as he looks at it but then shakes his head. "Great idea, but who would we invite?"

I guess he's not wrong. Maybe when she's older and has made a few more friends.

"Okay, fair enough, but we're definitely putting our name down for this basket of assorted wines." I type the item code assigned into the app and place a bid.

"Do you ever win?" he asks, taking a sip of his drink and then grimacing.

"Not once." I laugh. "But I'd like to think I'm doing my part in donating by upping the price on all these items."

He walks a few paces over and sets down the glass.

"I'll get something else in a bit. Let's do it," he says, waving his hand out toward all of the items.

We bid on cooking lessons, a full lobster fishing kit for Tyler, a trip to Disney World where you stay overnight in Cinderella's castle, a pair of Jet Skis, and a Gucci handbag. It was fun, and within minutes of each bid, the app dings that we've been outbid.

Eventually we stop in front of the Tarpons display, which is full of fun things and tickets, and I point at the poster and the football in front of us. "Look! It's your signature," I tease him by bumping my hip against his.

"It's not just mine," he fires back. And he's right. A bunch of the team members have signed these items.

"Still, it's cute." I grin at him.

His hand slides down my back and settles just below my waist. He leans down and murmurs, "Cute is when you're blushing while I talk about burying my face between your legs."

I jerk back so our eyes can connect, and sure enough, I blush, and he gives me a wicked grin.

"You are going to be trouble tonight. I can tell already."

"Do you blame me?" he asks as he moves to stand directly behind me, and his hands skate over my butt. "This dress has me wanting to do all kinds of things to you. Here. There. Everywhere," he says, leaning over so his lips are next to my ear for only me to hear and swaying a little to the music that is playing.

I glance back to find his eyes hooded and one side of his mouth tipped up. "We are not sneaking off," I tell him, shaking my head, but I do push back into him a little. His size and heat surround me, and he slides one hand around my hip to my stomach. I'm so happy to be here with him.

"Yet," he teases. Then he looks over my shoulder down at his watch and frowns. "I hate to leave you, but I'm being summoned for team photos."

He steps away, and I instantly want to step back in his arms.

"Go. Do your thing. I'll stay here and do mine." I'm certain I can bet on more things that I know someone else will want more.

My smile turns mischievous, and his eyes drop to my lips. Leaning down, he gives me a lingering kiss next to my mouth. He runs his hand over my arm and down to my elbow, where he gently squeezes it, and then he's gone.

Of course I watch him walk away. With long legs wrapped in black, shiny black shoes, and formally styled men's hair that's been parted and slicked over, he doesn't give me butterflies, he gives me dragonflies.

"Dr. Black," someone says from my left, and I peel my eyes off Jonah to turn and find Dr. McLeod walking my way. "I did wonder if I would run into you today," she says, all smiles in her greeting.

Dr. McLeod was one of my favorite professors during my residency. Her accolades are long, and her CV even longer, and she's currently the vice dean of research here at the College of Medicine. While she's not a super warm and fuzzy person, she is dedicated and widely respected for her active research programs.

"Dr. McLeod, it's so nice to see you. And I must admit I'm surprised to hear that you were thinking of me." My back straightens, and I lightly clasp my hands in front of me. Dr. McLeod always stressed the importance of posture for surgeons, and well, old habits die hard.

"Nonsense. You were stellar during your residency, and I've been thinking about you a lot. I was actually planning to give you a call this week."

There's no way to hide the shock I feel over this, and my brows rise.

"Really? I must admit this feels a little surprising, but I would have loved to have received a call from you."

"I'm happy to hear that." She adjusts her clutch and tucks it up further under her arm. "I have an upcoming opportunity I'd love to run by you."

"An opportunity for you or me?"

"You." She smiles. "Also, I'm not going to lie. I do miss seeing you around."

"I'm flattered."

"You should be." She smiles at me. It's rare to see her smile, and she's done it several times now during this conversation. "Email me tomorrow with your availability this week."

"I will. Thank you."

"Don't thank me yet." That's her warning. "But I'll see you this week."

She walks off, and as she does, I spot Jonah directly across the room. My heart skips a beat as I take him in. He has one hand back in his pocket, the other is holding a new drink, and he's laughing as he talks to his teammate Tyler Quinn. Other teammates are around him, but he quickly glances my way, which lets me know he's watching me too.

He raises his glass in my direction, and I give him a tiny wave. I feel stupid but giddy at the same time.

Jonah has somehow infiltrated my system. Just the sight of him alone makes my heart beat faster, and somehow, my nerves feel calmer. I'm not sure when this happened, but I'm starting to wonder if it was that night almost two and a half years ago. I'm realizing I haven't been the same since I met him. He may not know this, but I do. I waited and waited, for months, even though I told myself I wasn't, but looking back, I was. Waiting for what, I don't know. I got stood up. He didn't come back, but maybe it was the fairy tale that he would. Or perhaps I was just waiting to meet someone new who would light my soul on fire like he did.

It shouldn't come as a revelation to me that no one else did.

Just him.

Breaking me from my thoughts, Isaac steps into my line of sight. "Your glass is empty, so I got this for you," he says, holding out a glass of champagne. He too is wearing a tux, but in typical Isaac fashion, he has on a black vest, and his tie is black-and-red polka dots. It's endearing to me, but that's the extent of my affection for him.

"Thank you," I tell him and take a sip. In many ways, this glass feels like he is holding out an olive branch too. "I didn't know you were coming tonight."

"Yeah, I'm sorry about that. I guess we haven't really talked that much lately." He lets out a sigh. "I try to come every year. There's a group of us who gets a table." He turns and looks toward the far side of the room, where he must spot his friends. "You look beautiful tonight."

"Thank you, and I guess I haven't really tried to speak to you much either," I tell him, owning my part of how we ended.

"It wasn't you. It was all me," he says, running his hand over the back of his neck. "You never gave me any inclination that we were going to be more than what we were. I guess my pride took a hit because I was hoping we would. I'm sorry about that night in the restaurant. I think about it often, and I was out of line."

"No, you were fine. I definitely needed to hear what you were saying. You weren't wrong. I had stalled, and I needed that kick in the behind to pull myself back together."

"I hope we're still able to be friends. I know it was a little awkward at first. It was never my intention to make you uncomfortable at work."

"So you did see and hear how the staff were treating me."

He looks away sheepishly, and there's my answer.

"Were you hoping that I would leave the practice?"

"No. But I'll admit, I was licking my wounds a bit. It was Laurie who ripped me a new one. Her exact words were, 'Get your professional shit together.'" He chuckles. "She wasn't wrong."

I am definitely taking Laurie out as a thank-you. I had no idea she'd done this, and although I know we've become friends outside of work, this now makes it so much more.

"I do love her," I tell him.

"Apparently, she loves you too. Friends?" He holds his hand out.

"Friends," I tell him, slipping mine against his for the shake. "Don't think that I didn't notice you have a date tonight, too," I tell him as our hands drop.

He turns and looks toward where his date stands. She's speaking with a few people I don't know and smiling from ear to ear. She appears to be in her thirties. She's wearing a red dress, which I assume is to match him, and she's really pretty. I'm happy for him.

"Yeah. Interestingly, I met her the day after things ended with you. It did take me a bit to get out of my own way, but once I did, things have been good."

"I'm glad to hear this."

And that's when I feel heat at my back and know who it is without even having to turn and look. Isaac's eyes slide up over my shoulder and land on Jonah. They widen just like they did back in the office, and the moment Jonah lays his hand on me, I see it register with Isaac.

I turn and give Jonah a small smile.

"Jonah, this is Dr. Isaac Bradley. He's a colleague of mine. Isaac, this is my friend Jonah Dallmann."

I know Jonah recognizes the name, but he doesn't give anything away. Instead, he reaches his hand forward in greeting.

"It's nice to meet someone from Sophie's work. She's talked about a lot of you."

Isaac's gaze dances quickly between the two of us.

Isaac cringes a little and then laughs. "I'm really hoping that's a good thing. Big fan of yours, by the way."

"Thank you. I mean that," Jonah kindly tells him.

"How do you two know each other?" Isaac curiously asks.

I glance up at Jonah, but he lets me answer. "We first met about two and a half years ago through mutual friends."

His eyes flare with understanding as they come back to mine. "Wow, you never mentioned. I'm sorry to do this here, but you have to go for it when the moment arises. Jonah, how do you feel about meet and greets? Our group works closely with several lower-income high schools as the team physicians. We like to bring out professionals to inspire them to want more. Would you be open to that?"

"Of course. Just tell me when and where. I'll bring a few others too," he tells Isaac. I love that he shows no jealousy or possessiveness regarding me. He has no reason to be jealous. I am all about him and only him.

"That would mean a lot. Thank you." Isaac looks at me and grins. "I guess I'll have my people reach out to your people."

Jonah chuckles. "Perfect."

"Well, I'll leave you two. I hope you both have a wonderful evening," he says, and it's so sincere I know that things at work will be just fine. Glancing back and forth between us one more time, he takes a step away, looks at me, and says, "Roses."

I nod.

He presses his lips together in a closed-mouth smile and then shakes his head.

"I do see it," he says.

"See what?" Jonah asks, but Isaac only answers me.

"How you look at him versus how you looked at me."

"And how do I look at him?"

His smile grows. "This time, I'm going to let you figure it out on your own."

Chapter 32
Jonah

Since the gala, Sophie and I have spent every moment we can together. This week has flown by, we've eaten at two new pizza places, we've visited three different dog parks with Vivi and Molly, and every night after Vivi goes to bed, we fall into each other like we're starved. This thing between us, it isn't casual, and although we haven't had the talk yet, I'm certain she knows it too.

It's now Friday afternoon. At two fifteen, Sophie texts me that she's leaving work early and heading home. She asks if I'm free to come over, and damn, the girl doesn't need to ask me twice.

I've barely knocked on her door when she swings it open, fists the front of my shirt, and drags me inside.

"Happy to see me?" I ask as my hands wrap around her head and my fingers thread through her hair.

"Very," she says as she stretches up on her toes, sucks

my bottom lip between her teeth, and runs the palm of her hand right over my dick. It's so unexpected and not at the same time that I moan into her mouth and am immediately hard.

Up and down, she strokes as I taste every corner of her mouth, then she drops to her knees.

"Soph," I groan, leaning back against the door and looking down at her.

"All day, I've been thinking about this," she says, slipping her fingers under my waistband and dragging everything down.

"Why?"

It's not that I don't think about being with her just about every second of the day, because I do, but this . . . it's surprising.

She tilts her head to look up at me. Long eyelashes wave at me as she blinks and then smiles. My fingers run over the curve of her jaw and her mouth, my thumb dipping right in and rubbing along the inside of her bottom lip. "I was thinking about what you did to me here at this door, and once I started, I couldn't stop."

One half of my mouth tips up. "Well, who am I to deny you?"

She smiles, and her eyes drop to focus on the task at hand.

Dragging one finger around the tip, she runs it over the edge and all the way down to the base, causing my stomach muscles to clench. She's so incredibly sexy; my fingers tangle in her hair in anticipation, and she doesn't make me wait any longer. She runs her tongue straight up me, her hands up the backs of my thighs, she bites my hip bone, and then takes me fully into her mouth.

"You're going to be the death of me," I groan. "But in the best way."

This doesn't take long. How can it when the perfect girl is on her knees in front of me? Her mouth is warm, her hands know how to work me in the perfect way, and her hair is so soft as my fingers get tangled and grip her to me.

Instantly needing more, I yank up my shorts and throw her over my shoulder. She squeals as I smack her on the ass and take off for her room. I have to pick Vivi up at five, so we've got some time for a round two, maybe even a round three.

"I think I like you getting off work early," I tell her as I toss her onto the bed and reach for her shorts.

"I think I like you being available whenever I want," she teases back as she shimmies out of her shirt and her bra.

"Whenever you want, huh?" I ask, leaning over her.

"Yes." She smiles up at me, then hooks me around the neck to pull me to her and kisses me.

Yanking my shirt over my head, I lie back down on top of her and soak up the feel of her warm skin against mine. She smells like candy, and she tastes just as good.

"What is this scar here?" I ask her, running my tongue over the small silver line just under her jaw.

"Roller-skating, I fell," she whispers as she pushes my shorts down and hooks her foot into them to drag them off.

"How old were you?" I mumble, moving my lips lower to the middle of her chest.

"Eight."

"I think I would have liked to have known you when you were eight," I tell her as I drag my tongue from one breast to the next.

She laughs. "I was a very studious child. Loved to read, and I wore glasses."

"No glasses now?" I glance up at her.

"No. Lasik," she says, running one foot over the back of my leg.

"You do have beautiful eyes." Eyes that are happy I'm here. Eyes that are hungry for what I'm about to do to her.

"So do you." Her hands wrap around my head, and her thumbs run under each eye once and then over each eyebrow. "Your lashes are so long, I'm envious."

"You can have them. I'll go without," I tell her, nuzzling my face against her skin.

She giggles.

"Come here."

Climbing up higher, I wrap my hands around her face and do the same to her, under her gorgeous eyes and then over her eyebrows. She's watching me, and since we're so close, I swear she can see straight down into my soul.

Her hands run over my lats and down to my butt, where she pushes, trying to get me closer.

"Impatient?"

"Desperate."

Now I can't have that. Rocking my hips forward, I

push inside, and a small gasp escapes her. She draws her legs up next to my hips, opening herself up more, and I pull back only to sink in farther. She feels so good. My lips drop to hers, and slowly, I mimic the movement of my hips with my tongue. In and out. Deep and shallow. In and out. Deep and shallow. I want her to come undone for me like I have for her. Undone in every way.

"Jonah," she whispers, and I don't need to be told anything more. I know what she needs, and I shift to make it happen. With my hands under her hips and my mouth savoring her skin, her whole body sings for me. I listen to her melody. I keep the beat, and as her song crescendos, I do the same. How could I not?

I will never get enough of this.

I will never get enough of her.

With no words being said, I set my alarm. I wrap my body around hers, tucking us in, and almost instantly, the two of us fall asleep.

I'm so content, and I know deep down I'm so in love.

In love with her.

The truth and honesty in these words, there's a rightness that heals a broken piece of my heart left behind after John, and I feel so blessed to have been given another chance with this girl.

Eventually, the sound of the alarm wakes us. Picking up my phone from the nightstand, I see there's a missed call from Vivi's dance teacher. Putting the phone on speaker, Sophie and I both sit up and listen to the message.

"Hi, Jonah. This is Kelli from the dance camp. I just

wanted to let you know that Vivi isn't having the best day. There's nothing to be alarmed about, but I wanted to call you and let you know she's more withdrawn and not giving me her usual best. I know she's supposed to be here until five, but if you're free to come and get her, I think that would be best."

"Oh, no," Soph says, looking at me with large concerned eyes.

"I have to go," I tell her as I slide off the bed and grab my clothes.

"Of course you do," she tells me. "Do you want me to come with you?" She scoots to the edge of the bed, wrapping the sheet around her.

"No, it's okay. Let me go get her and see how she is, and then I'll call you," I tell her, pulling on my shorts.

"Okay, well, if I can help, please let me know."

It takes me less than one minute to get dressed. I lean over and kiss Sophie, then take the stairs two at a time.

Walking through the townhouse, I spot a FedEx envelope on her table and next to it is a navy folder that's open, and a trifold pediatric orthopedic flier sitting on top. I don't know what has me stopping to pick it up, but I do, thinking it's from her current group, and I want to see her picture. As it turns out, it's not from her group but from a group in Minnesota. Why would she have this? And why is it out now?

And that's when I remember what Reid said weeks ago while we were sitting out on his back deck watching Vivi and Izzy in the hot tub. "Yeah, she's biding her time and not dating anyone seriously." For some reason, it just didn't occur to me that biding her time might not have been here in Tampa, but given her relationship with her dad, I suddenly realize it's possible.

She also hinted at my house that night that her plan was still to get back to Minnesota.

An ache forms in the pit of my stomach, and my chest seizes. Just like the possibility of her leaving Tampa didn't occur to me, it also didn't occur to me that she and I might be temporary. I thought fate was pushing us back together, but maybe I was wrong.

Glancing down at the folder, there's a cover letter tucked into the right side pocket. The date is from yesterday, and the first line says, "We are excited to offer you a position here at Minneapolis Children's . . ." The words blur, and I stop reading.

What the fuck.

This can't be happening.

I don't even know what to do.

Behind me, I hear Sophie coming down the stairs. She freezes on the last step when I assume she sees what I'm holding. I turn to face her more squarely and hold up the trifold. Silence wraps around us, her eyes grow large with worry, and that's when it hits me.

"You didn't go home to just see your dad, did you?"

"No."

Rocks roll down my throat and land in my stomach.

Painful rocks.

"And they offered you the job?" I ask even though I just saw the proof of it with my own eyes.

"Yes," she whispers.

My arm drops, and my whole body tingles with adrenaline.

I feel so stupid.

"Right."

"Jonah," she says, taking that last step and moving across the room toward me. "I want to talk about this with you."

But we can't. Not right now.

Vivi is my priority. She always will be.

And it's with this thought that the pain I have doubles at what this means for her.

I hold up my hand and let out a shuddering breath. "I need to go pick up Vivi."

"Okay," she says, our eyes holding on to each other, but no more words are said.

Slamming mine shut, I drop the pamphlet and turn to make my way toward the door. I don't even know what to think right now, as every part of my body is recoiling and protesting. Why wouldn't she just tell me? Does she not trust me? One of the things that stings the most is that I've been completely open with her, and it hurts that she wasn't with me.

But I know I can't leave like this.

Looking back over my shoulder, I see she hasn't moved. She's standing next to the table with tears in her eyes. Are these tears about me finding out? Are these tears because she knows she's about to break my heart? Or are these tears because she knows she's about to break her own?

"Sophie"—my voice is hoarse against the lump in my throat—"I do want to talk about this with you too, okay?"

She nods, and with my heart pounding in my chest after one final lingering look, I pivot, walk out her front door, and leave.

If she leaves, what will I tell Vivi?

She's already suffered a great loss, and she's finally starting to open up and show more of her personality that used to shine bright. I don't know if she'll take this okay or view it as something worse.

Abandonment.

On the entire drive to the studio, the weight of grief, loss, and uncertainty as to what to do or say next nearly make me immobile. But when I walk into the studio and see Vivi sitting by herself off to the side, all my worries disappear, and I focus on her.

"Uncle Jonah," Vivi says when she sees me, then she takes off running.

Squatting down to her level, I catch her when she throws herself into my arms and starts silently crying. It's not hard or loud, but just enough so I know that today is a bad day.

Kelli comes up behind her, sets Vivi's bag down on the floor, and gives me a look that lets me know she's sad for my girl.

"Come on, Wildflower. Let's go home."

I grab her bag and pick her up. She never removes her face from my neck as I carry her out.

Chapter 33
Sophie

It's been an hour and a half since Jonah left, and I feel worse than I ever have before. When he realized I had gone to that interview and not told him, the look on his face wasn't anger but complete and utter sadness.

Sadness that I felt ricochet through all of my bones. A sadness that's a result of my decisions. A sadness he doesn't deserve.

I didn't lie to him. It was an unexpected flight and I did go see my father, I just didn't tell him the whole truth. I wasn't ready. I know people say that omission is lying, but I wasn't sure what I was omitting. I wasn't afraid of jinxing the situation by telling him, I just didn't know what to say. Would our conversation have been about the interview? Or that my dream was never to stay here, but has always been to end up back in Minneapolis? How would any of this make him feel? I can tell you, it would have made him feel terrible.

Turns out I made him feel bad anyway.

I guess there really isn't a way to prevent that, I just wasn't ready. I wasn't ready to discuss what all of this might mean with myself, my future, with him, with anyone. Especially when I don't know.

I feel like I'm at a fork in the road. I'm living two separate lives. There's this life that I've worked toward for my entire adult life, and then there's this beautiful life that unexpectedly came out of nowhere. With his career, with mine, and add in Vivi, I don't see a way for us to be able to make both roads work and that's what leaves me completely frozen. Emotionally stunted as well as tongue-tied. It's like everything I have ever wanted is right in front of me, and I just don't know how to grab it.

But as I stare down the two different roads, I have a sinking feeling there's one path I don't even want anymore, and I'm still trying to reconcile that. What does that mean for me? What does that mean for my dad? What about all our plans? Am I just going to blow it up for someone I've not even been with that long? This dream that I wanted so bad? I'm thirty-three. Long distance isn't something that I want, but a family is. Jonah and Vivi could be my family. At least, I think. He hasn't said it, but I feel it deep in my bones.

Lying in bed, I'm flat on my back in the starfish position when my phone rings. Jonah's name flashes across the screen, and panic streaks through me. I still don't think I'm ready to have this conversation with him yet. How can I when I'm trying to figure things out myself?

But I can't ignore him either. I respect him and quite frankly like him too much.

"Hey," I say to him, trying not to sound like the sad person that I am even though I'm certain I've failed.

"Hey," he says back, his voice thick and heavy.

"How's Vivi?" I ask, really hoping to try to avoid the elephant in the room for as long as possible when it comes to us.

"She's had better days. Can . . ." He pauses, and my stomach tightens anticipating what he's going to say next. "Can you come over? She's asking for you."

I sit up straight and push my hair over my forehead and out of my face.

"She's asking for me?"

"Yes," he says on an audible exhale, and my heart starts racing.

"Of course I'll come. Is there anything I should bring?" I ask as I slide off the bed and head for my bathroom to make myself somewhat presentable.

"Nope, just yourself."

Pulling up to Jonah's house, I'm equally nervous as I am concerned for Vivi.

What happened to her today?

I knock on the door, hear Molly bark, then step inside without waiting for it to be answered. I find them curled up on the couch, under a blanket, and they're quietly watching some animal show on the television. Both of them track me with their eyes as I make my way across the room to them.

Gently, I sit down next to them on the couch, giving Vivi my full attention. Her sweet little face is puffy, and her eyes are red from what I'm assuming are tears. Slowly, I stretch my hand out in front of us for her to take, but instead, she scoots over and climbs into my lap, dragging her stuffed dolphin with her. I pull the blanket over us, wrap my arms around her, and lock eyes with Jonah.

His are a mixture of failure, sadness, and worry. The hazel in them is dull, and I hate whatever this is for both of them. I also can't help but wonder how often this happens.

Sitting in silence, Jonah moves over next to us and he runs his arm along the backside of the couch to tuck us up against him. The three of us are cuddled together, and while I have no idea what's happening, I'm guessing this is what she needs.

Turns out the animal show is an old show about a pet dolphin named Flipper. My heart squeezes with fondness for Jonah. It doesn't surprise me that he's gone out of his way to find every dolphin show for her there is. That's the kind of man he is. Always putting others' needs before his.

Once the show ends, Jonah pauses the streaming. I take this as my cue. He wants me to try to get her to talk, so I shift us in my arms and look down at her.

"You want to tell me what happened today?"

She shrugs her shoulders and looks down at her stuffed animal.

"It's okay if you don't want to. But I find I always feel

better after I've talked to my friends. Our friends and our family are our safe space. I also feel better when I'm baking cookies. Do you want to help me bake some cookies?"

She looks up at me with her big hazel eyes, leans in a little to hug me, then nods. She slides off my lap and takes my hand as we walk toward the kitchen.

From behind us, Jonah lets out a deep sigh. He doesn't say anything, he just posts up at the large kitchen island and Molly circles, curious as to see what we're up to.

"Do you want to help us? Might be fun to watch you crack some eggs with those big hands of yours?"

Both he and Vivi look at Jonah's hands, he holds them out in front of him in a dramatic way, and then Vivi lets out a single giggle.

It's not much, but we're getting somewhere.

Together, we find all the ingredients needed to make peanut butter cookies since Jonah doesn't have chocolate chips in his pantry. Using a recipe we found on my phone, we find flour, butter, peanut butter, brown sugar, regular sugar, eggs, vanilla, and baking powder. Vivi pulls a stool over that Jonah has specifically for this, and one by one, we follow the instructions to make the dough. It's when we're rolling the dough into balls for the baking sheet, she finally says, "I couldn't remember them today."

She glances Jonah's way, almost like she's afraid to tell him, and he gives her the softest, most understanding smile. It's not full of condemnation, pity, or "there, there." It's one that says, I understand, and it's going to be okay.

"I have that problem sometimes, too," he tells her.

"Really?" Her eyes fill with new tears.

"Yes."

"But I don't want to forget them."

"Wildflower, you will never truly forget them. Sometimes individual memories fade. There's nothing we can do about that, but the big ones, the big things, like how much they loved you, we always remember that."

"Do you still remember your mom?" she asks me.

"Of course I do. I don't remember all the little day-to-day things we used to do, but I remember how she used to brush my hair, just like your mom braided yours. I remember how she used to tuck me in at night, how I felt when she hugged me, and I love to look at her pictures to see her smile."

"I don't want to forget them," she says, tears from her innocent little heart spilling over.

"Oh, sweetheart, you won't," I tell her as I pull her into my arms, and some of the tension in her back leaves.

Hugs with children are such an important thing. I specifically remember a lecture that I attended which spoke about hugging and child development. The benefits are endless from emotional bonds, reduced stress, increased self-esteem, as well as boosting their immune systems.

At this, Jonah gets up, walks around the island, and enfolds us both in his arms. I know what we look like, and I definitely know what this feels like, I'm just not sure what I'm supposed to do from here. My heart aches for all of us, especially for Vivi, so I do the thing where I take the moment and lighten it.

"You know what we've just made, don't you?"

Both of them look at me.

"A Vivi sandwich."

Vivi smiles, and Jonah tightens his arms for another long beat before he releases us, and then his stomach growls.

We both laugh.

I guess we did work up an appetite earlier.

"I'm thinking cookies aren't going to be enough for him. I mean, look at him." I eye him up and down. He's still wearing what he wore to my house and still looks good. "He's kind of huge."

Vivi giggles again. This time, it's noticeable that some of the dark cloud that was hanging over her is gone.

"Can we make grilled cheese?" she asks him.

"Of course, but you'd better make me two." He smiles at her, and I melt just like the cheese.

After dinner, cookies, and more Flipper, Vivi and I make our way upstairs to get her ready for bed. Other than sneaking in and out of Jonah's room, I haven't been inside any others, including hers. Which is absolutely beautiful. I shouldn't have expected anything less, but what I find takes my breath away. The room is painted a pale pink, she has two windows on the outside wall draped in gauzy white, her canopy bed sits against one wall, and the other has a huge floor-to-ceiling painting that is a field of wild-flowers. It's bright and stunning, and just gorgeous.

As Vivi starts changing into her pajamas, I take the time to look around at the rest of the details. She has the standard things I would expect to see in a little girl's room —a dollhouse, a craft table and easel, a soft pink rug, a bookshelf loaded with books, a ton of stuffed animals, she has a pretty chandelier, there are a few dance posters, but it's the framed photos on the wall that leads to the bathroom that have caught my eye.

"Come here and tell me about these," I say to her once she's dressed.

Vivi walks over and I pick her up. She lays her head on my shoulder as she looks at them.

"That's my mom and dad."

"I recognize them from the pictures downstairs. You look like the perfect mixture of the two of them."

She doesn't say anything. She just stares at the photos.

"How old are you here?" I ask, pointing at the first one.

"One," she says sweetly.

There are six pictures. Four in a row and then two are underneath them. It's easy to see that it's one picture for every year starting at one. What's beautiful about the pictures is that each family photo is taken in a different field of wildflowers. The first four are of Vivi and her parents, and the next two are of her and Jonah.

"This is such a great idea. Whose idea was this?"

"I don't know," she says. "But Uncle Jonah thought we should keep them going. That's why he's in those. He planned trips for us both summers."

"That sounds like a super fun tradition. And I bet it

was your mom's idea. From everything you and Jonah have said about her, she sounds like she would be sentimental and artistic."

"She painted those, too." Vivi shifts her weight and points toward the large painting of the wildflowers.

"She did?" I'm shocked. I thought this was something that Camille had found for her or Jonah had commissioned.

"Yes. It was on my wall in my old house. When we moved, Uncle Jonah had them cut the wall so we could bring it."

Oh, my heart.

I love that he did that.

"Will you read me a story?"

"Of course I will."

Chapter 34
Jonah

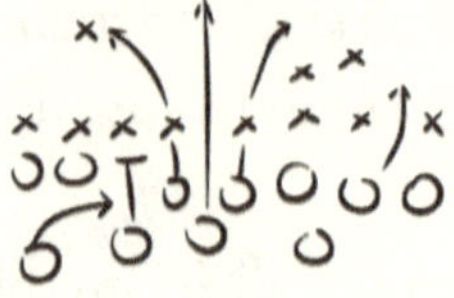

Ishouldn't be hovering in the hallway, leaning against the wall next to her door listening to them, but how can I not? Do I want to be in there with them? Absolutely. But after what I saw at Sophie's place earlier today, I can't stand there as a unified front in Vivi's eyes with Sophie knowing that we're not. Well, I don't know that exactly, but I'm leaning more toward not. It was hard enough to call her over here when I don't know if that's the right decision or the wrong one. Then to sit with her on the couch, with Vivi snuggled between us and have them both in my arms in the kitchen, it's too much. I can't be a part of a bedtime routine too. I can't start the image of what life could be like in Vivi's eyes, knowing that we might not end up that way after all. Because if we were as solid as I thought, why would she have ever gone to that interview?

An interview she didn't even bother to tell me about.

I don't think I've ever given off the impression that she can't tell me things. I want her to, just like I've been one hundred percent open with her. It feels really shitty knowing that I'm not the person to her that she is to me.

I guess in some twisted way it's only fair. The first time, I broke her heart. The second time, she breaks mine.

Am I going to be one of these people who indefinitely has their heart broken? How many people need to leave me before I finally say, "No more."

By the time she comes out of the room, I've already moved to mine. Sophie follows the light and finds me sitting propped up against the head of the bed. She pads over and climbs up to sit next to me.

"Thank you for calling me over," she says, tucking some hair behind her ear. She's so beautiful, my chest aches fiercely at what it's about to lose.

I swallow hard. I hate that I've allowed myself to be in this situation. That I've allowed myself to become so invested in her. "I wasn't sure if I should have. Probably not, but it is what it is." I run my hand over my face and then through my hair.

"Jonah—" she whispers.

My eyes find hers. "No more tonight, okay?"

I can't. I'm emotionally shot. I feel like I'm being pulled in six directions, and it's too much.

"Okay," she says, moving to mimic my position. The two of us sit side by side in silence. We lean against the headboard with our legs stretched out in front of us and crossed at the ankles. She's wearing tiny navy shorts, and my gaze zeros in on our differences. My legs are significantly larger and longer than hers, but her skin looks so smooth and so soft, and my feet are giant, whereas hers are perfect and her toenails are painted pink. Just like her cheeks, she has freckles dusted across her thighs, and they're still tan from our trip to the beach. I love her legs. I love everything about her.

How am I going to tell Vivi she's leaving?

How am I going to say goodbye?

Pulling me from my own internal meltdown, she asks, "How did the whole Wildflower nickname come about?"

"When she turned one, I flew home for her birthday party. Of course I'd seen daily pictures of her from my brother and on social media, but I was shocked at how much she had grown. I made the comment that she's growing like a weed, and Ashley looked at her and said, 'Not a weed, but maybe a wildflower.' It kind of stuck after that, and I've called her Wildflower ever since."

"It really is a cute nickname," she says, fidgeting with the hem of her shorts.

"Ashley thought so too, and the older Vivi got, the more they incorporated wildflowers into her room and everyday life. She used to have a wildflower backpack for school, I have no idea what happened to it."

"I can't believe you had the wall cut and transported to Tampa." Both of us look toward the doorway as if we can see into her room. There was no way I was leaving that wall behind. At five, she didn't understand why I had to have it, but I know she'll want it as she gets older and one day moves into her own place.

"Yeah, that wasn't the easiest, but money talks."

I knew a guy from college who had a younger brother. I hired a contractor to cut the wall and then replace the missing piece. He carefully wrapped the portion of the wall and I rented a U-haul. That friend's brother drove the wall from Boston to Tampa and took it to a framing place I contacted. That day, I put him on a plane and sent him home, the wall became artwork for Vivi's room, and with the help of a few of the guys from the team, we got it hung up where I wanted it to be. I wanted her to have a piece of her mom and her home so things wouldn't feel so new and different. I have caught her staring at it quite a few times, and I always wonder what she's thinking.

"Are you okay?" Sophie asks. I can feel her looking at me, so I look back and wonder how she can ask me that.

"No," I answer honestly, shaking my head.

She looks down at my hands sitting on my lap and whispers, "I'm sorry."

"Me too," I tell her, knowing that even if she does take this job and move, I've made her decision harder. It would be an easy transition if Vivi and I weren't in the picture, but now that we are, it just sucks. For all of us.

Her eyes shoot back to mine. "You have nothing to be sorry about. This is all me."

"It doesn't feel that way." I hold out my arm as I lie down. As much as all of this hurts, I just need to hold her. To feel her next to me. "Come here." She makes her way over to snuggle into my side, and my eyes slide shut. Her head finds my shoulder, her hand falls to my chest, and one of her legs drapes over mine. Does she feel how hard my heart is beating? Does she not realize that it beats for her?

"Does this happen a lot with her?" she asks.

"No. Mostly, she's not been herself since they passed. They say time heals all wounds, and while I have seen more of her personality shine through lately, I'm not surprised today happened. It hasn't been easy."

"That makes me sad. I know it's easier said than done, but I don't want her to hurt anymore. She's so young and should be enjoying her childhood."

"I don't think any of us wants that anymore, but you're right, it is easier said than done. Grief has its own timeline."

Grief that will flare up again when I tell her that Sophie is moving.

My eyes burn, and I let out a deep sigh. It feels like I have an elephant sitting on my chest.

She must want it. I have to believe she wouldn't have gone if she intended to stay. And now knowing that the offer is out there, I suddenly feel like we're on borrowed time. Job offers don't just linger. There has to be a start date, and I'll bet it's pretty soon.

Her hand starts rubbing up and down my rib cage, and I bend my arm so I can run my fingers through her hair. Tilting my head so it's lying against hers, I breathe her in. Citrus and sugar, she smells so good. My eyes fall shut, and I try to memorize the moment. Eventually, her hand slips under my shirt and presses against my skin. Did I have her a few hours ago? Yes. But I want her again. Rolling, I put her on her back, my hand wraps around her waist, and I hover over.

"This okay?" I search her eyes for any clue that it's not.

"More than okay," she replies, her hand fisting my shirt to pull me closer.

Our lips brush once, twice, and then the third time, I seal them together.

I suddenly need to be with her more than I need my next breath, and it seems she feels the same. Her hand slides up the back of my shirt while her other slips underneath me and wraps around my waist to pull my weight more over her. My hips settle in the cradle of hers as she pulls my shirt off, and wasting no time, I do the same to hers and her bra. Her chest connects with mine, and I push my arms underneath her, with my hands coming over the top of her shoulders. I want her as close as possible. I want to hold her as tight as possible.

Dipping my tongue into her mouth, I kiss her with everything I have.

Can't she feel how much she means to me?

Can't she tell how much I crave her? This?

Not to be left out, her hands slide down my back and under the waistband of my shorts. She grips my ass and pulls me into her. Our hips rock together, and through my shorts, I can feel the heat pouring off her.

That's all it takes.

Sitting back on my knees, I stare down at the beautiful

girl beneath me. Her lips are swollen, her cheeks are flushed, and her skin quivers as I run my hands over her chest, only stopping to squeeze once.

"Jonah," she moans as my thumbs drag across her nipples and my large hands surround her torso. She's not petite. I'd say her size is average, but my fingers damn near touch each other on her back.

I lean forward, and my mouth replaces one thumb as I lift her a little off the bed. Her head falls back and her knees squeeze me tighter as I work one breast and then the other. She tastes so good and feels so good, my dick aches to be involved.

Releasing her with a pop of my lips, I quickly unfasten her shorts. She shifts her hips and lifts her legs in front of us so I can pull everything off. Immediately, her legs return and fall open for me.

So. Fucking. Beautiful.

Just once, I run my fingers over her, slip one inside, and my mouth goes dry as she clenches around me.

I want this. Her. For the rest of my life.

Pulling my shorts off, I climb back above her and settle in with my lips on hers and our hips perfectly aligned. Easily, she welcomes me, and it only takes drawing in and out twice to bottom out.

There is no place in the world that is better than this, and as I make love to her—yes, I do fully know that's what I'm doing—my heart does its best to speak to hers. "Don't leave," it whispers. "I'm in love with you," it damn near cries, but I refuse to voice any of these sentiments. Not today, and maybe not ever. Do I want to beg her to stay? Of course, but there's a feeling deep in the pit of my stomach that says, "Don't do that. It's not fair."

I can't be the one to prevent her dreams from coming true. I just wish more than anything that I was her dream, like she was mine.

Chapter 35
Sophie

Sometime in the early hours of the morning, I wake and find Jonah's side of the bed empty. I stretch my hand across the sheets, and they are not warm. They're cold. He's been gone for a while, and the nerves in my stomach instantly awaken.

Slipping out of bed, I find his T-shirt on the floor and pull it over my head. The fabric is soft, and it smells just like him. I feel like I'm being hugged by him, even though he isn't here, and I really need that right now.

Looking around his room, I soak in the details that are his, as it's quite possible this might be the last time I see them. From the bookshelf that holds travel books, sports books, a few classics and photo albums to the Tom Brady autographed football and a picture of him and his family at a Patriots game from when he was a boy to another draft photo of him and his brother both wearing Carolina gear. There are mementos of his life, athletic shoes scattered on the floor near the chair in the corner, and a sand dollar on the far nightstand that I know if I flip it over, it'll have the date from when we were at the beach. He is a good man, but I don't know if he's meant to be mine. I want him to be. I'm just not sure yet how to make this work.

Quietly, I tiptoe down the stairs not to wake Molly or Vivi, and I find Jonah sitting on the couch in the dark with his elbows on his knees and his head bent forward, resting in his hands. He's only wearing a pair of shorts. A half glass of water is sitting in front of him and the room is dead silent.

Not to scare him, I breathe a little louder and drag my hand across the couch so he hears me. He doesn't lift his head. He doesn't even acknowledge me.

Tucking one leg underneath me, I gently sit next to him and wait.

I know seeing that folder and the offer letter hurt him. It was never my intention to hurt him, and I was careless about not making sure it was put away. I was also reckless in not figuring out how to discuss this with him before we got to this point.

Time passes, and he sniffs a few times. Eventually, he leans back on the couch and drops his head to rest it behind him. He's not staring at the ceiling; his eyes are closed, but the stress on his face is so evident, my heart aches more than it did upstairs.

"I don't know how to do this," he whispers.

"Do what?"

"Any of it," he lets out, and then he swallows, the lines of his throat moving.

The large windows in this room let in enough moonlight for me to see him through all of the shadows. His chin trembles, and his nostrils flare just a bit as he inhales air.

Oh God.

He curls his hands into themselves as they rest on his lap and pulls his arms closer.

"All night, I've asked myself, if I had known from the beginning that you were not planning on staying, would I have done things differently? And I don't think I would have. In fact, I'm pretty sure I would have put together some type of 'Win Sophie Over' campaign, just to try to convince you to stay. Although, I'm not sure if that is what you would have wanted or if it would have mattered. I'm thinking it's the latter as we never once talked about this."

Of course he doesn't know. I didn't really want to talk about it with him. We skimmed the surface one night over dinner, but I never led him to believe that there was a possibility that I might not be staying. I can see how from his vantage point that might look different, but we haven't been together that long. Who's to say we would have even gotten along? I didn't know, and neither did he.

Was it wrong of me? Seeing his reaction right this moment, most definitely. But up until this point, he might not have wanted me for anything more than what we are. Fun during the day, and sneaking around at night. Any sane person wouldn't make life decisions based on that, but

I kept this from him. I can try to justify this any way I want, but it doesn't matter. I hurt him.

"I didn't mean for you to find out like you did. They told me they were interviewing several people, so I wasn't even aware of the timeline. I'd somehow convinced myself that I wasn't going to get it. After all, I'd been inquiring off and on for over a year now, but I had to see it through. I got the call from them earlier today, and then the FedEx package was on my doorstep when I got home. I was going to tell you."

"I'm sure you were," he grumbles, but not in a sarcastic way, just resigned.

"Jonah . . ." I say quietly, but he just shakes his head, keeping his eyes shut.

I scoot a little closer and place my hand over his on his thigh and watch his chest rise and fall in the darkness. He doesn't try to lace our fingers together, something he's always done since we started spending time together. In fact, he pulls them in tighter, and a stab of pain pierces through me.

"I'm so overwhelmed, I don't even know where to begin," he says as a single tear leaks out of the corner of his eye and runs down his face.

Oh no.

Instantly, mine swell as well.

"Talk it out with me, please," I beg him softly. I'm sure that Vivi's meltdown is a lot of what has him twisted up inside, but I'm certain that I am part of the reason he's feeling like this, too. And I hate it. I never want to hurt him.

"I just didn't see it coming," he says.

"See what coming?"

"This. You. Vivi. Us. All these weeks. I've been so blinded by the opportunity to finally get to know you and actually spend time with you, that it never occurred to me that this wasn't going to become something more. You live here. It's been over two years. Why would I ever think you were trying to live somewhere else? I had convinced myself that fate had brought us back together, but how fucking foolish is that?"

This time, he does turn to look at me. There's devastation and heartbreak etched into the muscles on his face.

"I don't think it's foolish. I had those thoughts, too," I tell him. I have so much to say, so much I want to express to him. "Jonah," I start, but he cuts me off.

"No. Don't. I'm not mad. I understand, I do. You have goals and dreams, just like I do. You're so smart, and I'm so proud of you, but Vivi," he chokes out while more tears start to leak from his eyes. "She's already suffered enough loss in her lifetime, and now I've let her get close to you, and you're going to be someone else who leaves her."

When it comes to children, men are just a different breed. Would Jonah have ever cried in front of me before? I don't know. But most guys that I've met over the years would not. Add in their love of a child and every wall comes down. It's sexy, it's pheromone overload, but when they're worried or hurt, it's devastating.

"No matter what happens between us, I will never leave her," I state firmly, my own tears falling.

He lays his head back against the couch and closes his eyes again. He doesn't want me to see him, and that's when it hits me. He's hurting because it's not just about me leaving Vivi; he thinks I'm leaving him, too. He opened himself up to me, allowed me into a place I'm not sure anyone else has been, and now this. His father left, his mother died, his brother died, and now me.

How did I not see this sooner?

This makes my process for how I've handled this and how I've tried to sort through it even worse.

I feel so atrocious to have made him feel this way, it hurts to breathe.

More tears fall from both of us as I watch this beautiful man and sit with him while he tries to shut out the world. A world that I made more damaging, even after all the disappointment and loss he's already experienced.

"I try so hard to be what she needs, and I selfishly and quickly allowed you to fill a role in her life that isn't yours to fill. I should have kept our relationship separate, at least until we had some kind of discussion about where we were headed."

My heart plummets because we did have a little bit of this discussion that night, and I take full responsibility because I kind of led him on. He was very upfront when he said, "This is our life, and I need you to decide sooner rather than later if you want to be a part of it." For weeks,

I've let him believe I did, and the worst feeling slithers into my chest.

Guilt.

Shame.

And suddenly unworthy.

"She was never meant to be mine." He looks back at me, his eyes watery. "But now she is, and although I will mess things up as we go, she's my number one responsibility, I hope you understand that."

"I do," I say, hoping to convince him that I really do.

He frowns as he looks at me. His expression is so sad and so resigned, I can't help but continue to cry as I stare at him.

He sniffs and blinks once. The pain in his eyes moves behind a wall as he layers the bricks to block me out, and very calmly but firmly, he says, "I need you not to be here when she wakes up."

And the hammer falls, smashing my heart to pieces.

I've never been here when she wakes in the morning. We've always kept our romantic life separate, but right now, at this moment, he's politely asking me to leave.

I suddenly feel awkward, like I'm imposing, and it feels terrible.

"Of course. Let me just run upstairs and get dressed." I scramble off the couch and make my way toward the stairs as my heartbeat pounds against my chest wall.

Why did I let this happen?

Why did I allow us all to get so close?

From the moment I accepted the interview, I should

have told him, so he could make up his own mind or let them go.

Tears keep falling as I pull off his shirt and slip on my clothes. It takes me no time at all, and I'm back down the stairs, my shoes are on, and I'm headed for the door. He follows, but as I go to pull it open, he places his hand on the top, keeping it shut. I glance over my shoulder at him and find him a little bit open, which has me turning to face him.

His free hand reaches up and tucks a few strands of hair behind my ear before he sweeps his thumb over my cheekbone to wipe away my tears and cradles the back of my head.

"I'm sorry," he says.

"For what?"

"I don't even know anymore. I just feel bad. I don't like seeing you cry."

"You have nothing to feel bad about," I tell him, taking a step closer, tilting my head to see him. Without asking and without a warning, I rise on my toes and brush my lips over his. He holds us together with my lips pressed to his until he tips his face so his forehead can rest against mine. His hand drops to my waist, and he pulls me closer.

And then even closer as he wraps both arms around me and hugs me.

No one ever talks about hugs. It's always kisses or unexpected touches, but hugs, they're probably more important than both of those two combined. It's a moment between two people when the need to be as close as possible to that person takes over, and two hearts are pressed together to become one. A hug is an exchange of affection meant to show support, whether it's due to a celebration or through grief, and a hug is the thing that everyone needs when most of the time they don't realize it. A hug is small, simple, yet it can be everything.

And this is.

"Will you come over for dinner on Friday?" I ask him. We still need to talk.

He pulls back and looks at me.

"You're going to cook for me?" he asks, raising his brows, the mood lifting just a bit.

"Yes." I give him a small smile even though he knows I'm not the best. Can I cook? A little, but for him, I would try anything.

Jonah gives himself to everyone and everything he cares about. Whether it's football, his friends, Vivi, even me. I haven't left yet, and I definitely want to do something just for him.

"Okay," he agrees. "Text me what time."

Chapter 36
Team Chat

Reid: If anyone wants to stop by, I'll be on the grill

Miles: Sweet. Ryder and I are in

Darius: Ah, look who's bonding

Reid: Grab steaks or burgers on your way

Miles: Fuck off, D

Rico: Count me in. I'll bring the fireworks

Sully: No fireworks

Rico: What do you mean? It's the 4th of July

Ryder: It's against the code

Reid: Camille says no fireworks

Sully: Holla! Look who finally did their job

Darius: I guess we know who wears the pants in your family

Rico: What do you mean against code?

Sully: Bro, it's one of the no-gos in your contract, like hoverboards and snowboarding

Dylan: Always thought that was a stupid rule

Sully: It's a rule for a reason

Reid: Damn straight. She looks good in pants too

Camden: Most common injuries for hoverboards are fractured hands/arms and head injuries

Rico: Why do you know this?

Marcus: Clark Kent in the house

Titan: 😂

Camden: Firework burns account for
32% of the injuries in July

Rico: Bro.

Sully: Rico thinks he doesn't need his
fingers to play

Rico: I don't. I don't need them at all to
play, if you catch my drift

Sully: Deep sigh

Marcus: Why is he even in this chat?

Rico: You love me, that's why

Marcus: If you say so

Miles: Where's Ty, he's always down
for food

Reid: Tyler?

Reid: You coming over?

Camden: Ty?

Sully: T?

Rico: Fine, I'll bring Tammy instead

Chapter 37
Jonah

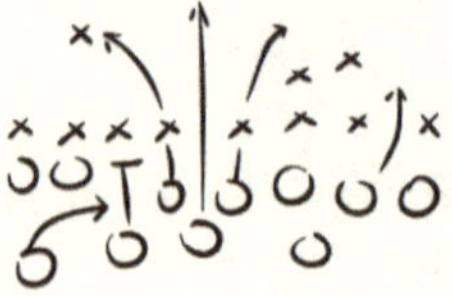

I t's the Fourth of July, and my need for a holiday or to celebrate is sitting at less than zero. But having a kid who thinks holidays are special means we have to honor every one.

Every. Single. One.

Not that I wouldn't for her anyway, as these years are the magical years. Once she becomes a teenager and then older, the allure will shift and change. I know us together creating these memories isn't ideal because she should be with John and Ashley, but the least I can do is still try to make her childhood idyllic.

"Thanks for taking us out today," I tell Tyler as we take off toward St. Petersburg. All around us, boats are heading in the same direction. American flags are waving proudly. People are laughing, dancing, and in general having the best time. I wish I could say the same for us.

Last year, Tyler bought this boat. He had mentioned

wanting one prior to that, but it wasn't until the Tarpons gave him a three-year extension that he pulled the trigger. This boat, well, technically it's a yacht, is thirty-four feet and designed for fishing and water sports. While it can hold a nice-sized group of people, I'd say six to eight is best, especially considering our size. Two to three in the front, two in the middle, and two to three in the back. And of course Tyler wouldn't be Tyler if he left off a Tarpons flag and a pirate flag.

Vivi thinks the pirate flag is funny, but he's like, "Hey, you never know what we might find." Her seven-year-old imagination has run wild.

The boat bounces a little as it picks up speed, and I watch as Vivi holds on to Molly to keep her from losing her balance. I appreciate him letting us bring her because, inevitably, she will pee on the floor. It's too long in one place, and well, she's a puppy. He just shrugs and says, "This boat has seen worse," and hoses it down like it's no big deal. Worse meaning fish guts. While I might tease Tyler about eating at our house all the time, every time he takes the boat out, he always brings back fresh fish, Gulf shrimp, and lobsters when they're in season.

"Of course." He glances at me because he knows something is wrong, but doesn't want to ask. He's learned by now that if I want to talk about it, I will, if I don't, I won't. He and I are alike in that sense. He's also had something going on this past week, which he hasn't talked about, but I'm certain of it due to the permanent scowl on his face. Tyler is happy all the time, so his mood shift is noticeable.

The weather is beautiful today. The humidity hasn't taken over, the skies are a deep shade of sky blue with just a few clouds in sight, and I find I'm angry that it doesn't match my mood. Of course, this is Florida, so later in the day, we will have an afternoon summer storm, where the sky darkens and then lets its tears flow just like mine have been, but for right now, the sunniness irritates me.

Tyler turns on some music, he readjusts his hat, which he's flipped on backward and Vivi smiles at us as it pours out of the speakers. The other day when she was talking to Sophie, I heard her ask if she ever learned how to play the piano. I didn't even realize Vivi had an interest in the piano, but I guess I should start thinking about these things too. Little girls seem to like dance, piano, violin, cooking, art, theater, and some sports. I need to make sure I'm not forgetting anything that she might want to learn or do.

"Vivi, want to do some fishing today?" Tyler asks her. She's sitting in the front of the boat, and I'm in the middle with him. She loves to feel the wind on her face, and I let her stretch out across the benches.

"Sure, Uncle Tyler. But no crying from you when I catch the biggest one," she taunts him without even tearing her eyes away from the horizon.

He turns to face me, and silently, his expression says, "Did she just talk smack to me?"

I chuckle because it sure sounded like she did.

"As long as you know the rules. You catch it, you clean it." He smirks.

We can see her thinking about this, and then she looks at us and shrugs.

"Okay."

I'm not sure if she's ever seen anyone clean a fish, so I'm thinking in her seven-year-old mind she's just giving it a bath.

"We'll get to a good spot in about twenty minutes," he tells her. "I brought you some snacks too if you get hungry. Uncle Jonah might have a thing for fruits and vegetables, but I know what you really want." He winks at her. "Pringles and Oreos."

Her eyes widen as she glances at me, then her face splits into the largest smile.

"Yep, this is why I'm the favorite uncle." He wags his brows at me. "So are you ready to report in two weeks?" he asks. There's always this dueling sense of excitement and dread over a new season. Excitement over doing what we love in front of a house full of fans, yet dread because we know the long hours and work we're about to have to put in. Plus teams always know when they're going to be good or bad. This year, we're predicted to be good. Bryan has been on fire over the past couple of years, with one Super Bowl win. Who knows, maybe we can do it again.

"Yep," I tell him, frowning.

He laughs. "You don't look it. Your face is screaming, 'Please don't make me,' when it should be lighting up with, 'Can't wait!'"

"That's not it. I just have a lot on my mind right now, and reporting in isn't one of them."

I did text Sophie earlier today. I wouldn't say we've "broken up," but things are just uncertain at the moment. She's on call, so no barbecuing or joining us for fireworks tonight. If anything, she said all her fingers and toes are crossed for an uneventful night. Fireworks can go either way. Some years, there are hardly any accidents, and other years, there are dozens. Yeah, we're all told to be responsible around fireworks, but I've never given it much thought to how many aren't.

"Bro," Tyler says, getting my attention. One eyebrow pops up over the top of his sunglasses. That's his silent way of asking me to spill something, anything and I let out a deep sigh.

I don't want to say too much in front of Vivi. Little ears seem to hear everything. I don't know exactly what is happening. We're going to talk about it at her house later this week, and it just sucks. Sucks for all of us.

I swallow once and then push the words out. "Job offer." Just saying them makes my stomach ache.

Both brows pop now. "Where?"

I pause, not wanting to put it out into the universe, but damn if this doesn't hurt to say on a deep exhale. "Minneapolis."

He frowns and shakes his head a little like he doesn't understand.

"Yeah, my sentiments exactly," I tell him as I pull my hat down a little farther over my face.

"Did you ask her to stay?" he asks as he increases the speed of the boat.

He makes it sound so simple when it's anything but.

"How can I? This is her dream."

A dream I didn't even know she had. All those hours together when I poured myself out to her, yet she chose not to tell me this. This thing that impacts us all.

"Since when?" he asks like he doesn't believe me. Water sprays up over the front of the boat, and Vivi squeals.

"She's from there. Her dad is there."

He shrugs in a way that says, "So what?"

I don't know how to explain it to him. Hell, I'm still trying to explain it to myself.

Silence falls over us as we glide across the water. Both of us are lost in thought. Eventually, we approach the bridge leading us out into the Gulf, and he slows.

"Dreams can change," he says without looking at me.

I know he's not wrong, but have hers? If they had, wouldn't she have canceled the interview? And what happens if I do ask her to stay and she does out of some misguided sense of obligation because of me or Vivi? Resentment is a real thing, and I refuse to layer that between us as well.

I've thought of everything too. Asking for a long-distance relationship. It's not ideal, but I would do it if she agreed. Homeschooling Vivi so she and I can go back and forth between Tampa and Minnesota during the on and offseasons. Moving there and leaving them during the season so Vivi can have stability. And retiring.

I've never considered retiring early. After all, who

turns down that kind of money, but at some point, it's just money, right? We have enough to live comfortably, and with the right investments, it could even grow. I just don't know if I'm ready. My heart isn't there yet, but I suppose it could be for her.

I do recognize that it is okay for each of us to have a dream. It's how badly we want each other to make it work.

"Your turn," I state, returning the raised brow and shifting in the seat so I can reach behind us and into the cooler for three sparkling waters.

His expression sours and drops into a deep scowl, and I almost laugh. Seriously, what could be so bad that he turns into this?

"New roommate," he says, and the shock on my face has his ears turning red and his lips pressing into a flat line.

"What? Who?"

To my knowledge, the only roommate he's ever had was his buddy Lance all through college. While Tyler is definitely one of the guys, what he's not is someone who shares his space. Even on the road, he has some agreement with management that usually gets him his own room, unless it's not available. He likes being alone.

"No one I'm ready to talk about yet." He continues to frown, and this has me even more intrigued.

I try to think back to what family members he has, but I can't come up with any. His parents are happy in Jacksonville, he's an only child, and while he's mentioned a few cousins in passing, none of them were frequent enough to become a roommate.

So who is it?

"You know you won't be able to keep this a secret for long. Someone will find out soon enough, and word will travel." I pop the top on the can, and Vivi turns at the sound. She stands to grab the drink as I hold it out for her.

"No one will find out if you keep your trap shut. Besides, it's not a big deal. She won't be there long."

"She?" My jaw drops.

He keeps his head facing forward and his eyes on the water in front of us as he completely ignores my question.

Chapter 38
Sophie

Pulling onto Davis Islands, my heart aches, knowing that they're close. As many times as I've driven to Camille's, I've always loved the feel of this quiet little slip of a neighborhood in downtown Tampa, but now it feels different, it feels more. As much as I hate to say it, it feels like home.

A home that's not mine, but with each day that passes, I'm wishing more that it was.

As I pass the hospital, my phone rings throughout my car. It's my dad and instantly I feel better at seeing his name.

"Hey, Dad," I say as the road curves. The late afternoon light streaks gold through the tree branches, and it's so beautiful and inviting.

"Hey, kiddo. How's it going?" His voice is warm, familiar, and I already know I'm about to spill all the tea.

"It's going," I tell him, uninterested in trying to mask the sadness I feel.

"Uh-oh. That doesn't sound too good," he says. He's moving through the house, and after a beat I hear him close a door.

"I don't know what it is, but not good sums it up." The road forks, and I veer to the right.

"Well, are you going to tell me, or will you make your old man worry."

I let out a deep sigh. Just like I should have told Jonah about the job interview, I feel like I should have told my dad about Jonah when I was back home. I thought I was doing the right thing by compartmentalizing the different areas of my life. As it turns out, I wasn't.

"I met someone," I tell him, suddenly feeling nervous and relieved at the same time. I've never spoken about a guy to my dad, so this is uncharted waters, and while I'm not sure what his reaction is going to be, I am proud and excited to tell him about Jonah and Vivi.

There's a long pause and then he says, "And?" Like he's confused as to why this is a problem.

"He lives here."

My dad chuckles. "You live there, too. I'm not sure what the problem is."

"I got the job," I tell him, my heart thumping hard in my chest. I've waited so long to be able to tell him this, and now here I am with tears of sadness filling my eyes instead of tears of joy.

"Oh. I see now," he says, the bed squeaking as he sits

down. I can totally picture him too. I've seen him sit on this side of the bed, his side, my whole life.

"Yeah," I tell him as I make a few more turns and pull onto Camille's street.

"Is it serious?" he asks, and unless I'm reading more into his tone than there is, it almost sounds like he's hopeful.

"It's still kind of new, but it has the potential to be." Who am I kidding, it's already serious. I know it, Jonah definitely knows it, and I'm guessing Vivi does too by the way she's taken to me.

"And now you're second-guessing yourself."

"I am."

But I don't know what I'm really second-guessing. Is it taking the job or staying here?

"And you don't think he would want to move with you? Can't be that serious if making a sacrifice for you isn't on the table."

I pull up to the small gate at their house and let myself in. A while ago Camille gave me the code, she said it would be easier for me to have it, versus having to call her and wait every time.

"It's not that simple. Does the name Jonah Dallmann ring a bell?"

"The wide receiver for the Tarpons?" The surprise he has is evident, but I'm not sure why. He knows I'm friends with Camille and am frequently around the players.

"Yep." I pull through and park under the massive oak tree that covers their front yard.

"That's who you're dating?" He sounds completely incredulous.

"Why do you sound so shocked?"

He doesn't answer me but says, "Now I see how that complicates things."

I park my car and push the seat all the way back so I can prop up my legs.

"Did you know he has guardianship of his niece?" I glance over to my passenger seat where there is a picture of a dolphin that she drew and colored for me. It's been there for a few days and I love it.

"Now that you mention it, I do remember seeing something about that a few years ago. Someone died, right?"

"Yeah, his brother." My heart aches at what Jonah has gone through.

"So not one, but two complications."

"I don't really like thinking of it that way. They aren't complicated, but being long distance would be an obstacle."

"Do you love them?" he asks, as if it's that simple.

I don't need to think or even hesitate. "Yes, I do."

It's the first time I've admitted this out loud, well, even to myself really. Sure I'd felt it pushing in at the edges, but I wasn't acknowledging it on purpose. But now it comes so easily, just like taking my next breath, and with it comes peace. Peace from a struggle that I've been dealing with for weeks that suddenly doesn't feel like a struggle at all.

"Then there's your answer. Life is short, and unexpected things can happen. You know this, so why would you leave them?"

"What about you? We had a plan."

"Sophie," he says in his unique way, which tells me he thinks I'm being ridiculous.

"I know. But it's all we've talked about for what feels like my whole life. You and me."

"Yes, it is what you've talked about, and I just went along with it because I know you. You like plans, you like feeling secure. Uncertainty makes you nervous, and there's nothing wrong with that, but you can't close yourself off from the possibility of great unexpected things because you made a plan. Plans can change."

I know he's not wrong, things change all the time, but this isn't small. It's huge. I'm pivoting from a dream that I've had for more than a decade, and this new direction suddenly makes me want to jump out of my skin as it looks like the adventure of a lifetime.

"But how does that make you feel? You're my family, don't you want us to be together?"

"Of course I do. But, Soph, if I'm reading between the lines here, it sounds like between you and me, our family might be growing by three. It's not just the two of us anymore. You don't need to worry about me, I have Chrissy now, so it will be the five of us. Doesn't that sound amazing?"

When he puts it like that.

My eyes prick and blur with tears.

"Yeah, it does."

Jonah and Vivi as my family . . . suddenly my heart calms as it floods with more love for the two of them and all those worries and fears I had for disappointing him subside. Not that I thought he would ever be disappointed with Jonah and Vivi, but more so that he might have been over the loss of our plans. A plan that apparently was just mine.

"I look forward to meeting this young man of yours. Make sure you tell him it's not personal, but I'm a Vikings fan until the day I die."

I laugh.

"So what's he like? What's the little girl's name? How did you meet?"

I tell him everything. Well, almost everything, and after twenty minutes of sitting in Camille's driveway, I finally let him go, knowing that everything will turn out okay.

"You good?" Camille asks. She's popped her head out and stands in the doorway, swaying back and forth like a new mom does. "The camera went off a while ago that you were here."

I'm more than good.

"I'm good," I tell her. "Was just talking to my dad." I climb out of my car and make my way over to them, my heart suddenly so full, as I realize I'm not going to be leaving her either. "Look at you, little mama," I say, smiling, as I wrap her and baby Claire in one giant, gentle hug. She's glowing with happiness, even though there are deep dark circles under her eyes.

"Isn't it so surreal?" she says, as she looks down at the sleeping bundle in her arms.

"She's so tiny. I always forget how small babies actually are," I tell her as we make our way back into the house. Izzy comes running over and I bend down to give her a pet too.

"Tiny, but as much as she eats, she'll be growing soon enough," she laughs, patting her bottom.

"How's it going?" I ask as we make our way toward the kitchen.

"It's going. When Reid and I got home from the hospital, he set her car seat bucket down on the couch over there. Claire was sleeping and not moving at all, and we just looked at each other like *Now what?*"

"That's funny. I guess I've never really thought about it."

"We just sat there and stared at her until she woke up. So how are you doing?" she asks again, while reaching in the refrigerator and pulling out a sparkling water. This time her gaze is a little more thorough.

"I feel like this is a trick question." I grin, feeling lighter than I have in the last month.

She laughs. "I'm just asking because Reid mentioned that Jonah has been a little more quiet than usual. Kind of reminded him of the Jonah he was two years ago. What happened?"

"I got a job in Minneapolis."

She gasps. I can tell she's not certain if she's supposed to be happy for me or upset.

"He found out because I left the offer letter and a flier lying on the kitchen table."

"But didn't he know that has always been your goal, to end up back there with your dad?"

"Nope. It wasn't that I was withholding it from him, I just never had anything to tell him. When I saw him at the beach, I had already inquired to see if there was an opening, and nothing was happening between us. Then suddenly it was. And then I received an email asking for an interview. So I went, and here we are now. All of it happened so fast."

"So what are you going to do?" she asks, moving toward the living room and I follow.

It's funny, after speaking with my dad, I realize I always thought of Minnesota as my home, but it's not. My singular focus for so long has been to get back there, and to be with him. He's right, it was the safe and easy choice. But, if I'm to really break down that thought of home, at the core of it, what I wanted was to be with my dad, my family. It really had nothing to do with Minnesota. If he had moved, I would have sought a job in the new city, not Minnesota.

Family.

Family of five.

For so long, I've traveled on the path I designed for myself and the one I knew. And if another path popped up at any point in time, regardless of how good it sounded, I refused to take it. It wasn't worth the risk.

But they aren't a risk. They are so much more than that.

And the thought of leaving Jonah and Vivi nearly breaks me. Why would I break my own heart when I can have everything that I want right here? And I know without a doubt that if Jonah and I had been together this whole time, the past two and a half years, I wouldn't be trying to move. I would be here with them . . . indefinitely.

I look at Camille as we settle onto the couch and smile. "I have a plan."

Chapter 39
Jonah

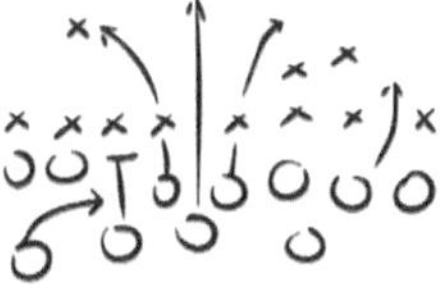

Over the past couple of days, I've done nothing but dread tonight.

Not because I don't want to see her, I absolutely do. But I know that tonight will most likely be our make-or-break night. We have to have the tough conversation about where we're going, if anywhere at all.

"It smells good in here," I tell her after she opens the door for me. I lean in to kiss her on the cheek and follow her inside.

"Thanks," she says, making her way toward the kitchen table. The same table that might inadvertently be changing my life.

I do love her place. Whereas some might expect it to be super feminine, it's anything but. She has stormy-gray and dark-wood furniture, a white and stainless-steel kitchen, wrought-iron barstools, huge television on the wall, and shelves overflowing with books. So many books.

Trendy country music plays over the speakers, and it's not lost on me that she remembers I said I love it at the beach.

"Growing up, there were several things my mom made that I loved, so my dad and I have been trying to perfect them over the years. I know you are particular about what you eat, so I skipped the tater tot hotdish and made the wild rice and chicken soup instead. Seems healthier, but I did buy bread to go with it, and I made you a bundt cake." She smiles at me sheepishly.

"A bundt cake?" I ask as I take a seat at the table and run my hands over my thighs to dry them. I don't eat a lot of sweets, but for her I would eat anything. My nerves are all over the place, and as much as I tell myself it's all going to be okay, I can't help but feel anxious.

"Yeah." She grins. "It's the official cake of Minnesota." She picks it up off the kitchen counter and brings it over to the table.

"Okay. Never met a cake I haven't liked." I smile at her.

"There's a salad for you too. I've seen you eat before, but I wasn't sure if the soup and the cake would be enough."

"Thank you, it's all perfect," I tell her, when really I have zero appetite and don't want to eat at all.

She takes a seat next to me, and I look around at all of the thoughts and details she put into tonight. The table is decorated with placemats, chargers, pretty napkins, two glasses of wine, water, fresh flowers, and candles. She's wearing a cute navy-and-white-patterned dress that's a little loose and has three-quarter sleeves. Her hair is styled and down, and she has on a full face of makeup. I'm thinking I'm not the only one who's nervous.

"How's Vivi been the rest of the week?" she asks as she picks up my bowl to ladle me some of the soup.

"Okay, actually." She sets the bowl back in front of me. "She bounced back pretty quick, and I'm certain that has a lot to do with you."

Her eyes connect with mine, and she lets out a deep breath. "Good, I was worried about her. Where is she tonight?"

"At home with Tyler. He said he'd stay as long as I needed him to."

She nods her head, then picks up her own bowl, filling it almost to the top. I add some salad to my plate, cut us both a piece of bread, and we both sit in silence as we go through the motions.

"Wow, this is delicious," I say after taking my first bite. And it is. I can see why this is a family favorite and easily know it could become one of mine.

"Thank you. I was worried that there wouldn't be enough salt."

"You have nothing to worry about," I assure, and I feel these words in the deepest part of my heart. I hope she reads between the lines. If she wants this, us, there's nothing I won't do to make it work.

"Want to see something funny? Here, look at this." I pull out my phone and pull up the video from yesterday.

She takes it from me and hits play. I watch her, but she doesn't say anything. Instead, she touches a few things on the screen and then her eyes come back to mine.

"What is this?"

"It's Vivi teaching Molly to dance." Did she not see? It's such a cute video too. Vivi holds her hands in the air, palms facing down and she waves them up and down like she's pounding on a drum. Molly stands on her back legs when she does this and starts dancing.

"I see that, but what site is this?"

Oh, now I understand what she's asking.

"I made a website for Vivi. Well, I guess it's for me too."

She looks back at my phone and then at me. "Why?"

I want to tell her I don't know, but I do. "John was always taking pictures of her. I used to make fun of him and he took it in stride every time. He used to tell me that one day I would understand. That all the little moments are what mean the most. When he died, I don't know, I kind of became obsessed with making sure I documented every little moment. I was afraid I would miss something, for him, for me, or for her. And then one night, after scrolling through hundreds of photos, I decided to create a website. I guess it's my version of a photo album, but I've tried to capture everything. Maybe she'll want it someday; maybe she won't. Maybe John can see it wherever he is; maybe he can't." I shrug. "It felt important to me."

Her eyes turn glassy.

"You titled this website, *Wildflowers and Wide Receivers*."

"I did," I answer, blushing.

"Why is it plural?"

I chuckle. "Because *Wildflower and the Wide Receiver* didn't sound good to me. It sounds hippie and, I don't know, intimate. It felt wrong, and the plural version felt better. Plus, wildflowers aren't just her nickname—they're kind of a mascot for our life. The memories, the painting, the annual pictures, they're all around us. As for wide receivers, outside of me, we've received a lot of love from far and wide over the last two years. I tried not to be so literal with the title."

"I'm speechless," she whispers as she looks back at my phone and scrolls through the images.

Other than Vivi, Tyler, and my uncle, I haven't told anyone else about this site. It's not that I need to keep it secret, I just want to. It belongs to us, and I don't need the world to know it exists.

"Am I on it?" She glances back at me.

It never occurred to me that she might not want to be, and uneasiness burns its way into my lungs. Everyone I've put on the site has a tag: Sophie, the guys, Kelli. That makes it easy to pull each one.

"Yes," I tell her hesitantly, again rubbing my hands across my thighs. "I can take you off if you don't want to be."

Please don't make me remove you.

"No, that's fine. Jonah, I think this is one of the

sweetest things I've ever seen." She slowly hands me back my phone. Now that she knows the site address, I wonder if she'll go on and look at all the photos? Deep down, I hope she does. I want her to know everything about me.

I scoff. "You won't think that once you see the one I posted of you eating that giant slice of pizza from Madison Avenue Pizza."

She smiles a real smile and leans back in her chair.

"Obviously, I've seen you taking photos and wondered what you were doing with them. I thought maybe an Instagram account or something, but this is so much better. This is thoughtful and amazing."

"Thank you. I know a lot of parents have scrapbooks and such, but I get lost when I see how many pictures there are and this makes everything so much easier. I can make categories for each school year, one for back-to-school photos, Halloween costumes, holidays, all of it. Every night before I go to bed, if I have a photo, I upload it. It takes no time at all. Like right here." I lean over and show her where the categories are and the tags.

"For her whole life," she whispers. "Does she know?"

"Yes. I also have categories for John and Ashley. She likes to look at those."

"You never cease to surprise me."

Picking up her spoon she takes a bit of the soup. I do the same and can't help but wonder what's going through her head.

Setting the spoon down, she takes a sip of her wine and then turns to face me.

"I know I shouldn't be nervous to have you over tonight, but I am. And after seeing that, I somehow am even more."

"Soph, I don't want you to be nervous. It's all going to work out as it should."

"You don't understand . . ." She hesitates.

"But I do."

"I've thought about what I want to say to you. In fact, I've rehearsed it. I just don't want to forget anything or get it wrong."

"Sophie, you haven't done anything wrong." I turn so I'm facing her too and our knees are touching.

"We'll have to agree to disagree on this one," she says, looking down at her lap.

"Listen, was I hurt at first? Yes. But once I took the time to think about it, I understand why you didn't tell me. But I need you to know I will never be someone who holds you back from following your dreams. And I know that if it were just me in this scenario, things might look a little different, but that's not how it is."

"Jonah—" she says, wanting to tell me what it is she's rehearsed, but I need to talk first. I have to.

"Please, just let me get this out."

"Okay," she says, reaching over and placing her hand on mine. I flip mine so our fingers can lace together. I love holding her hand. I want to grow old holding this hand.

"While I never want to stifle you from your dreams, I also feel strongly that you deserve a man who will fight for you. Because you're worth it. You're more than worth it. So this is me asking you to stay. Here. In Tampa. With me. Give us a shot. I know this probably feels sudden and wild to throw out there, considering we haven't been together that long, but, Sophie, I'm in love with you. I didn't need six days to tell you."

"Six days?" she says, looking at me confused.

"And I can't promise I'll always be in Tampa, but I know right now I am, and I want you with us. Down the road, if you want to move back to Minneapolis, we'll go. I promise. We will follow you to the edge of the world if that's what you want. I can't see myself having more than five or so years left anyway. So for now, I'm asking you, please . . . please stay."

"You love me?"

I lift our hands and kiss the back of hers.

"Of course I do."

Chapter 40
Sophie

He loves me.

I should have known this already. In fact, if I'm honest with myself, I knew he did. Since the night I met him, he hasn't been able to hide his emotions, but hearing him say it is entirely different.

His lips brush against the back of my hand, and if I wasn't already sitting, I'd swoon, and he'd have to catch me.

"I've never been one to believe in love at first sight, but if that's not what happened to us, then I don't know what to call it. From the very first moment I saw you step out onto the back patio at Reid's that night so long ago, you were it. I wasn't interested or looking for anyone either. All I'd wanted for my life up until then was football—that was my singular focus—but then there you were, and my world tilted, shifted, whatever you want to call it, and I was certain the trajectory of my life was changing. And when I walked out of your place that following morning, I knew deep down in my gut I was right. I was a different man, and I was completely yours."

"How did you know?" I ask him, inching my way closer to him on my chair and loving hearing about how he fell in love with me.

"Call it a gut feeling, call it cheesy, whatever, but for the first time in my life the word soulmate struck me."

Soulmate.

Tingles of love race down my spine, as my very being has a visceral reaction to this word and indefinitely tethers itself to him. Our connection, the feeling of wholeness, the mutual understanding and respect of each other, my best friend, and the unconditional love and my lover all wrapped into one. Is there anything in this world more treasured than this? My throat tightens, and I blink back the burn in my eyes.

"But how did you know we would get along?"

He gives me a flat look.

"Come on." He holds up his hand and glances at his pointer finger. "Well, first of all, you're friends with Camille. I happen to hold her on a pedestal, and she's very particular about who she lets in. She let you in." He adds the next finger. "Second, you laughed a lot, which told me you had a great sense of humor, which I value." He adds the third. "You were down for whatever that night. We could have driven to Georgia and back or just ended up at your place, and you were happy to go along. This told me you were adventurous." Now, he holds up four. "I saw your place. You weren't hiding fourteen smelly animals or a closet hoarder. And fifth." His whole hand is open now. "I could go on and on, but you were kind, sweet, and so damn beautiful it hurt to look at you. I couldn't find any red flags, not that I was really looking. You had me spellbound, but unless something off the wall emerged, my mind was not changing. There is no changing my mind. But then Vivi happened." He drops his hand. "I grieved the loss of my brother, but I need you to know I also grieved you."

"Jonah . . ." I take both his hands and wrap them in mine. "I still wish you would have reached out and told me. I'm sorry I let my hurt feelings get in the way of being there for you. I will forever feel terrible about this."

He shakes his head.

"No. I don't want that. A relationship shouldn't start like that. I was so overwhelmed by it all too. I was twenty-four years old and knew nothing about shutting down someone's life or taking care of a five-year-old. It wouldn't have been fair to you."

"I hear what you're saying, and we've talked about this before, but it doesn't change the fact that I wish I could have been there for you both."

"You're here now," he says, dropping one hand and leaning forward to tuck some loose hair behind my ear. I love it when he does this, he always runs a finger down the side of my face when he's done.

"Can I ask you something? It's completely random, but I am curious."

"Of course," he says, now inching his way closer to me.

His knees brush up against mine as they bracket them on the outside. We've completely forgotten about dinner, not that I wanted to eat anything until this conversation was over anyway.

"When is your birthday?" I ask him.

His brows pop, and he lets out a single chuckle. "May eighteenth."

So I just missed celebrating it with him.

"So that makes you twenty-seven." I'm feeling oddly nervous that he might now realize our age gap.

"Last I checked. When is your birthday?"

"November sixteenth."

"Hmm," he mumbles like he's committing that date to memory. "And how old will you be on November sixteenth?"

My stomach clenches. I just need to spit it out. "I'll be thirty-four."

He chuckles again, this time his smile stretching across his handsome face.

"I always did like older women." He winks, flirting with me.

The admiration I have for this man is endless, but then I remember my speech. There are things I want to tell him —no, I need to.

"My father is getting married," I announce, which might feel out of nowhere for him, but it doesn't to me.

His eyebrows rise. "Okay. That's good, right? You did mention he was hinting around to it."

"Yes. But it's official, and get this, they bought a small RV."

One side of his mouth quirks up. He doesn't understand, but he sits patiently as he wants to listen to me.

"All these years, I wanted to be there to be with him. That's what family does, right? They stick together. But then he tells me he and Chrissy bought an RV and are planning to travel during the winter months. Like snowbirds."

He frowns. Now he's catching on.

"Snowbirds. So you're going to move back to Minnesota and he's going to turn around and leave you there?" He shifts in his chair, not happy with the picture he's just painted.

"Basically, that's what I was thinking and how I felt too, until he tells me that his plan was to spend the winter months down here with me."

He tilts his head as he thinks about this, and in an instant, his eyes widen and flash to mine.

"So regardless of where I live, here or there, I'm getting him for half of the year."

Hope suddenly surrounds his aura, and I can feel it floating in the air. Color rises into his cheeks and the hazel in his eyes intensifies.

"So you could choose to stay here, then?"

There's so much emotion in his voice that I nearly choke out the answer he wants to hear, but I have to finish the story first.

"I took a job offer."

He inhales sharply. His face falls, but then he masks it because he's that kind of man who'd put how he feels aside to show me support.

"But not there . . . here." I lean a little closer to him and place my hand on his thigh. His solid warm thigh.

"I don't understand. You already have a job here."

"Well, at the same time I was interviewing for the position in Minneapolis, one of my old attendings reached out to me and asked if I would be interested in teaching. You saw me talking to her at the hospital gala. It's not a full-time position, as I do already have one, but I'll be an adjunct professor, specifically helping students publish different articles of research within their field of specialty in orthopedics. This professor just received a large grant, and she needs additional help while she starts a new study of her own."

"And this is something that you want to do?"

"Yes, very much. I've realized that I like to be stimulated and challenged. I don't like being stagnant, and that's what I've been over the past year. But, Jonah, I don't want to move to Minnesota. I don't know what will happen between us down the road, I just know what's happening now."

"And what is that?" he asks, that hope trying desperately to drip back into his tone.

"That I'm in love with you. Both of you. You're my family too and I don't want to leave you. I can't."

Silence settles over us as he stares at me. His eyes turn watery and his nose flares once as he breathes in. His shoulders fall forward as he exhales and he takes both my hands in his. Looking down at them, he rubs a few of my fingers until he drags his gaze back to mine.

"I feel like I've been waiting a long time to hear someone say that they love me," he says quietly.

"What do you mean? So many people love you." I tangle our fingers together, because I want to feel his hands too. Hands that have calluses from all the hard work he puts in at the gym and with catching the ball.

"Yes, but until this moment, they weren't the ones who I wanted to hear it from. You, I wanted to hear it from you."

Leaning forward, I cup his cheek. "I love you. Very much," I tell him again, and his whole body shudders. It's wild how such small words can have such a profound impact. "All this time, I've been so focused on my plan, this antiquated plan I put in place years ago before I even lived any life to figure out exactly what I want, so it shouldn't be surprising that somewhere along the way, my plan changed. You became my plan. You and Vivi. I love you both so much, I can't imagine not being with you. The two of you are stitched into the very fiber of my being and I would give up everything and move anywhere as long as I get to be with you. It's not about the location, it's about the people I love, and I love you so much."

"I don't know what to say."

"You should know it wasn't just you. That night, your soul spoke to mine and together they whispered soulmate. I felt it too and I wanted it so bad. I still do. I want you and

Vivi. Sweet Vivi who I want to shower with so much love. You both deserve it and I feel lucky to be the one you chose."

He slowly blinks at me, those dark blond eyelashes sweeping up and down, but they do nothing to hide the array of emotions coursing through him. He's happy, he's humbled, he's hopeful, and he's in love. With me.

"Move in with us." He's so serious, but then the corners of his mouth lift too.

I blurt out a laugh. "Don't you think that's a little fast?"

"No." He sits up straight. "I know what I want, and it's you. It's always been you. You should be with us. You complete us. And if there's anything I've learned from John's death, it's that tomorrow isn't a guarantee."

Should I take more time to think about this? Probably. But do I want to? No. I want to be there with them in Jonah's beautiful home, too.

"Okay," I tell him.

"Okay?" He looks at me with shock and so much optimism.

"Yes." I laugh.

He reaches over and yanks me off my chair and onto his lap so I'm straddling him. I laugh again as he wraps his long arms around me and hugs me fiercely. Minutes pass as the pounding of his heart slows, and my weight gradually settles onto him. Pulling back, he drags his lips across my face until they press against mine, and that's when I realize I get to kiss this man every day, multiple times a day, for what I'm hoping is the rest of my life.

"I'm so happy, I don't know what to do with these feel-ings," he tells me, kissing me all over my face.

"I can think of something," I breathe out as I run my hand down his back and my feet curve around his legs.

"I like the way you think," he mumbles against my mouth as his hand runs up under my dress and his fingers slip under the edge of my underwear. "But what about dinner? You worked so hard on it."

"It'll be here when we get done."

He groans into my mouth, tilts my head, and then kisses me in that all-consuming way of his. I love it. I love him and dissolve into him, knowing he loves me too.

"While I do love this position, what I'd love more is you, in my bed, and naked."

He pulls back to look at me, and he narrows his eyes. "Technically, it's no longer your bed. There is no yours or mine. It's all ours." He grins and then stands with me wrapped around him. I hook my ankles on his lower back.

"Then I guess we should enjoy this bed since we won't have it too much longer," I tell him.

"I have a plan." He smirks.

"Do I get to hear this plan?"

As he starts walking toward the stairs, I start undoing the buttons on his shirt. His skin is so warm and so golden, and the bone doctor in me can't help but to appreciate the strong lines of his clavicles.

"Remember when I said I wanted a beach house?"

I push his shirt open so I can run my fingers over the

bones in his shoulders and then around to the back of his neck. "You want to move my things there?"

"Yes. At least your furniture. We'll keep whatever you want." He pulls on my dress and it's loose enough that it pulls straight over my head. He drops it on the stairs and then his large hands slide under my butt where he lifts me so we're eye level. The heat in his gaze is enough to raise my temperature a few degrees.

"You really are something else," I whisper, leaning in to kiss him. He kisses me back and there's no hesitation in the glide of his tongue against mine. He groans as I finally free him of his shirt and the sound reverberates through his chest and into mine as I thread my fingers through his hair.

"Since we're on all the subjects," he mutters against my skin. "Should we just get married too?"

I throw my head back and laugh. This man. What am I going to do with him?

"I'm not opposed," I tell him, and his eyes get all excited. In the past I would have had a wave of nervousness or anxiety over his question, as it's change, but since I firmly decided that he and Vivi are my plan indefinitely, I'm open to anything with them. Anything and everything. How could I not be? "But I'd like my proposal to be somewhat of a surprise."

"And this isn't?" He grins as he nuzzles his face against mine.

"Where's the ring?" I tease.

He smiles that beautiful smile of his at me, and my heart flutters.

"I hear you, and when you least expect it, it's coming."

With that, he tosses me onto the bed and ends all of our conversations.

Sometime in the early morning, I wake and roll over to find him asleep on his stomach. His long, muscular arms are folded and up under his pillow, his hair, which is starting to get just a tad bit too long, falls over his forehead, and his full, delicious lips are slightly parted as he steadily breathes in and out.

So many nights over the past couple of weeks have been spent with one of us sneaking out that I never get to see him this way. To admire how perfect he is. The sheets are lowered so his long, lean back is on full display. There's the way his rounded shoulders smoothly transition and guide my eyes to travel over the bumps of his spine, and his waist narrows just so that it's perfect for me to slide my fingers around. I won't, though, because I want him to sleep. He needs to sleep. And the best part is, I know he's mine.

And he loves me.

Just as I love him.

Chapter 41
Team Chat

Sully: Just call me matchmaker

Miles: Bro, what now

Titan: 😂

Sully: Jonah and Sophie. I take the credit
for this

Darius: You would try

Bryan: I'm thinking Reid is the catalyst
for this

Sully: How so?

Bryan: He hosted the party where
they met

Sully: Two years ago! I'm talking about now

Miles: Also, if we're being specific, I remember Jack had a hand in this too

Bryan: No way. Jonah was locked in at that party regardless of Jack

Sully: Still. That was forever ago. I'm the reason he texted her and they reconnected

Tyler: Bro. No. That was all him

Bryan: Still giving it to Reid. He and Camille schemed to get them to the beach house

Rico: The beach house where he wooed her and not with his words but his magic peen

Titan: 😆

Darius: Do you ever stop?

Rico: Nope

Sully: He's going to be begging me to stop after I put him on suicides for his stupidity.

Rico: The fuck? What for? I speak the truth

Sully: You speak like an idiot

Tyler: Still beach house or not, Jonah knew what he wanted

Sully: And what is it that you want? Don't think we haven't noticed your mood shift

Miles: I haven't noticed anything

Sully: You wouldn't. You're too busy looking up at him after he puts you on your ass

Darius: Oh, snap! Bro's throwing shade

Sully: That's right. Miles feels the shade of Ty standing over him

Miles: One time. That happened one time.

Ryder: False

Titan: 😂

Miles: Shut it, Rookie. Suicides are looking good in your future too

Ryder: Geez. Rough crowd today

Sully: Earth to Tyler

Jonah: Leave him alone

Sully: He speaks. Tell them I'm the matchmaker

Jonah: Tell them you're a pain in my ass

Rico: Truth

Sully: Ouch. You wound me

Jonah: Doubtful

Sully: You defending him just tells us there's something up

Jonah: You're fishing

Sully: You took the bait. Can't keep secrets from this group

Tyler: Watch me.

Epilogue
Three and a half months later

Jonah

Life is good.

But then again, I knew it would be with her.

One week after she agreed to move in with me, my teammates—my friends—helped pack Sophie's stuff. They loaded it up, and then delivered it to either a storage unit or our house. We wanted it done quickly since the team was getting ready to report in for the new season. We didn't want it hanging over us. Of course, Vivi was over the moon when we told her, and each day, just like the therapist said, I've watched the heaviness that she's carried for the past two and a half years lighten. She still has her moments, but having that second person around every day to love and support her has made a huge difference.

"I don't know why, but I didn't expect it to be so hot today," Sophie says, as she rounds the back of the Tahoe to join me and peeks up at the sky. Last week, the humidity was low, and this week, it is not. And at three in the afternoon, there's no way to make it from the car to the door without sweating.

"Really? Because even though it's the end of October, it feels just like it did yesterday, and I'm sure it will be the same tomorrow."

She glances my way with narrowed eyes, and I smirk as she mouths, "Smart-ass."

One month after Sophie moved in, she and Vivi flew to Minneapolis to watch me play in a preseason game. It was the first time Vivi and I met Dan, and they instantly bonded. I don't know if it's because it's Sophie's dad and that makes him special to her, or if it's something they created on their own, but even I can't come between them. They are as thick as thieves.

"Papa, you're going to love this," Vivi tells Sophie's dad, looking up at him with hearts in her eyes. She's walking with Sophie's dad and Chrissy, and Vivi's damn near skipping she's so excited to bring them here today.

To our family favorite pizza place.

"Is that so?" he asks, looking down at her adoringly. "What would happen if I didn't like pizza?"

She scrunches up her face. "Who doesn't like pizza?"

"I don't know. There's got to be someone out there."

"That's dumb," Vivi says, and all of us laugh.

As for calling him Papa, she just started one day, and that was that. She knows that Sophie is an aunt to her, and technically, that makes her dad a great-uncle, but if you step back and look at our family as it is now, his role is most definitely one of a grandfather. They are two peas in a pod, and as for Chrissy, it's hard not to love her too. She's gentle, nurturing, and completely open to being whatever we need her to be, which Vivi recently decided is Nana.

Also, while we were in Minneapolis, I found a photographer who agreed to meet with us on a Monday afternoon. She knew of a meadow not far from the city, filled with late summer Minnesota wildflowers. There were shades of purple, white, and yellow, and it was so idyllic that while Sophie was in awe over the scenery, she never saw it coming, me dropping to one knee. She gasped, and her dad teared up because how could I leave him out of this special moment for her? Vivi jumped up and down, the photographer captured the whole proposal, and in front of all of them, I professed to love her forever.

This year, the family picture hanging on the wall in Vivi's room is of the three of us and Molly. Yes, the dog was there, too. At one time, I thought these annual photos might be sad for her, but now all I see is the years of our life together. We've added Sophie, and who knows, maybe in a few years, we'll add a baby, too. I'm in no rush, but if it turns out to be something that Sophie wants, who am I to tell her no?

"Here, let me get that," I say, reaching for the door to hold it open.

A bell rings as each person enters, and I can't help but squeeze Sophie's ass as she walks by. She's wearing a yellow sundress with short cowboy boots, and I'm counting down the minutes until we're home and I can bend her over.

She swats at my hand, but I know she doesn't hate it. In fact, she loves it, just like she loves me.

We're met with the face of the same hostess we've seen several times now.

"Good afternoon." She smiles at us with recognition and waves at Vivi. Vivi doesn't drop Dan's or Chrissy's hands. Instead, she just smiles real big back.

"Dallmann, party of five," Sophie tells her.

"You all are officially becoming regulars," she says as she gathers the menus to take us to our table.

"That's because you're our favorite," Vivi announces.

She's not wrong. It did score highest on the chart. However, as it turns out, each one of us prefers some place different. I like Madison Avenue Pizza, but Sophie thinks their sauce needs a tad more salt. Sophie has declared she likes my grilled pizzas the best, the ones we make at home, and Vivi likes any that aren't burnt on the bottom. She is not a fan of coal-fired pizza.

Two months after Sophie moved in, on a Tuesday afternoon, along with Vivi, Dan, Chrissy, and Tyler, we stood in front of a judge at the county courthouse and said, "I do."

Neither one of us needed a big wedding. Our family is small, so we decided to keep it that way. We just wanted to be married anyway. To celebrate, we booked a private room at Bern's Steak House, where a few other of our friends joined us. Sophie loved this being her first experience at the restaurant, loved the dessert room, and we both agreed there wasn't a more perfect place for us to drink champagne and start our life together.

Three months after Sophie moved in, we closed on our beach house. While we weren't in a hurry to buy just any house, I had reached out to a real estate agent to keep us updated as things became available, and this popped up unexpectedly. The owners were ready to simplify their life in retirement, and instead of dealing with rental upkeep, they decided to let it go. It's five houses in from the water. Close enough that we can still hear the waves, and only two streets over from Reid and Camille.

In front of me, I hear Vivi gasp, and that's when I know she's spotted her party.

"Surprise!" everyone yells, and she whips around to look at me with big, happy tears in her eyes.

It's been three and a half months since Sophie moved in, and it's Vivi's eighth birthday.

I can't believe she's already eight.

While we could have had her birthday party anywhere, it seems appropriate to have it here this year. I don't know that she loves pizza as much as Sophie does, but it's the memories we've made, the laughter, the love. It's sentimental to her, and that means so much more.

Tyler is the first to break free from the group as he scoops her up.

"How's my girl doing today?" He grins at her.

"Great!" she says as she ruffles his hair and then gives him a big hug.

"Who told you that you were allowed to get older?" he teases, and she just giggles as he lets her down.

"Papa, come meet my friends." She grabs Dan's hand and drags him over to Heather and another little girl named Jillian. Both are in her class at school and her level-three ballet class at Kelli's Dance Studio. While Vivi isn't ready to sleep over at anyone's house yet, we did host her first slumber party. Sophie found some company that came out and set up individual bougie glamping tents in the living room, and the theme was movie night—all hot pink, yellow, and teal. There was a large screen set up, each kid had their own beanbag chair, and there was a candy bar. They had a great time.

I lean close to Sophie. "I want to make a prediction."

"Oh, yeah? What's that?" She shifts her weight so she's angled toward me too.

"Eighteen months. That's how long it takes for your dad to decide to sell the Minnesota house and move here permanently."

We both look at Dan as he's sitting at the table with Vivi's friends, and she's sitting on his lap. I pull out my phone and snap a quick picture. While I don't think they had originally planned on starting their snowbird season until after Halloween, there was no keeping him from Vivi's birthday once we told him when it was.

Sophie huffs. "I never thought I'd see the day he'd leave Minnesota, but I think you're right."

Her tone is soft, and my need to be closer has me wrapping my arm around my wife.

Wife.

I love saying that.

"So how did I do?" Sully asks as he noisily pushes his way past a tall bundle of bright pink balloons.

"You did so good!" Sophie tells him, rubbing his arm affectionately.

Sully, Tyler, and Camden were in charge of the decorations. The restaurant graciously accommodated them and helped set up. It looks like a balloon factory exploded in here, and I'm not sad about it. I'm sure they're not either as this will get them some free publicity from the social media tags and mentions.

"I wanted to do a theme, but Camden told me no. He's such a stiff buzzkill. He said the pizza place was the theme, and we only needed some bright colors to announce the event."

Camden's not wrong, but I don't bother to tell him that. Bringing in unicorns, dolphins, or some princess balloons would just look out of place.

"It looks perfect," Sophie tells him. "I had little goodie bags made for the three of them, so the bright colors match just as they should. Did you see the cake?"

Tyler was in charge of the cake.

"Yes. Although if you think my balloons are a lot, just wait until you see this thing. It's set on a wooden cutting board and looks like a giant eight-inch deep-dish pizza. It's covered with vegetables and pepperoni made of icing, and he tells me the layers are filled with strawberry jam for sauce. He got a number eight candle and sparkler candles to go with it."

"Why are you over here running your trap and ruining my surprise?" Tyler has come up behind Sully, and he's scowling. Sophie covers her mouth as she tries not to laugh.

"I think Camille is calling me," she says as she quickly bolts away from the guys. We have a tendency to bicker with each other, and she's smart to flee. We all watch as she picks up Claire from Camille's lap and smiles so bright, it's like she's shining.

Sully shoves me in the arm. "That will be you soon." He nods in their direction.

"I hope so," I tell them because it would be a welcome blessing.

A server walks out from the back, and he's holding two large cheese pies.

"Who's ready to eat?" he asks.

Vivi cheers, "Me!"

These guys, their wives and children, her dad and Chrissy, none of them will ever understand what they've come to mean to us. They say sometimes the best families are a found family, and I firmly stand behind that.

Life is better than I can ever remember.

As for Sophie, she doesn't even realize that by coming into our lives, she not only stole our hearts but she mended them too. Vivi and I were broken, but now we are not. Do we look different than we did before the accident? Yes. But nothing is ever exactly the same after it's been repaired. Bumps, bruises, and cracks represent having lived life and being loved. And I can tell you, from personal experience, I like this version of me better.

While I'm still a work in progress, I no longer worry about what can happen tomorrow. I still take as many pictures as I can, but only to remember today. I didn't understand why John felt the need to capture every little moment at the time, but now I do. Sometimes the days are long, but I realize the years are short. Soon she'll be ten, then thirteen, driving at sixteen, and then off to college at eighteen. The little moments are memories, and with Sophie by my side, I plan on loving and cherishing every one.

Thank you so much for reading Wildflowers and Wide Receivers. If I am new to you, I appreciate you taking a chance on me and if I am not, then I hope you know how much I love and adore your continued support.

If you liked Wildflowers and Wide Receivers, please come tell me and consider leaving a spoiler free review. If you didn't like it, well don't tell me, but I promise we'll still be friends LOL... 🫣

If you're like me, then you were left wanting to know more about our guys on the Tampa Tarpons Football Team. Especially Tyler. Do you want to know who shows up on his doorstep? I'll give you a hint, it's his best friend's little sister, Lily. Only she's not so little anymore, and she needs a place to hide out from her ex and the world.

Here are a few of the other Tampa Tarpons players who also have a story...

Wide Receiver, Reid Jackson, in **Chasing Clouds**. This is an opposites attract, marriage of convenience contemporary romance that will have you on the edge of your church pew when the minister asks if there's anyone who objects at Camille's wedding, and Reid stands up and says, "I do."

Quarterback, Bryan Bremen, in **Last Slice of Pie**. She's a small town girl. He's a household name. Off the field and out of the kitchen, will they break and crumble, or finally get their second chance at the biggest game of them all . . . love.

Acknowledgments

First and foremost, I have to thank my husband and my boys for allowing me the opportunity to follow my dreams. Writing a book is no small feat, and it goes without saying that it is time consuming. Time that is spent not with my family, not helping to keep our house clean, or cooking all the delicious food. I appreciate how much you all love and accept me for me, and how you're always my biggest cheerleaders. I am lucky and love you more than all the stars in the sky.

While writing this book, we unexpectedly lost my father-in-law. It was a definite blow to our family, as he was such a strong presence for all of our boys. Thank you, dad, for loving me and always being so proud. There are hundreds of moments over the last twenty-five years I will never forget, but there is one I will always remember the most. Love you, with my whole heart, and as Matty said, "Fly high, man . . . Fly high."

Kelli B, thank you for always listening to me and encouraging me to keep going. This job is hard, and for all the times I wanted to quit, you stood next to me and told me no. I appreciate you and I love you.

Karla S and Kandi H, every day you continue to

inspire me. Your love, wisdom, and overall positivity shines brightly and I am grateful to be the lucky one who gets to soak up your light.

Megan C, no story is ever complete without your magic touch. Thank you for always being available to me and selflessly spending hours of your time trying to make my stories better. I value your opinion so much, I'm certain I'd be lost without you. Love you...

To Julie, Jenny, and Judy, thank you for helping me create my vision for the cover, and for cleaning up all my grammatical errors. I appreciate the attention to detail, the flexibility, and the care each of you give to help me make the best story possible. It takes a team and I am so happy to have all of you on mine. Thank you. Thank you. Thank you.

To the readers, whether you've been with me for a while, or if you are brand new, thank you for taking a chance on Wildflowers and Wide Receivers. I am always so grateful to those who choose to take the time to read my words. For those of you who are new, I can't wait to give you more. More words, more magical moments, more stories. Happy reading . . . much love, Kathryn.

About the Author

Kathryn Andrews loves stories that end with a happily ever after. She started writing at age seven and never stopped. Kathryn is an Amazon Bestseller for her much loved Starving for Southern series, Chasing Clouds and is a contemporary romance, women's fiction, and Southern fiction writer.

Kathryn graduated from the University of South Florida with degrees in biology and chemistry, and she currently lives in Tampa, Florida. She spends her days as a sales director for a medical device company and her nights lost in her love of fictional characters.

When Kathryn is not crafting beautiful worlds that incorporate some of her most favorite real-life places, she can be found with her husband and two boys while drinking iced coffee and enjoying the sun.

Website: www.kandrewsauthor.com
Facebook: Author Kathryn Andrews
Instagram: @kandrewsauthor
TikTok: @kandrewsauthor

Also by Kathryn Andrews

Standalone Titles
Chasing Clouds
Hats off to Love
Where the Light Shines

Starving for Southern series
The Sweetness of Life
Last Slice of Pie
Lessons in Lemonade

Horizons Valley Series
Blue Horizons
White Horizons
Gold Horizons

The Hale Brothers Series
Drops of Rain
Starless Nights
Unforgettable Sun